WEESQUACHAK

WEESQUACHAK

Ruby Slipperjack

Theytus Books Ltd.
Penticton, BC

Weesquachak

Library and Archives Canada Cataloguing in Publication

Slipperjack, Ruby, 1952-
Weesquachak / Ruby Slipperjack-Farrell. -- Rev. ed.

Originally published, 2000, under title: Weesquachak and the lost ones.
ISBN-13: 978-1-894778-23-7
ISBN-10: 1-894778-23-5

I. Title.

PS8587.L53S43 2005 C813'.54 C2005-906846-9

Copy Editing: Melva McLean
Cover Design: Suzanne Bates
Layout: Leanne Flett Kruger
Interior Graphics: Julie Flett

www.theytusbook.ca

Printed in Canada

We acknowledge the financial support of the Government of Canada through the Book Publishing Industry Development Program (BPIDP) for our publishing activities.

We acknowledge the support of the Canada Council for the Arts, the Department of Canadian Heritage and the British Columbia Arts Council.

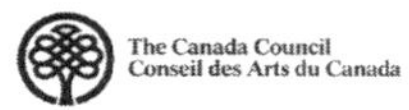

WEESQUACHAK

Chapter One

Walking along the sand beach with my bag of songs over my shoulder, I long for the old days when people use to talk about me. They acknowledged my existence then. I am Weesquachak or the Trickster as other people call me these days. I have been around since the beginning of time and was always an integral part of the people's lives for generations. Now, I feel very much alone.

I can hear the children laughing over by the train station; dogs barking over at the dock. It is quiet at the cabin by the bay. I stop and notice Channie closing the cabin door behind her. I think she is going somewhere. I shall take flight and see what she is up to.

My suitcases were on the ground on either side of me. This was as good a place as any to rest. From the hill where I stood, I looked around at the quiet stillness of the morning. The lake lay dark along the bay and melted into a steely grey along the horizon past the island. The sky was heavy with low grey clouds, and a few flies fluttered over the dead flowers and bushes. It was the end of September and everything had pretty much ended.

The seagulls were ready to fly south, and I too was on my way south to the city in search of a job. I was going to find a job. I had said that with such confidence but in all truth, all I had was a high-school diploma. I wasn't proud of that because I knew that I couldn't even do grade eleven math. They had just passed me along, and no one cared if I could actually do things at that grade level. Oh, I hated high school. A large raven swooped over my head, emitting a loud squawk as if he too agreed with me. Stupid bird. What does he know anyway?

It was 1969. I was nineteen years old and I felt trapped in my life. I was suffocating. But, I was on my way to find out what I could do for myself. Dad was starting to have that worried look on his face, as if he had just discovered he had another mouth to feed. I knew it would soon occur to him to find me a husband as quick as he could to get me out of the house. Well, I hung around as long as I could. I had nowhere else to go. When I graduated from high school last summer, I got a summer job in the city and came home in the fall just when everyone was headed to the traplines. My sister-in-law seemed so pleased to see me that it didn't take long to figure out that she was pregnant and desperately needed an extra pair of hands. So, I used my savings to buy all the things that I would need out there, like hand cream, toothpaste and deodorant, and spent the winter out at the trapline with my brother and his wife. We came back in late May and the baby was born a few days later. That was too close. It occurred to me then that she could very well have had the baby earlier when we were still in the bush. What help could I have been then? I stayed around in the community until the end of June and then went to live with my sister and her family in Nipigon for the summer.

I arrived there at the end of August and was asked, "Who are you going to marry? Who are you going to marry?" so many times that I finally answered, just that once, and said, "The Pope." It might have been funny I suppose, but it was the Priest who was asking. Every time I stayed somewhere for more than a month, the guessing and speculation would start, and then the rumours would begin about why a young woman could possibly be just drifting around. I smiled and heaved a big sigh. There was never an end to that.

There's that raven over my head again. What does he want with me? Stupid thing.

I picked up my suitcases and continued on my way past the creek to the path along the railroad tracks. I paused and looked down one of the many trails that veered off to the lake. I could hear someone running toward me. I continued walking and then I heard Ron calling and soon he fell into step beside me. When I glanced at him, he looked like he had just got out of bed. His hair was sticking out all over the place. I smiled at his matted bed-head. I had heard his girlfriend from another town had moved in with him. His parents were bragging about Ron's new girlfriend at Mother's place the other day. It was supposed to make me feel bad. I smiled.

"How did you know I was leaving?" I asked.

"Oh, I got up to go to the toilet and saw you standing there on the hill."

I felt my face go red. He always had a way of embarrassing me. What did he go and say that for? He was about as sophisticated as a piece of driftwood. No, that was an insult to the driftwood. I didn't say anything else as I continued walking. He said nothing more until we came to the shim-shack where he suddenly pulled me to a stop. With a smile, he gave me a big hug and whispered, "C.B.T.M. Charlie." It was a short form he began using when we were teenagers so other people by the station wouldn't understand. He had always said that every time I left for school. It stood for "come back to me." I giggled as I watched him disappear back down the path.. I smiled as I walked on. This time I wasn't going to school. And, maybe I wouldn't be coming back.

The people forgot about me. Their children have never even heard of me. The adults don't remember anymore. The old have no one to listen but I... I will not be forgotten. I will make them know that I still exist. I will make them get to know me again. I exist. I am here, always have been – right among them.

Now, I've been watching this girl. There was something different about her. Right from the moment she was born, I knew she was an old one. She could become the bridge from the past to the present. I don't quite know how that is going to work. I just have to wait and see. She comes and goes and doesn't seem to know what she is supposed to do. She seems lost. I have never actually followed her when she gets on the train. Maybe I will. Good-looking girl. Interesting... but I don't think she likes me. Maybe she doesn't like ravens. Hmmm. Perhaps she will like me better soft and quiet.

I continued down the path to the C.N. Railway stop. We had long since stopped calling it a station since it was no longer a station as such but more like an open shack. Strange, there's that black and white dog again. It meets me when I get off the train and it comes to meet me when I'm about to get back on the train.

I put my heavy suitcases down and reached to scratch the dog's head. Yes, yes, my welcoming committee and my last farewell. I didn't know whose dog he was. Strange that. I used to know the name of every dog in the community, and the few cats there were.

My hand came away gritty. Yuck! I patted his head. He walked me to the train stop and sat down beside my suitcases. There was absolutely no one around except me and this dog.

There were a few dogs barking somewhere by the shoreline. Soon, the postal clerk showed up with the morning's mailbag. Nothing much passed between us other than a nod. We waited as the distant hum of the coming train became louder. Soon, the train came to a hissing stop and I brushed the top of the dog's head one last time and picked up my suitcases. I boarded the train, determined that I would not be coming back again.

It was mid-afternoon when I got off at Sioux Lookout, Ontario. It was beginning to rain. I walked briskly across the cold parking lot and across the street to the Sioux Hotel. After paying for a room, I lugged my suitcases up the stairs and down the hall to the room at the end. Just as I turned the key, I heard a voice across the hall that sounded just like Fred's. It couldn't be! He should be at his trapline by now. I entered the room and made a beeline for the tub.

When I was up to my neck in warm water, I heard Fred's voice again from one of the rooms.

Freddy...

I happened to be on my way to the store in June when I noticed a baseball game going on in the field by the railway tracks. I sat on the store windowsill with several other ladies and watched the game for a while when I noticed Freddy among them. I had heard that his wife had died in a car accident the year before. I never heard if they had any children. Now, there he was looking so handsome in that t-shirt. I could hear him laughing. Then, during a break, he came running toward the store, and his face lit up when he noticed me. I got very shy for some reason. He walked right up to me and gave me two dollars saying, "Get two pop for me. I'll come and get them in a while." He turned and ran back to the field. I became aware that the ladies were giggling and whispering together. I knew it really looked like Fred and I were so familiar with each other that he would come up to me like that and ask me to get something for him. I had not seen him for several years and, oh, I was so embarrassed. I went into the store though and bought the pop then put them down beside me on the windowsill and watched the rest of the game.

Sure enough, Fred came running over after the game and stopped in front of me. He handed me one of the pop and sat down on the windowsill beside me. The ladies retreated into the store where I was sure they continued whispering. He talked about the game for a bit and nothing much else that I could remember because my heart was thumping so loud. I was afraid he could actually hear it. Later that evening, Mom told me that Fred had come by later when I wasn't home.

That was the evening I went paddling in the canoe and met a bear in the lake. I never knew bears swam that fast. I had just paddled around the bend into the bay when I met it. His eyes looked bug-sore, yet he swam with such speed and determination, and with a loud "humph" veered away from me. He sounded exactly like Hugh, my stepfather, though now I call him Dad, and everyone else calls him O. I back-paddled and drifted while I watched the bear reach the shoreline, saw him shake off the water, turn to take a last long look at me then disappear into the bushes without a noise. I wished I had some food in the canoe with me. I could have thrown it into the bush where he went in. That sounds just like me. It is only when something is over that I wish I had said or done this or that.

Anyway, back to Freddy. I met Freddy once more after that — quite by accident. I had gone to look for a scarf I thought I'd dropped somewhere along the railroad tracks the day before when I had been out collecting flowers of all sorts the day before. So, I went to retrace my steps. Mom hated the flowers, saying it brought in the bees. But, I liked to have flowers on the table. I knew she was just disappointed that all her preaching to me since I was a child about not picking wildflowers had not done any good. There I was with a handful of wildflowers of all kinds and the scarf I'd found was threatening to blow away again when I saw Freddy sitting on a rock by the rock cliff. He just stared at me for a long moment then he smiled but never said a thing. I continued walking along the railroad until I was parallel to him and stopped. I turned and looked at him, but he just sat there smiling. I smiled then started to laugh softly. He looked so silly sitting there, totally tongue-tied. I was just about to ask him what he was doing there when I saw a movement off to the side through the bush. A lady with a paddle still in her hand was coming up the path from the portage. It was Karen. She had two small children at home and her husband worked out of town. I saw the look on Freddy's face just as I turned and skipped over the railroad tracks, ran around behind the rock cliff and on to the path that lead directly to Mom's place. My knees were shaking when I came to a stop behind the cabin. Karen would not have seen me. That was why he didn't do anything. He knew she was coming. He simply had not known what to do.

Now, I laughed softly as I got out of the tub. Oh, you never know. Maybe there were other people with her and they had just gone out for a canoe ride. Yeah. Then what was he doing there? Why didn't he say anything? I knew back then that I had caught him red-handed. That was the same evening I got the call from my sister in Nipigon saying she was working and wanted me to come babysit for the summer.

I got out of the tub and dressed. After lounging around in the room for several hours, I decided to go out for supper. I had to go to the bank to take out some money and I still needed to pick up some food and snacks for the daylong ride to Port Arthur the next day. Although, I would end up paying more to get a taxi from Fort William to get to Port Arthur... it was cheaper just to pay the extra and get off at Port Arthur. See? It was when I got just like this, that I would drive my mother crazy. "Enough, Channie!" she'd sigh. It had got to a point where I could never carry on a conversation with her. That skinny runt of a stepfather always got his measly whiny voice in, cutting me off, as if I had not said anything at all. I yanked on my coat and looked up at the blotch-stained ceiling for a few minutes and took several long deep breaths. I always ended up getting angry about things I could do nothing about. And, since when did Dad become my "stepfather" again? Man, he did have a way though of letting you know that you were not wanted.

I came away from the bank with three hundred and sixty dollars in my purse. It was all of my savings from after-school jobs and summer program jobs and babysitting money. I was feeling carefree and happy as I wandered slowly down the street, looking at the store window displays. Coming back from the grocery store, arms loaded with paper bags, I glanced at the theatre sign. It showed a movie there that I might like to see.

After depositing the bags on the table in my room, I went slowly back down the stairs, out of the hotel and down the street to a restaurant. I settled into a corner booth and ordered my supper. I always travelled with a pen and piece of paper, so I took it out and started writing about what I would do when I got to Port Arthur. I always did that before I went somewhere just to see how close or way off I would actually be. I signed Janine at the top corner of the page before I flipped the page over. That's my proper name. Mother and the older people called me Channie or Channine. The kids I grew up with just called me Charlie.

Sipping at a cup of coffee, I saw a man get up from the other side of the partition and knew from the back of his head that it was Fred. He turned but I pretended that I was very busy writing something important on the piece of paper. Sure enough, I could feel his eyes on me. I heard footsteps and then there he was sliding into the seat across from me.

"When did you come in?" he asked with a broad smile on his face. He threw his head back to get the left droop of his hair away from his eye. That slow grin seemed to light his eyes into mischievous glints of dark brown pools. I dropped my gaze.

"Got in this afternoon. What are you doing here?"

My paper forgotten, I looked into those dark brown dancing eyes again. I don't know what it was but I always felt that tingle go down to my toes when he looked at me like that.

"I came to get some trapping supplies. Where are you going?"

The waitress came and took my order and refilled my coffee

cup and then she was asking if he wanted more coffee. Now he had a cup of coffee in front of him too.

"Port Arthur. When did you get here?"

"Yesterday. How long are you staying?"

He sure made a lot of noise clinking the spoon in his cup as he deposited another teaspoon of sugar. I watched his fingers tightly holding the spoon, stirring and clinking the cup a few more times, as he seemed to be thinking very hard about what he should say next.

"I'm leaving tomorrow. When are you leaving?"

He was putting in some more sugar and rapidly stirring his cup again.

"Can't you stay here tomorrow? Stay another day?"

There went another spoonful of sugar into his cup. I started to smile. How much sugar was that now: five teaspoons? I glanced up into his face and my smile disappeared. He thought I was smiling because I liked what he said.

"We can rent a boat you know. We'll go for a boat ride and maybe go fishing."

His face was all lit up and smiling broadly when a lady stood up at the table he had just vacated. Oh my, he was with someone. She turned and gave him a dirty look as she marched down the aisle and stormed out the door. That was bad.

"You left someone sitting there by herself?" I asked, looking over the top of my cup. Steady. My hands were shaking. Keep your eyes down, I thought to myself, concentrate on the cup.

Looking sheepish now, he said, "Just someone I was talking to. She was waiting for her husband actually. He had to go to the bank or something. They have a trapline."

I knew he was lying to me.

"I am leaving tomorrow," I said.

I watched him take a sip of his coffee and pause before he swallowed very slowly. The waitress came and I smiled and tried to concentrate on the food she placed before me as Fred asked for another cup of coffee. I had to sit there and try to eat with him watching everything I put on my fork, watching it travel to my mouth and watching me very intently as I tried to chew and swallow. I was very hungry but I soon lost my appetite. I was so nervous and uncomfortable with him watching me so closely.

Leaning forward over the table toward me, he asked, "What are you doing after this?"

I had moved until the back seat was pressed flat against my back and now I looked around, trying to distract myself.

Any answer I gave him would sound like a suggestion or an invitation, so I just said, "Nothing."

"Then, let's go see a movie, eh? Come on, just this once."

That means I would spend the whole evening with him. I felt like running away at the moment. Now what? What was I going to do? The waitress came and put the bill down on the table and Fred put it in his pocket. This was going too fast, the situation was getting away on me.

I leaned toward him and said, "That is my bill. I'll pay for my food."

He was leaning toward me again, bringing his face very close to mine, and looking right at me, he said, "No, I am paying for your meal. My treat. Then I am taking you to the show and we'll have a nice evening. Alright?"

I leaned back wondering how I was going to get out of this.

Fred was on his feet now. "Come on. Let's go for a walk."

I stood and followed him to the counter and watched him pay. I hated this feeling, like I was his wife or something. The way he paid my bill. Then I followed him out the door and into the street. I felt his hand on my elbow as he started telling me a story about his life in Auden. He led me down the street that went under the railway tracks and on through toward the lake.

He was saying, "One spring, I was cutting wood behind my cabin when these crows started creating such a ruckus over my head. I figured maybe they had a nest close by and wanted me out of there. I just ignored them. Then, the next minute, just as I swung my axe to split the wood, one bird dive-bombed me, knocked my hat off and it fell just as the axe blade came down, right on top of it, and I split my hat in half."

I laughed as he continued.

"And then there was another time I had a tug-of-war with a seagull. I was fishing down by the lake and had caught a tiny four-inch pike that had my small jig hook so far down its throat that I couldn't reach it with my fingers. So I left it flipping around on the shore and went up to the cabin to get the pliers. As I was coming back down the path, I saw a big old seagull circling around my fish. 'Hey!' I yelled as I ran down to the lake. Too late! He had swooped down and grabbed the fish. I saw my fishing rod flip around and dove for it. But by now that bugger had swallowed my fish. The fishing line was just singing as I got a good hold of the rod and started reeling in. He was flapping his wings, getting really ticked off, but I just kept turning the handle. He was flapping and flapping his wings then finally he skid-landed on the ground. I kept reeling in and he kept hopping and skidding closer toward me when finally, his head shot forward and that little fish whizzed by just missing my face."

I didn't know whether to believe him or not. The hand on my elbow had slid into my hand and firmly held mine. He told me about his deceased wife, his relatives and his aunt. It was evening now and I found myself relaxing at the sight of the lake. I knew his mother had died and he mentioned the relatives he had heard about living all over the place. Some he didn't know and others he happened to meet briefly. All he had left that he cared about was his aunt.

I had a fall coat on but the wind was blowing from the north. We stopped by the beach and he stood leaning against a tree.

My voice shook from the cold as I asked, "Do you have any children?"

Quite unexpectedly, he reached out and pulled me to him. I felt instant warmth as his arms went around me. He acted like I had always been there and that it was quite natural for him to push the hair from my face before brushing my forehead with a kiss. He drew me close once more.

It was a few minutes before his voice, close to my ear, said, "Not that I know of. My wife was two months pregnant when she was killed. I didn't know about that until they told me after the accident. Nobody else knows. I didn't bother telling the family. I thought it would only add more grief."

I stood perfectly still, not knowing what to say. I was in

unknown territory and didn't know how to get out of this situation. I only knew that I wanted out. I wanted to be in control. I didn't like things "happening to me." I wanted to "do" the things that happened. Oh, never mind. I thought.

I pushed myself away slowly and said, "Let's get back. It's getting cold."

He did not object but took my hand again as we retraced our steps up the street. He wanted to know about my life.

My story was short, punctured with a few funny events in the bush at the trapline. Nothing was said about the incident by the railroad tracks. There was still a half hour before the show started so, back into the restaurant we went. This time, the conversation was a bit more relaxed. I watched him put one and a half teaspoons of sugar into his coffee. I made no comment about the coffee with the five teaspoons of sugar.

An elderly couple beside us caught my attention. The old man was saying in Ojibway, "We'll eat a big meal tonight. We have a long day tomorrow." Freddy was talking about life at home and how difficult it was without any of his family left. When the waitress came, the old woman, being the one who spoke English ordered steak and potatoes. When Freddy was into his second cup of coffee, the food for the old couple came. After a while, when Freddy was talking about being at the end of his rope and that he had just up and left his job and that was why he was at the baseball game during the summer, I heard the old woman ask, "Why do they feel they need to put these big green leaves on our plates with the food?" "Oh," said the old man, "They're probably to wipe our hands with." He proceeded to wipe his fingertips with the lettuce.

I smiled, thinking that if there can be finger bowls, then there should be finger-wipe leaves. The only problem was, no one had thought about the "finger-wipe" leaves in restaurants like we use when we eat in the bush.

"What are you smiling at?"

Freddy was looking right at me. Since I really did not have an excuse why I wasn't listening I just said, "I'll tell you when we leave."

A few minutes later, the story brought out a loud laugh from him as we headed to the theatre. There were only a few people at the show, mainly teenagers up in the front rows. I kept my hands busy with pop and popcorn until about half an hour into the movie when I felt his hand over mine again. He seemed intent on slowly feeling every single one of my fingers. I jumped as the crashing train in the movie thundered onto the screen and came to a grinding halt right in front of my face. Feeling silly, I turned to Fred and giggled. He leaned very close to me. I pushed him back with my elbow and pulled my hand away to resume eating my popcorn. Without being too obvious, my elbow kept him at distance and I kept my hands out of reach by slowly munching on the popcorn throughout the whole movie.

When the movie was over, I knew I had another problem. His arm was still around me as we left the theatre.

"Would you like to stop at the restaurant for a cup of coffee?" he asked.

"Are you kidding? I'm full of pop and popcorn. No, you go. That's it for me tonight."

I tried to distance myself from his body but his arm stayed

firmly around my shoulder. He made no comment as we made our way to the hotel. When we came through the door, the manager at the desk said, "Hello there, Fred!" I caught the look that passed between them as I went up the stairs with Fred behind me. Darn him anyway! I hated being made to feel like this. I sensed him at my back when I stopped at my door and waited for him to move away before I opened my door. When I finally turned, his hands came up to my arms.

"That's it? You don't want to sit and talk?" he said.

I shook my head.

Quite persistent, he continued, "Are you going in? Or, would you like to come to my room for a minute?"

I smiled and shook my head, "No, Fred. It was nice of you to spend time with me. It was good to talk to you. But, I have to go in now. Take care in the bush. Goodbye."

I turned to unlock the door but he still stood behind me. I held the key in my hand and said, "What are you waiting for? Go."

His hands came down on my shoulders and were turning me around when a loud burst of noise came from the bar downstairs. People were coming out and making their way up the stairs.

I moved back quickly and said, "Goodbye, Freddy. Take care." I opened the door and slipped inside just as I heard a woman cry, "Fred, oh Fred! Where have you been? Come here."

I unpacked the groceries and listened to their noise in the room down the hall before I heard them thunder their way back down the stairs. I got my stuff ready to pack in my suitcases and went to bed. The train to Port Arthur would leave before five o'clock in the morning. I thought about the strange evening while drifting to sleep.

In what seemed like only a few minutes, I heard a commotion on the stairway and knew it was Freddy. I looked at my travel clock. It was just after one o'clock. Oh, no! His footsteps were coming to my door. I heard a shuffle against the door and then a hesitant knock. A second later came another knock. I heard him whisper loudly, "Aw, come on, Charlie. I just want to see you. Just for one second. I just need to look at your beautiful face once more. I just thought . . . please Charlie! Keep yourself for me! You are mine you know, remember our parents? They had an agreement you know. Remember? You are mine, Charlie. Don't you ever forget that, okay?"

Another knock. What was I going to do? My heart was pounding. Fear? Yes. I was scared. I was always afraid of drunks. Suddenly a thought occurred to me, which made me grin. If you could only hear yourself, Fred? "Charlie, I want you, Charlie keep yourself for me!"

As I giggled softly, I heard another voice coming up the stairs. It was the woman. Footsteps were coming close to my room, when I heard her say, "Fred, you silly man, that is not your room." Then I heard a door open and the murmur of voices coming from the room across the hall became quite muffled. They were *both* inside the room.

Well, you know where you can go, Freddy. What was he talking about . . . our parents? Yes, I remembered hearing something like that. I smiled. Keep yourself for me. And what was he doing now? Stupid man!

Chapter Two

The next morning, after only three hours sleep, I was at the station boarding the train to Port Arthur. I found a seat on the side away from the town and sat with the trees and bushes outside my window. I pulled out the sheet of paper and what I had written on the train to Sioux Lookout the day before. I read:

This is going to be a long day, but I look forward to all the stops to see if I know any of the people. I will watch them looking out their windows and from their porches. I will wave from my open window. I knew how much a wave from the train meant to me when I watched one go by.

I put the paper down and looked out the window. It was beginning to rain outside. I was not going to be waving at people from any open window today. I sat with my head down. I was very tired. I could feel sorry for myself for a while. What can I write? I began:

Nothing can penetrate the heavy cloak of loneliness that I am feeling. I said goodbye to my community yesterday, knowing that I may not be coming back and that I had not told them about it. The hurt is more intense about leaving Mom, but then I always felt that I had lost Mom when my stepfather moved in. What actually hurt more? Losing Mom or leaving Mom?

No, it was not Mom; it was □home□. I lost my home when he moved in. Either way, as long as she was alive and well, she was still Mom whether I was with her or not. The problem here Janine, is that you just don□t like your stepfather. There. I said it. I hate the measly whiny skinny weasel. I know that I am trying to blame him and the community for my sadness and trying to shut out the pain I am feel-

ing about Freddy.

Now, wait a minute. Why am I feeling bad about Freddy? Because I□m a hopeless romantic that□s why. I loved the way he was when we went to the beach. I liked the way he laughed and I loved the sound of his voice. But wait. No. The last voice I heard was the drunken slurred voice at my door. Then there is the suffocating misery and desperation of feeling very much alone, hopeless, and helpless to do anything about anything. I have nowhere to go, no one to love or to love me. What do I feel about Fred? I liked the feeling I had when he was with me. He made me feel loved and wanted. I wanted him to love me. Then it would be okay to love him back. Okay? I do not like the feeling I got when other people were around. Ah, this is too depressing!

I paused a moment, put my pen down and looked back out the window. That feeling which had nearly choked me to death the night before was back. It was a dream that descended on me nightly . . . a big black cloud that clamped around my throat and choked me while I struggled for breath, until I discovered a deeper strength from somewhere within me to live. What was this thing? At other times, I would dream about being seated with an elder by a shoreline. I could never figure out if the elder was a man or woman. Not that it mattered. He or she was intent on showing me different sizes of bones laid out in a row on a piece of leather. I would remember that, although the language sounded ancient, I had no problem understanding. Then I would wake up. Sometimes weeks or months would go by before the dream and the instructions continued where it left off. Weird! I wish I knew someone to ask about what these dreams meant. But, I had no one.

The train was moving now and the conductor was making his rounds. When I handed him my ticket he said a very cheerful, "Good morning." I nodded, and looked out the window while thinking how much I hated cheerful people on mornings like this.

I dozed off and on throughout the day, briefly looking around at each stop then going back to sleep. It was still raining. What was left of the leaves was blowing around everywhere. I watched the telephone poles march up and down the hills all the way to Lake Superior. The conductor kept stopping by my seat trying to carry on a conversation, but I didn't feel like talking. At one stop, an elderly couple got on the train and sat down on the seat opposite me. They appeared to have been drinking. The old woman talked about a grandson, their only grandson, who it seemed was not much interested in the plans they had for him. Suddenly, the old man focused his attention on me and asked me what my name was, where I came from, and where I was going. That I was not married and never had been was of quite an interest to them.

The old woman leaned close to me, locked her steely black eyes at me and asked quite seriously, "Would you marry our grandson? We have a mine. It is a nickel mine and he is going to be a very rich man. We don't have any other children, you see. We raised him since he was a little boy. Would you marry him?"

If I had ever thought of receiving a proposal for marriage, this way was definitely not in my dreams. I just smiled and turned to the window. This situation was getting really bad and for some reason I got a weird sensation that I was about to burst into uncontrollable laughter. I blinked back tears and continued to stare out the window.

To my relief, they got off at the next stop. I never did know what their names were.

I picked up a newspaper that someone had left on the empty seat across the aisle and read every section of it. I never realized that so many things went on in the world.

It was evening when the slow leisurely ride finally came to an end and the train from Sioux Lookout to Port Arthur finally reached its destination. I got my snack bag and coat together with my suitcases and stood in line with the few other passengers and descended to the platform amidst blowing wind and rain. I walked with my head down into the waiting room to make some phone calls. There were a few people I could call to see if they could put me up for the night. It was Thursday, so they should be home. Then, suddenly there was Linda grabbing the suitcase on my right.

"What are you doing here?" I asked in surprise.

She laughed, "I was waiting for you. Come this way. I'm parked over there."

I followed her out of the building and to her little car. We got the suitcases into the trunk then got into the car. It was quiet inside, while outside was the sound of freezing rain pelting against the windshield. When Linda started the car, the heat came on.

"You couldn't have waited long. The car is still warm," I said.

Linda laughed as she backed up. "I came tearing down Red River Road trying to beat the train otherwise I'd have had to wait to cross the railroad tracks."

I giggled. "Oh yes, I forgot. How did you know I was coming in?" I asked as we sat at the railway crossing, waiting for the same train to go by.

"Tom the mailman called me."

I smiled and said, "And how did Tom the mailman know where I was going when I saw him at the train stop yesterday morning?"

Linda laughed outright as the train went slowly by. "Your mother was in the store later that morning. She told him when he asked then he called me."

I laughed, "How news travels fast."

Linda lit a cigarette and blew the smoke out the window. She said, "I heard all about last night too."

I turned to her as the car sped up the hill. "What about last night?"

She giggled and gave me one of those "sideways glance lift-of-the-shoulder" things she does when she goes into juicy gossip.

"Well, the guy that works up there saw you with, what's his name? Fred, isn't it?"

I heaved a big sigh and watched the lights go on at Hillcrest Park as down we drove into one of the side streets.

"He said he saw the two of you walking hand in hand to the beach and when he was coming back from his mother's place, he saw you coming out of the theatre with Fred's arm around you and then you both went into the hotel."

I leaned over to look at her, "Are you saying this with a straight face or are you eating your cigarette?"

At that, she actually broke into a coughing fit as she parked in front of the driveway of her apartment building.

"Fred or no Fred, you really should stop smoking those little cigars," I said.

Linda stomped on the cigarette and said, "They are not little cigars, they're cigarettes and they're light, not as strong as cigars."

I smiled, "Same difference. They're just shaped a little different that's all."

Now she was really laughing. "Oh, you really get me. We're not talking about cigarettes are we? We're talking about Fred. Oh you clever girl."

She grabbed one suitcase. I grabbed the other one and followed her down the four steps to her basement apartment. Wondering what on earth she had meant by that last remark, I watched her bang my suitcase along the sides of the stairs and down against her leg which was tightly encased in purple pants.

Chapter Three

Several days later, I got a job at Indian Affairs. Linda worked at the Counseling Unit in Port Arthur and I got a position as a temporary receptionist in the Fort William office. We sometimes saw each other at lunch hour, but only if she was coming my way. We also had some pretty interesting suppers together at her place that first month. She brought in take-out food to supplement my "home-cooked" meals. One time, we ended up with a supper of egg rolls, bologna and macaroni with tomato sauce. Another time, we had pizza with fried fish and bannock. One time we decided to go out for supper and Linda suggested we order lobsters.

"I don't eat lobster," I said.

"Why not?" she asked.

Quite seriously I looked right across the table at her and whispered, "Because they're too much like me. They turn red when they're thrown into hot water."

Linda laughed until she wiped tears from her eyes.

But for all her good heart, I knew Linda needed some privacy. I overheard her saying over the phone that she couldn't go out that weekend because she had company. That was it. This was her place and I was in the way. I doubled my efforts to find my own apartment.

At work, I began getting calls from people from my own community who had moved to Port Arthur and found out where I worked. They called at all hours of the day, which soon began to aggravate my supervisor. I explained that the first thing a city dweller discovers is that whenever a person from your community knows you are in the city, you can be assured that they will call on you to help them out. It is expected of them to do so and it is expected of you to provide the assistance. However, I never got more than one phone call from each person. I take it I was of no help to them whatsoever because I didn't have a car. Now, I'm not saying that I didn't help in other ways.

Some time during the second week, I came home late from work with an armful of groceries, or "greens and fruit" as I called the only fresh things that Linda kept in the refrigerator. Any milk she ever had in the fridge was always sour or in the process of turning, so I, being a non-fresh dairy intake person, being what she called a "natural bush-Indian" couldn't stomach fresh milk. The only thing she ever did have in the fridge was the "greens and fruit." She never said she was "going for groceries"; it was "going for greens and fruit." Anyway, I had just shut the door with the heel of my high-heeled shoe when I heard her say, "Charlie? Channie? Channine? No, you got the wrong number," before she dropped the phone back on the hook.

She came into the room, glanced at me and asked, "What's wrong with you?"

"Who was that?"

"I don't know. Same guy. He calls once in awhile. Wants to talk to Charlie first and then says Channie or Channine. What?"

"Did you ask him his name?"

"Yeah, said his name was Fredrick and that he wanted to talk to Channie or Charlie or something. Why?"

Deep inside me, a deep rumble of laughter started. It slowly travelled up my chest and burst out of my throat before I could take a breath. I was right into a belly laugh when I managed to gasp, "Fred... rick! And he wants to talk to Char...lie."

Through the tears of my hysterical laughter, I could see that Linda thought I had surely lost it. When she started her hesitant laughter, it was as though she were trying to gauge if she should be laughing at all.

Suddenly, as if she had snapped, she turned me around and plopped me down on the kitchen chair and said, "Now, you stop this nonsense! Tell me who this Fredrick is! Is this the Fred at Sioux Lookout? And who on earth is this Charlie or Channie he's been asking for?"

I crossed my arms over my middle and laughed, doubling over until I was able to lean back on the chair. She was seated across from me with another cigarette going up in quick puffs of smoke. I wiped my eyes and said with a resigned sigh, "Fredrick is the 'Fred' who happened to be in Sioux Lookout while I was on my way down here, and 'Charlie'. Well, when we were kids my family just called me 'Channie' but to the others I was known as 'Channine' because there is no 'J' sound in the Ojibway language for 'Janine'. It becomes 'Ch' and it soon became shortened to 'Channie', which sounds exactly the same as the Chanii they use for the name 'Charlie'. Chanii is the Ojibway translation of Charlie. Since there are no 'r' or 'l' sounds in the Ojibway language they become 'n' sounds in Ojibway. Therefore, I am Charlie."

At that moment, a runaway tomato shot out of the bag and rolled across the kitchen floor and then bounced against a potato skin in the corner of the bottom cupboard. I hadn't noticed the potato skin there before. I saw Linda reach over to pick up the shrivelled-up brown remnant. She didn't touch the tomato but seemed intent on studying the potato peel as if trying to determine how old it was, or how long it had been lying there.

I continued, "Fred has been trying to call me at the office since I got here. I was hoping he wouldn't find out where I lived because I don't want to talk to him. If he calls again, just tell him I don't live here and you don't know where I am."

I actually saw her shoulders slump as she shot another puff of smoke into the air and said, "Well now how the heck was I supposed to know these things, eh?"

"I'm sorry, Linda. I just didn't want you getting mixed up in this. It felt good to know that I could disappear after work to somewhere in Port Arthur and that he couldn't find me."

Linda smashed her cigarette into the ashtray. "Well, now he's found you. So, what are you going to do? Does he know that you don't want to talk to him?"

I felt my body sag against the chair. "I'll find a place of my own and . . . no, I haven't talked to him yet. Because if I talk to him, I'll never get the chance to tell him that I don't want to talk to him and that I don't want him to call me anymore."

Linda jumped up and threw the potato peel into the garbage, grabbed the bags off the counter and dropped them over by the kitchen sink while saying over her shoulder, "You are not moving out just because you don't want to talk to the guy. If you want me to tell him, I will."

I saw the tomato gush its guts out under her shoe and heard her swear as she stood looking at the mess on the floor. I started giggling and reached down to pick up the tomato pulp but by then she was there with a wet cloth to wipe up the mess. Both of us were squatting on the floor when she suddenly faced me, looking at me eye to eye. My eyes dropped to blink back the tears. Finally, I just threw the tomato into the sink and settled down on the floor with my back against the cupboard.

Linda flopped down on the floor with her back against the stove and we sat facing each other on the kitchen floor. She said, "Talk!"

This was always the hardest thing she asked me to do. I remember that it was in my second year of high school when she was first assigned to me as a counselor. It was at a time when I thought I was near the breaking point. Linda had parked her car on the side of the road and just sat there waiting for me to talk.

"Talk!" she had said.

It sounded so simple but telling was something that I had never done in my whole life. I didn't know how. How could I possibly tell her what I was going through? Or what I was feeling? Or what was happening to me? I would sound stupid, ridiculous, self-defeating, self-pitying, confused and totally dumb. And, who would care anyway? Nobody cared! What could she possibly do to help me? I remember getting angry with myself when I began to cry. Later, I'd blown my nose, taken a big sigh and stared out the window.

She'd lit a cigarette, opened a window and said, "Now, talk."

I remember asking, "About what?"

She had replied, "Not 'about what', tell me why? Why do you cry? Why are you feeling the way you do? Why do you not tell anyone what is bothering you? Why don't you tell me, now? Don't worry if it makes any sense or not, just get it all out."

I had laughed at that. And then for the first time in my life, I'd talked. I talked and talked and talked. When I was finished, I'd waited for the big "slam down" that never came.

When I'd glanced at her, she'd smiled. Later, she drove to a fast-food place and bought some food. We were munching on the hamburgers near the park when she'd asked, "Do you know what you need to do?"

I remember saying, "About what? I can't do anything. What can I do?"

No. Yes. I hadn't known until it came out and then by the time it crashed against my brain, I'd known what it was. "Yes, I'd known then what I needed to do."

She had said, and continually reminded me over the years, that she was there whenever I needed help. I remember feeling emptied out, lighter and clean. Now, here she was asking me to "talk" again.

"It's nothing major," I began.

Linda interrupted, "No. No judgments remember? Just talk, straight out."

I smiled at her and said, "Yeah. If I remember correctly, the first time I 'talked' it was like throwing up and cleaning it up after. And you just sat back and watched."

She smiled at me and sent another cloud of smoke to the ceiling.

I took a deep breath and began again, "I don't have a home anymore. I have nowhere to go. I mean I don't belong anywhere. I feel like I'm trapped when I am at Mom's and I need to escape. I am terrified that one day I may never be able to leave there. So, when I come to the city, I feel such a relief that I can disappear and they can't find me. I like who I am, when I am here. I am independent and I want to be on my own. I need to know that I can make it here in the city, all by myself. I need to know that I can take care of myself. I think I don't want to talk to Fred because he is very authoritative and I become instantly shy, quiet, and turn back into the obedient girl that I am . . . or have to be when I am back home. I don't want to be reminded of that girl and I don't know if I can be that 'me' in the city and be able to talk to, never mind face, a man who only knows me as the girl back home. Sometimes I have dreams of Fred or somebody like him and I am his wife. Suddenly I am like my mother and then a black cloud comes down and tries to choke me to death because . . . I am not like my mother. When I'm at home, it happens night after night – the black cloud, I mean. Or sometimes, I dream I am at the train station and the train is coming but I can't find my ticket anywhere. Or I dream that I have absolutely no money at all to get away and I get this horrible cornered feeling like I'm a caged animal. I can't get away and that is when this oppressive black cloud comes down and tries to choke me to death. I get so darned scared that I might not wake up ever again. At times, I actually struggle with both hands at my throat trying to pull or push the black cloud off my neck and face, and then I'll wake up just gasping for breath and sweating buckets."

Linda sat there looking at me for a second before she jumped up and made for the table saying, "Gotta have a smoke."

I got up off the floor, rubbing my backside and glanced at Linda as I said, "It's too hard a floor for this bony butt."

Linda giggled as she turned around. She walked toward me then slowly put her arms around me and gave me a big hug. I froze. I was not used to being hugged like that. I had never experienced a sister-to-sister hug or mother-to-daughter hug, let alone a friend-to-friend hug in my entire life. I didn't know what I was supposed to do. My arms came up and kind of touched the dead air between her shoulders. Then my arms dropped.

Linda stood back smiling as I shrugged. She blew another puff of smoke toward the darkened ceiling before she said, "I hate it when you do that. The longer you stay here, I'm going to forget to speak altogether."

That, coming from one who's always after me to talk. Let's face it, my sisters who had been raised in residential schools had raised me; and here I was trying to function as normal a human being as I imagined one to be.

I gave a weak, half-hearted smile at Linda as she gave my shoulders a little pat before we turned to the frying pan on the stove.

"I'll slice and fry the beef heart I bought. What did you bring, Linda?"

"Chicken chop suey. Well, that and greens... yuck!"

That night in my dream, I met the elder with the brown cape over his or her shoulder along a sand beach where I was instructed to dig a large pit and layer it with cedar branches. Over the pit, according to directions, I constructed a rack with more cedar branches. After more elaborate preparations, I understood that I was to do my last battle with that black thing which had plagued me all my life. I had no sooner finished than I felt a shadow loom over my head. After a very long battle, I threw the thing down into the pit and set fire to the rack. With an explosion of smoke and fire, it plummeted down on top of the thing. I heard a horrible screech before the black disappeared. In that instant, I felt a tremendous rush of strength and power flowing into my body. I awoke drenched in sweat with my heart beating hard as if I had actually been in a physical battle. A powerful sense of calmness and peace flooded my body as I straightened out in my bed. Lying on my back, I went right back to sleep.

Chapter Four

One day, I came running in from a pouring rainstorm to find a tall bald-headed thin man standing in the middle of the kitchen. I stopped dead still by the entrance and started to back out when he said, "Oh, I'm sorry. I startled you. I'm Joe. I'm just waiting for Linda."

Just then, Linda's voice came from the bedroom, "Is that you Janine? Oh, wait a moment, just introduce yourselves."

I closed the door and came in and deposited my wet shopping bag and purse, and peeled off my soaking wet jacket. What a sleazy type, I thought. What does she see in this guy? Oh, well, none of my business. She had never talked about her friends and there was no need for me to ask.

I went into my bedroom and waited. They left, with a shout from Linda, "Don't forget to leave the back light on for me."

"Yeah, sure. Have a nice evening!" I stretched myself out full-length on the bed. It was nice to be alone.

The next evening, Linda decided to pick up Joe on the way to dropping me off at the mall. I sat in the car and watched her walk up the few steps to a house on a very busy street. I noticed that the houses were so close to the street that the front steps came out on to the sidewalk. After what seemed like a very long time, they finally came out and Joe was wearing black- and red-checkered pants. Suddenly, he tripped on the bottom step and shot out full speed into the street with his legs trying to catch up with his head. He was almost to the other side before he got his balance. Four cars went by before he could come back to where Linda stood with her hand over her mouth and I heard her say, "Are you all right?" How he had missed the cars in the heavy traffic, I'll never know. I was near to killing myself laughing before they got to the car. I sat with a straight face

When the car finally came to a stop at the mall, I got out and thanked them for the ride and headed toward a bench. There was a big woman sitting there. I sat down beside her and she watched me laugh into my hands. Between gasps, I managed to say, "I'm sorry, but I just saw something very funny." When I finished laughing and sat there drying my eyes, she asked, "So, what was so funny?"

I told her and when I was done, I could see that she did not think it was funny at all. Oh, well, I thought, some people have absolutely no sense of humour. I got up and went into the store.

Three weeks later, I got a job interview at the Canada Manpower Centre in Port Arthur as a clerk typist. I remember that interview very well. I had been to the shoe stores the day before, trying to find shoes that would match my navy dress, but couldn't find any. My appointment for the interview was at one o'clock sharp and during my lunch hour, I ran across the street to a shoe store in a last-ditch effort to find a pair of dark navy shoes. Well, after trying on half a dozen navy shoes, none fit, and then the next thing you know, it was ten to one. I had only enough time to slip on my old black shoes, run to my office to deposit my coat and then run back across the street to the interview. I arrived all out of breath, but on time. I did really well, I thought. I answered all the questions; I was positive, full of spirit, knowledge and enthusiasm. It was only when I got back to the office that I sat back and let out a big sigh.

All the office girls gathered around me to hear how my interview went. Then someone asked how my lunch Keith had gone the other day.

Oh, yes, Keith, the guy who just showed up at the office one day. I sighed. I absolutely loved his sparkling bright blue eyes. His hair was light brown, flowing in gentle waves, and he had the loveliest lips I had ever seen on a man.

"Fine. Well, then at lunch today I went to the last shoe store on the block and tried on at least half a dozen shoes before I ran to the interview."

I put my feet up on the next chair and noticed in horror that I still had on one of the anklet "try-on-the-shoe-with-these" kind of nylons still draped down around my right ankle. I had gone to the interview with this thing on my foot.

I got a phone call the next day, saying that I had got the job. No one ever said anything about the strange stocking hanging around my right foot.

Soon after that, I found an apartment up on High Street in Port Arthur. It was in a nice location, tucked away from the main traffic but close enough to downtown. As the weeks went by, I would walk home and just tilt my head back to smell the fresh air. I knew that I could make it on my own. I had my paycheque in my purse and I had enough to pay my bills and set aside a bit each month. I always made a point of opening up an account at the nearest bank so I could accumulate enough money that would allow me to leave anytime I wanted to and go anywhere I wanted. Again, I dreaded being stuck in a place that I couldn't get out of because I didn't have money. For that reason, I always had what I called "get-out money" set aside.

It was around the end of November when it became obvious

that Keith was really going out of his way with the numerous lunches and quick coffee breaks with me, that "yes," he was getting my attention. He had started showing up at the office or just calling me on the phone to tell me jokes and, he never failed to make me laugh. He was the only one besides Linda who cared whether I was still alive in this city of strange faces. I wasn't clear about where he worked though. He always wore very nice business suits. All the girls went "gaga" every time he showed up. So, I was rather flattered that it was me he was interested in. He'd say something about the insurance business when I tried to press for more information and he'd quickly change the topic.

Took me awhile to figure out how to do this. To be a different kind of human, I mean. But, here I am. I am simply beautiful. Ha, ha, "those lovely blue eyes," eh? Silly girl. I will show you how lovely I can be, my little lost one. Ha, ha, ha. I am finding this very weird though, I mean being a white man and all. These people are deeply set in their ways, where you belong, what you should say, do, go, and who with. I am finding this very hard to understand. I also seem to be attracting certain kinds of white women and I'm not quite sure what to do about that either.

Trouble is, while I followed Channie to find out where she went when she left the land, I have come to want her for myself. I've always been known for that, you see. I love women, I especially love having sex with women and I find that I have come to want this woman more than anything I have wanted in a very, very long time. But, I also have a job to do.

One evening, Keith called my home number, which he got from Linda. He began calling every evening to tell me which funny movies were on TV. Then one night he called to ask if I liked Chinese food. Yes, sure I did. Anything was better than my cooking at that point. I even stopped by Linda's some evenings for some of her "bucket of take-out spaghetti and meatballs." They were fine. Not your everyday meal, but then neither was my macaroni and bologna. I agreed to meet Keith at a Chinese restaurant in downtown Fort William.

After over an hour bus ride, I entered the restaurant and paused at the door. I saw Keith at one of the tables talking to several people standing beside his table. I took no notice as I walked toward his table. It was only when I got close that I saw that the man and the two women were causing him some discomfort and then the blond-haired woman sat down across from him. It was at this point that I met his panic-stricken eyes. It was not the man and two women who were causing him this sudden discomfort; it was me! He didn't want me to be seen by these people. I turned around and walked back out. I continued down the street, crossed at the intersection, and stood for exactly three minutes by counting the usual thousand and one, thousand and two. He was a spineless worm! I rode the bus all the way home, thinking, "Yes, it was true. He was a spineless worm. We all know that worms have no spines, or do they? Now, I am not quite sure about that . . . I must look that up. Do worms have spines of some kind? There I go again!"

The following weekend, he called me saying, “Hi, how are things going at work?” “

Oh, fine,” I answered, then asked, “Aren’t you afraid someone’s going to find out that you are calling me?”

There was silence at the other end of the line before he said, “Janine, don’t get hateful. Please let me come and see you. You have not returned my calls. I’m sorry. I have been driving Linda crazy, calling her everyday because I don’t want you to get mad at me. Please, let me explain. It is not what it looked like at the restaurant . . . please, Janine. Would you like to go to the show with me on Saturday?”

I wasn’t doing anything on Saturday because I never do anything on Saturday. I hated the thought of sitting there again on a Saturday. I heard myself say, “I will meet you at the nine o’clock show, on Court Street, okay?”

Now, why did I say that?

I heard a big sigh of relief and then his voice full of enthusiasm came across the line, “Right on time. I’ll see you there. Wait outside; I’ll pay your way in. I’ll see you then. Good night, Janine.”

I mean, give me a break! Hey, I screwed up. I’m just not used to dealing with these pale-skinned, blue-eyed people. They play by their own kind of rules but I’m learning as fast as I can. Actually, I think I’m getting really good at this. I’ve already learned how to deal with those blond-haired women. I just say something like “I’m sorry but I am only interested in having a relationship with my own kind.” Ha, ha! The first time I said that, the woman’s eyes widened and she walked away without saying a word. Curious reaction. I still fly to my perch on the church steeple when Channie has gone to bed. I want her. I want her more than I have ever wanted anyone in a very, very, very, long time. I sense something from the familiar past, a past so strong in her presence that it emits an aura around her. I want that. I need that. That is where I once thrived in my full glorious and wonderful days of adventure, love and war. I want to be one with her so that I can be back in my old "home" even for a few slow minutes.

Saturday night came. I'd cashed my paycheque on Friday, paid my landlord the rent for the next month got my groceries for the next two weeks, put some more money in the bank, and still had a few dollars left. I did not want to be indebted to anybody so I arrived early for the show and paid my own way in. The show was close to starting when I finally decided to line up for pop and popcorn. He still hadn't arrived yet and I figured that whether he came or not, it wouldn't make much difference to me. I just thought that if he came, he could share with me if he didn't mind a large unbuttered popcorn and a large pop. As I stood in line, I heard a parka jacket zipper go up behind me and immediately felt the tension on my hair. When I went to move my head, I discovered to my horror that my hair was stuck to the man's jacket zipper stretched full belching over his big belly. I twisted to ease the tension as he struggled to push the zipper back down and I ended up with my nose directly against his belly.

We were involved in this weird attached dance with our four

hands struggling at the zipper and my hair, when the other people around us suddenly swarmed in, laughing and tugging. There was at least half a dozen pair of hands tugging at my hair. One hand hit me against the nose so hard I thought it was going to bleed. I twisted around again and saw Keith standing there, well away from all the people who were now gathered around us laughing. My head was pressed against the belly of the big man and I actually felt his belly jiggle against my face as he too began to laugh. I did not feel like laughing at all. The more he tried to pull the zipper up, the closer my head came up against his chest. There was no way the zipper was going down now. I thought to say something to Keith but the look on his face stopped me. His mouth was hanging open in total horror and he was very ashamed of me. He was even pretending he didn't know me. Then he started to shift to the left and right like a football running back trying to decide which way to go. In blind rage, I yanked my hair as hard as I could and felt it snap one strand at a time as it stretched and broke off against the man's hard metal zipper. With my hair now free in one big wad of tangles at the back of my head, I turned. There was no Keith in sight. I quickly marched out the door and ran down the street and just caught a bus heading toward home.

I entered my apartment, sat down on the bed and burst into tears. I cried like I had never cried before. It seemed the more I tried, the more things went wrong. What could I do? I had tried my best. In fact, what was hurting more was that I knew the problem with Keith had to do with my being an Indian. All he seemed to see when we were in public was the shade of my skin. Or, perhaps he thinks that was what everyone else saw. But, I knew that not all people were like that. I hurt so badly! I was not handling this very well. It just didn't make any sense any way you looked at it. I lay down on the bed and sniffled. I realized I was feeling sorry for myself.

I pulled out a sheet of paper and began writing:

Even getting groceries is getting hard. Last week I was at the counter when I came across one of the racists. I just left the groceries on the counter and walked out. I will never go back there again. Then before that, I was at a shoe store and the manager told me to come back some other time when there was a sale on. I never even got a chance to open my mouth. He clearly didn□t want me coming into his store. I remember another time just after that when I had stopped in front of the mall mirrors and looked at myself up and down and I could not see that I looked any different than any other shopper in the store. I had a long summer overcoat on, a dress and high-heeled shoes. And, they all matched. That seemed quite important to me. My hair was neatly styled and my makeup was all in conservative fashion. I thought I looked all right. Then another time, I went into a clothing store and the sales lady came up to me just as I came in and said, □I□m sorry, but we have nothing here for you.□ I never got the chance to even open my mouth, so I just turned around and walked out. That□s another store that I□ll never go back to. You know, at this rate I□m going to run out of stores to shop at.

I put the paper and pencil down on the night table and I slowly started to giggle. I was just trying to make myself feel better about what had happened earlier. Keith just wanted to go where there were no other people because he didn't like to be seen with me alone. Yet, I felt so flattered that he'd taken an interest in me, mainly because I liked being with him. But, all he seemed to be aware of was himself in his three-piece business suits. Me, no matter how businesslike I dressed, I still had my brown skin and black hair. If only he would get used to the fact that I am an Indian. I found out at the office that as long as I talked and acted like everyone else, they'd soon forget that I was an Indian. I was getting very good at acting, talking, reacting, and communicating like them. I was beginning to be just like them. I just wanted to fit in where I didn't always stick out. I rolled myself into a ball inside my quilt and fell asleep.

In my dream, I was running with a person straight toward a lone tree standing on the edge of a ridge. "You will fly" the person said. "I am afraid!" I replied. Then, just as we reached the cliff, I felt the person beneath me, holding me up and I was flying. Then the person was gone and I was flying on my own. I went swerving and diving and went headlong into a tunnel where I careened from one wall to the other, not quite getting the hang of balancing my wings and I nearly clipped something that was hanging on the roof of the tunnel before I came back out the other side. My stomach almost hit the back of my throat as I took a steep dive toward the ground before I figured out how to go swiftly back up. What an exhilarating experience! I knew that I would never dream about the black shadow anymore. I knew that I had killed it and that it would never plague me again.

All right! I am not very good at being a white man. How on earth is a person supposed to know what to do? When I showed up during the hair and zipper scene, there right behind her was the businessman who had introduced me to his daughter. I had to tell that woman too that I was only interested in my own kind. She too was aghast and quickly retreated. Hmm, very curious reaction. Very powerful words.

I must figure out something else . . . Oh, before I fly away, I must say that these city ravens are very nasty and aggressive creatures. When I first arrived and settled on top of that church steeple, Big Kaa came after me. How was I supposed to know that was his territory? He tormented me for so long, I finally got fed up. I clamped my beak on that old raven's wing and pulled him down to the ground where I became a wolf and I had him for lunch! Ha, ha, ha . . .

Chapter Five

The morning Charlie left Sioux Lookout, Fred was nursing a splitting headache, made worse by Gladys' voice coming from the bedroom, "Hey, Fredrick. What's taking you so long? I'm waiting for you, you know?"

He leaned over the bathroom sink and looked at himself in the mirror. He needed a shave, rather badly. He hated this. He hated the morning after, when there was a woman in the bed waiting for him. He grinned at his reflection. He was useless when he drank. So they waited until the next morning, at which time he wanted nothing to do with them. Then they would throw things at him or call him all kinds of obscene names. He looked at his crooked grin in the mirror. Just wait until he told Gladys that he would have to ask for another I.O.U.

Oh, Charlie! he thought, I wish you were ready, but you are not!

"Fredrick!"

He entered the bedroom and sank down at the foot of the bed with his head in his hands and moaned, "Sorry, Gladys. I can't seem to get this drinking and hangover stuff right."

He heard her give a big sigh behind him as she kicked the blankets off the bed and jumped up and stood naked in front of him. Then slowly, she began to get dressed. But, all he thought of was Charlie. This is really crazy, he thought. He knew that Gladys would not complain to anyone else because she would sound like she wasn't worth much if she couldn't even keep him, of all people, satisfied. He smiled. This business worked both ways.

Yesterday, he had had no idea that Charlie was still in the community. Her sister had told him the week before that Charlie was already in Port Arthur. He wondered now if she'd deliberately lied to him. But why? He crawled into bed and lay face down on the bed.

Eventually, he heard Gladys leaving the room. As usual, she made sure to bang the door closed behind her. He smiled and turned onto his back. So Charlie was now in Port Arthur. He had watched her since she was a child. His mother had told him that Charlie's father owed a debt to his father for saving Charlie's father's life when he had fallen through the ice with his dog team. He had promised his daughter to his son even though she'd been no more than three years old at the time. The men had left no doubt as to their children's future. But then they had both died. That had left his mother and Charlie's mother. Then his mother had died and that left only Charlie's mother who knew of the arrangement. He thought that she chose to ignore it and maybe she had not even told Charlie about the arrangement.

Well, one way or another, Charlie would be his. She had always been and always would be his. Whether she acknowledged it or not, she would be his. What bothered him now was that she no longer had a father to make sure that she was not touched by any other man. That left no one but him. Now, how was he supposed to do that without spying on her? He looked at the mottled ceiling of the hotel room thinking, I know I should not have married Mary. I married another girl when I was already spiritually married to another who was to have eventually become my real wife. I had done wrong. The Elders who approached me at the funeral that time told me so. Now, just yesterday, there I was facing the girl and I had no way to reach her. She would never have understood me.

He had tried once to tell Charlie about their future together, but she had been too young and she had not understood. He had also been drunk when he had gone to the cabin demanding that her mother open the door. She had. Charlie had been only thirteen years old then and she had looked so beautiful, fast asleep in the back room. He had bent over her for a good two minutes before he touched her face, then she had sprung to life, cursed him, screamed at him and hit him, and literally kicked him out of the cabin. Grinning now, he remembered that he had picked himself out of the snow bank in front of her doorstep and walked home quite assured that if he couldn't get near his future wife, and then no one else could either.

After seeing her again, he wanted her like he had wanted no other woman before. He was also beset with a fear that she would somehow find another man before him. Well, the deal would be off then. That was what he did not want. He wanted her and only her. And, he wanted her now. "Oh, Charlie, please don't forget me!" he said out loud.

He fell into a deep sleep. In his dream, she was with him. She was with him and she would be his but he would have to work hard. He saw her with an outfit more appropriate for the city and she stood in the middle of his trapper's shack at Clay Lake. He had felt embarrassed and sad that he could not provide her a better place. What hurt more was that she had looked so out of place. She deserved something better, to be somewhere better, better than what he would ever have to offer.

He awoke with a start sometime later in the evening. It was only a few minutes before the evening train came that would take him back home. He decided to scramble and make it to the train station on time. He would go to the trapline and get things ready for her. He got on the train that night determined that he would focus on her and nothing else would sidetrack him in the coming months. He would convince her to stay with him when all his plans were completed.

He got off the train and immediately his eyes swept over the crowd searching for Karen. "Out of habit," he thought as he picked up his boxes and walked to his cabin, determined that he was going to be alone this night. He must make an effort to stay away from Karen so he hurried away toward his cabin as quickly as he could. He unlocked the door. He hated coming home to this cold and dark home. Sometimes out at the trapline, he imagined coming home to a nice warm cabin, with the lamplight falling on Charlie's smiling face and the room filled with the smell of a good hot meal. He lit the coal-oil lamp and soon got the fire going. He didn't want to stay there, so he went next door to visit Sheila and Bob. He was sure to get a good hot meal there while he poured out drinks from the bottle of whiskey in his jacket pocket.

After several nights of partying and the nights spent with Karen, he finally got around to making arrangements and got ready to leave for the trapline. He got Sheila and Bob to set up his old community family cabin for Charlie. He promised them both that he would bring his long-awaited wife home for Christmas. When he got to the trapline he arranged the cabin as much as he could. He brought a vinyl kitchen tablecloth with red and pink flowers and draped it over the old wooden table. Next, he covered the exposed wooden shelves along the walls. He brought sleeping bags with flowery designs, which he threw over the double bed, along with two extra pillows. Finally, on his last trip, he hauled pails, frying pans, bowls, dishes and cups from his house at the community.

Around the first week of Christmas, Karen and her endless stashes of rum or gin distracted him. She demanded nothing, asked for nothing, and gave a bit of happiness for a few hours, before she disappeared into her cabin again. She had a certain dignity and maintained her position as the community "stay-at-home-wife" to take care of the kids while her husband was working in Winnipeg. When she had to get some wood, her neighbour came to look after the kids. She joked and laughed, perhaps her only chance to laugh after several weeks. "We all did what we could to survive," she always said. She was there for him and he had always been there when she needed him. But, Charlie, now . . . well, that could cause some complications. He had waited a long time but his time would come. He just had to make sure that all the things were there that she would need.

He had called several times to Indian Affairs and the Canada Manpower Centre, and then one day he got the number to Linda's place from his old friend, the postmaster. Still, there had been no answer until Linda picked up the phone. He knew then that he had the right house. Now, if only Charlie would pick up the phone! She never did. He could not afford to lose touch with her now.

In the second week of December, the cabin was all set and he had brought all the supplies for her, but he never got through to her on the phone. He went back to the trapline and worked hard at trying to accumulate enough pelts for him to come out again and to try to call her. He would remove all his traps, estimating the length of time he expected to be gone. When he got back to the community, he was on the phone again.

He tried calling her many times. She never answered until that one evening a week before Christmas when he was ready to go back to the trapline without her.

Chapter Six

I did not answer any more phone calls at home during the few days it took to get my number changed. Not until that night the week of Christmas. I had been feeling rather poorly, whether through a cold, depression, or loneliness, I cared not which. I wanted to go home so bad. Christmas was nearing and I still could not find a reason to go home at all. I had arranged a signal for Linda's calls. I would know it was her if she let it ring once, followed by three more rings. I would then pick up the phone on the fourth ring.

It was on one of these rings that I picked up the phone and said, "Yeah, Lin. Why don't you go home to see your mother? Why are you here calling me?"

There was silence at the other end of the line for a few seconds before I heard a voice say, "Charlie. I'm coming to get you. Get your bags packed. You are coming home with me. I need you with me this Christmas, please Charlie."

It was Freddy! His soft voice triggered something in me. I took a deep breath and then, gathering up my courage I quickly said, "I could see you in Armstrong on the 20th. Do you think you could be there around seven in the evening? I'll try to catch a ride with the last batch of students going home."

Freddy's voice came back saying, "I can't wait to see you again. Take care of yourself . . . and please keep yourself for me."

He always says that. I thought. What on earth does he mean by that?

On the ride to Armstrong, I sat at the back of the van trying to understand what I was doing. Why did I want him so? Why did I need someone so badly? More importantly, why did I feel such a tingling shock whenever I heard his voice? I loved the sound of him, the way he moved, talked, and the way he walked. At the moment, he was like a beacon flashing, calling me home. To go where I was needed, to where I would be loved. What about Freddy? There were too many things about Freddy that I did not like. I knew that he had women wherever he went. Another thing I could not ignore was that I did not like the feeling I had when I was with him in public. It was as if I was just one more woman, like the rest. Yet, I also knew that in spite of all the women he could have, he wanted me.

I arrived in Armstrong with some students and had just waved goodbye to them as they boarded the train when I felt a pair of arms come around my waist. When I turned, there was Freddy. I had never been so happy to see anyone. Never had I needed as much love and support as I did just then. After a slow meal and a lot of conversation in the restaurant, I actually welcomed the way he took control of the situation. Without hesitation, I allowed him to lead me to his room at the hotel where he made me feel like the most loved person in the whole world.

The next morning, I looked out the frosty window and knew that all I had needed was someone to love . . . and then, there was no mistaking it at that moment, I wanted to go back to the safety of the city. I had been a virgin and now, was no longer. For some reason, I felt quite empty inside.

I watched Fred roll over on to his back and heard him whisper, "Charlie, what are you doing standing there? You are shivering from cold. Come here. I will keep you warm. I will always keep you warm."

I slipped back beneath the blankets and instantly felt the

warmth of his legs and arms envelop me. I looked long and deep into his dark brown eyes, which were filled with wonder and perhaps a bit of disbelief. I slowly brushed his hair away from his forehead, thinking that ever since I was a little girl, I had looked closely at him but never touched him. I traced my finger down his nose, felt his lips kiss my finger, then I ran my finger over his chin and slowly trailed my fingers over his throat. I felt down his arms, his legs, and along his whole body. I adopted his body as part of my own; he became part of me. Never again would I feel alone.

We decided to go home to the community on the evening train with the boxes of groceries and trapping supplies. It was December 21st and we were still debating whether to head out right away the next morning to spend Christmas by ourselves in the bush at his cabin, or whether to hang around in the community and celebrate the holiday with everyone. I was all for getting away as soon as possible to the bush.

I hated to face my mother and stepfather. I could just imagine what they would have to say about Fred. My stepfather had no use for him. I remembered some comments he had made about Fred and his then new wife, which I had never understood and never cared to listen to. And then there were the others. How would they feel about his taking me as his wife? What about the other women in the community that he'd been with? I couldn't forget that. How could I look them all in the face and say I knew what I was doing? If and when I faced them, would I have the nerve to tell them that it was Fred I had picked to be my husband? My husband. The thought brought heat to my cheeks and an ache of fear in my belly. I knew right then that I couldn't do it.

We were at the train station waiting for the train. I had already come across some people from the community and the reaction had not been very good when they saw me with Fred. I looked at him standing there, so tall and proud. He always had a half-smile on his face as if the world was a pleasure for him to behold each and every day. I liked the way he always stood with one knee bent when he spoke to someone. I liked the way that one lock of hair always curled up over his left ear whereas the right side curled and tucked neatly underneath. There were things about him that I was picking out as personal acknowledgments that he was mine. He was my husband to be. When I looked at him when we were alone, I saw a life with a happy future. But things quickly got jumbled up when other people came into the scene. At those times, I was suddenly not quite sure about anything. Right now, I had only thought as far as the holidays. Yes, I would go and spend Christmas at his trapline but I'd head back to the safety of the city after the holidays.

My problem was that I wasn't comfortable being with him when we met up with people from the community who were also on their way home from a day of shopping. I felt as if the women knew what I had just found out. Also, I did not like the feeling I got when Fred deliberately put his arms around me in public. It was like he was showing off his most recent acquisition. They looked at me like I had done something wrong and they were deeply disappointed in me.

Right after we boarded the train and gave our tickets to the conductor, Fred got up and left the seat. I never saw him again until the train was coming to a stop at home. He appeared behind me with his breath smelling of liquor. My anxiety increased right after we got off the train when Fred insisted I follow him to this man's cabin. He had been drinking with him on the train. When I hesitated, he literally pushed me ahead of him.

As we neared the place, I could see from the shadows in the windows and the noise coming from the cabin that there was a party going on. I turned to say that I should perhaps see what was happening at Mom's when Fred firmly nudged me from behind — a signal that I was not to turn around. When he pushed me through the doors, I dropped my suitcases to the side. Fred took a firm hold of my arm and dragged me in past the table into the side room and on toward the other room. It was as if I was being pulled in every direction. We went past people sitting on every chair and in every space available.

All the while, Fred exclaimed, "Yeah, see! I went and got her and dragged her home! She is mine! Look! Isn't she beautiful? She's been getting more and more beautiful every year and now she's mine. She is going to be my wife! Eh, Charlie? You're all mine!"

I had such an ache in my stomach that I felt like throwing up. I was pushed forward again, ending up in the room where my suitcases were. I twisted around and grabbed my suitcases then went out the porch and quietly closed the door. I ran out the door and was at the railroad tracks in five minutes flat. I practically ran all the way down the uneven snow-trodden path along the railroad tracks toward the swamp.

Finally, I cleared the creek and ran all the way up the hill. When I paused a moment to catch my breath, I looked behind me and saw the black and white dog. The silly dog was coming up to me wagging his tail. I set my suitcases down on the snow on each side of my feet. Here I was again at my rest stop. I heard the dog's tail brushing the snow, the sound of my hard breathing, the loud thumping of my heart and then the tears came.

My stupid girl, what have you done? I am with you all the time and yet you always act like you don't see me. When you do see me, you don't recognize me. Your tear just landed on my nose and I taste the salt of it. Your arm pulls me closer to you. I feel your pain. My poor lost one. If you only knew what I had just arranged for your new fiancé. He'll pay for this. I will punish him. He has taken my beloved and caused her pain... pain... pain. He shall have double the pain!

I let the tears stream over my face until I became afraid of getting frostbite on my cheeks. What was happening to me? I did not like what was happening to me. Where was Fred? Why did Fred act like that with those people? Or maybe I should have asked why Fred was the way he was with those people? It was like he became different. He was not the Fred I knew in private; he was a different person in front of those people.

The moon was shining bright and it was a cool crisp night of December 23rd. I couldn't believe how much I had gone through in just two days. I picked up my two suitcases and continued down the path. I could see a light at my mother's cabin. They were still up. The dog followed me and the snow crunched unusually loud under our feet. As I approached the cabin, a dog next door started barking. I stepped on the porch and pushed at the door but it was locked. I pounded on the door and still there was no sound.

I pounded on the door with my fist once more. "Mom, it's me, Channie. Open the door!"

Still no sound. I put my suitcases down and stepped back. A light was on inside. I could tell from the light that the coal-oil lamp was on. Also, I could tell by the smoke coming from the stovepipe that someone had recently put fresh wood in the stove. I approached the door once more and noticed there was a stick of wood over the padlock loops on the door. I pulled out the stick, pushed the door open and walked in. The light was bright against my eyes.

I stood a moment then slowly walked toward the back of the room. There was no one in the front room where the coal-oil lamp stood on the table beside the double bed. I checked the back room where there was another double bed in one corner and several dressers flanked by another single bed along the back window. It was the bed I used to sleep on. I was standing at the doorway letting my eyes adjust and trying to collect my thoughts when I realized there was no one in the cabin. I went and got my suitcases, put them on the single bed and turned up the light. Then I threw more wood on the fire.

The two little squirrel-brained Groundhogs should be making their appearance now, I supposed. They usually did, since it was now way past the last train. The Groundhogs were my stepfather's twin sons from his first marriage. They would be around twelve or thirteen years old now and were here to stay. Good arrangement for his ex-wife, I'd say. Why didn't the boys see me getting off the train? They probably weren't there, which means they were probably going to the place I had already been since I got off the train. I boiled some water, made some tea and waited. It was exactly twenty minutes past twelve when Benny and Lenny came crashing through the door.

"Channine! Oh, man, Charlie! We're so glad to see you! Oh, man! You wouldn't believe what happened when Fred told Dad you were his wife and then there was no you, and then Fred had to prove that there was a 'you' before we came in and then your Mom said that you probably had gone home since Fred hadn't given you a home yet, seeing as he didn't have his own home to give you. Then Fred said that you definitely were his Mrs. Fred to be, and, well, that was, well . . . when she punched him full in the mouth."

I peered at the solid, thick brown-haired and chubby rosy-cheeked face in front of me. Was it Benny or Lenny? I felt the cup slip from my hand and, quite detached, watched it hit the floor as if in slow motion.

"Mother . . . hit Fred in the mouth?"

One of the twins – don't know which one – picked up the cup and then he was in front of me saying, "Oh, yeah, even Dad was really peeved off that you would choose Fred of all people."

The other one piped up, "Yeah, even Mam was really beefed that you would pick Fred. Come on, Charlie! You are the most beautiful girl in this place and all around. Everybody says so. And you are really smart, even Mam says so. Ah, come on now, don't cry!"

I said, "Just go away from me a minute," and got the mop to dry the tea off the floor.

No one ever said things like that to me before. No one ever told me I was smart. They never told me I was someone they cared about. It is only when we do something wrong, or when it is too late – always too late to undo things – that most people tell us they care. Well, it was too late for me. Why hadn't they told me before this? It might have made a difference. Maybe. But maybe not. Fred would have found me one way or another.

I kicked off my boots, moved my suitcases and curled up on top of the single bed. It was some time later that I felt someone put a warm blanket over me. I listened to the boys chatter for a good half-hour more before I heard them crawl into their double bed in what used to be my room. They had arrived last spring after their mother didn't want to look after them anymore, or so I had heard. I didn't think I would be able to sleep. I listened to every squeak of the logs and the snap of the oil lamp that was turned down low.

It was around seven o'clock in the morning when my mother and stepfather came through the door. I sat bolt upright, wide awake as they stomped in arguing about finding the perfect mate for Warts, then I promptly dropped my head back on the pillow and rolled over. A mate for Warts, the dog, was the least of my worries.

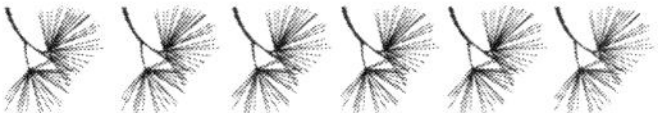

Fred walked along the path with the snow crunching under his feet. It had been an awful night. He thought back to a few nights earlier when he had called Charlie in Port Arthur. He had just been totally taken by surprise when she suggested they meet in Armstrong. She had come to him willingly like one who knew to whom she belonged. She was his and he was hers. With heartfelt thanks, he had discovered that he was the first with her. She *was* his. He whispered a silent message to the early morning sky, saying,

"You looked after her Grandpa. You saved her for me. Now, I ask you to help make her mine forever!"

It was only yesterday morning that reality hit him when he saw her standing at the hotel window. Oh, she had looked so beautiful, like an angel out of a storybook. She stood against the early morning sun, her form perfect against the light. Her hair hung in heavy dark waves down her back. She always seemed totally unaware of her beauty during the course of the day. He wondered if she was ever aware or had ever realized that people were always extra kind to her. He thought that maybe if there was a problem with her, it was that.

From the time that he could remember first seeing her when she was just a little girl, she had taken things for granted. She did not know that most people usually didn't act the way they did with others as they did with her. Yet, she seemed to always expect this treatment and not surprisingly, always got it. How did that happen? He didn't know anybody else who could do what she did to people. When he had seen her shiver in that cool hotel room, it had occurred to him that it was an awful place to have made her his. But soon she had been snug and warm in his arms again. How was he going to keep her there? When she found out that he just lived a totally humble existence, what was going to keep her to him? He couldn't expect her to love him as much as he loved her. No. No one could do that.

The next morning as they waited for the train at the train station, he had seen Old Henry of all people. There was Old Henry at the station platform giving him a dirty look.

Old Henry had walked up to him last month at the store in the village, bold as he pleased, and said for all to hear, "Don't you touch that girl. You're no good for her anymore! You know what you're called, son? You are a broken person. Let the girl go. Leave her alone! If your father was alive, he would tell you the same thing that I am telling you now!" He had been so infuriated that he had just looked at the old man, deciding that here was one life that would not last very long if he had anything to do with it.

On the train, the old man had sat down behind them. Fred had decided that he was going to be elsewhere for the length of the train ride and had left Charlie sitting alone while he went to the Club Car. There he'd met some drinking buddies from Sioux Lookout who'd immediately pressed drinks on him. One friend was indebted to him for help in a house repair at Allanwater Bridge. The other man had a very nice deck addition onto his home in Sioux Lookout that Fred had managed over one weekend last summer.

Fred loved helping people. There wasn't a thing he would not do for others. He was always full of joy and genuinely forthcoming in his offer of assistance, and he was well known to have a tremendous ability to help people in all situations. He prided himself in the knowledge that he could do anything he put his mind to. He never asked for money or anything other than that he would expect assistance in return, should he ever need it. People took him up on that offer, and to date, he had never asked anyone for anything. In some places, the people said, "If you need help, call Fred. He'll know what to do. He'll help you." So, right about that time, he did not want to see Old Henry. He remained in the Club Car until the conductor came by to announce the next stop.

He was determined to introduce her to everyone. They all must know that she was his. This was the night to stake his claim on her for all to see. But, it had not quite ended up like that. After pulling her through the mob in the front room then heading for the guys, Karen had pulled him aside.

Oh, she had a way of side railing him. He knew she did it on purpose, but the intrigue and play in public always fascinated him. Before he realized it, Charlie was no longer behind him. What was he to do? With perfect timing, Karen disappeared as Charlie's mother and stepfather materialized in front of him right as he was saying that Charlie would be married to him by spring. He had felt the push and a sting on his lips before he realized that Charlie's mother had hit him. He reeled back and stepped out of the room on the pretext of helping old Josephine out the door with her canes.

He walked the old woman to her cabin and then ran to Karen's place. That wench! That wasn't the first time she had deliberately gotten him into trouble. She was an expert at manipulating circumstances to give them time together before her husband came home. She held the door open for him when he arrived, brushing a kiss across his cheek as they went into the bedroom. She had been patiently waiting. He had taken a bit longer than she had expected. Well, it was old Josephine to blame for that, he had said, "Go ask her."

Now he was approaching Charlie's parents' cabin. What would she say? Would they let him in? He took a deep breath and knocked on the door.

Chapter Seven

I opened my eyes to find Benny, or was it Lenny, at my bedside smoothing the hair off my forehead as the pounding sounded at the door. He was gone and then Warts started barking next door. I heard my stepfather, or O as everyone called him, open the door and then I heard Freddy's voice. My heart bumped against my throat. Oh, what a complete turnaround. What a double-faced . . . he had brought bacon and eggs. I actually heard him insisting on making the coffee and frying the eggs while he waited for Mom to get herself on her feet. I imagined him watching Mom getting up off her bed beside the kitchen table and going into the shaded-off area to dress.

That was where I caught her with my insistent whispering, "What on earth are you doing?"

"What do you mean, what am I doing?" she whispered back.

"Why is he here?" I asked, perhaps too innocently because I flinched as I changed my clothes quickly.

"He is here to get the rest of you. By that, I take it he already got the first of you, so now he's here for the rest of you. If that is not true then you had better speak up. Otherwise, why is he here? You tell me that!"

I had no answer. It was almost nine o'clock. The train would be here soon. I had to get out. I was getting that suffocating feeling in me again. I threw my dirty clothes back into the suitcase, grabbed my jacket and put my boots on. Mom watched me but said not a word as I picked up my suitcases and walked out of the bedroom and into the kitchen.

Freddy was at the table with his back to me. I took a close look at him and somehow, for a moment, it was as if I didn't know him at all.

I started to panic deep inside and then he turned around and levelled those dark brown eyes at mine and said, "Charlie, please, don't disappear like that on me again!" He was off the chair and coming toward me saying, "I love you, Charlie. I need you."

He was in front of me with his arms closed around me tightly. My suitcases kept my arms straight and pressed against my legs but I refused to let them go. I had to be strong. I stood there not moving until he moved his face back to look at me. He smelled of stale liquor. Where had he spent the night? I had given him something pure and unused and he was giving me an old filthy used rag in return. I pushed hard and as he staggered back, I was out the door.

I did not pause but kept my feet moving one after another. I was up the hill when I heard him calling me, heard his footsteps catching up. I kept at a constant pace. Soon, he was behind me and he clamped his hands on my shoulders just as I was crossing the little bridge over the creek.

He stood there panting, "Why? Charlie, you can't leave like this! Come to the bush with me! Remember we had planned to leave today? What are you doing?"

I turned to look at him. "Why didn't you remember that last night Freddy? Where were you last night Freddy? What did you do last night Freddy? How can you stand there and ask me why?"

I whirled around and continued walking, thinking, as each step hit the soft snow that had fallen sometime during the night, "This is stupid. This is stupid. We are having a fight but we don't even have enough of a commitment to each other to have anything to fight about."

I stopped dead in my tracks as another thought hit me with

such force that I felt a shock go through me from head to foot. What if I was pregnant?

He was so close behind me, perhaps to say something else, so when I'd suddenly stopped, his teeth hit the back of my head so hard that I momentarily forgot my anger.

He exclaimed, "Gull darn it! Why the heck did you stop so suddenly? Oh, god!"

I looked back to see him leaning over spitting in the snow. There was no blood.

He said, "Come here. I'll check to see if your head is bleeding." He stepped closer behind me. "Your head's okay."

I turned to look at his face for a moment, noticing that the curls along his temples were sticking up in between the hanging strands of dark hair when he put his head down with such a dejected look. When I touched the top of his head I started laughing. Like a dam suddenly breaking, I was leaning over laughing, laughing as hard as I could. It was then that I heard him begin to laugh hesitantly before he looked at me. Wiping the tears from my eyes, I saw him standing there knowing that he knew that I knew something had come to an end before it had even begun.

I picked up my suitcases again and started to walk away. Still, he didn't move. I didn't want to leave him standing there, so I turned and, sounding a bit too chirpy or merry, said, "Go! Have a good time... have a good holiday! Take care of yourself. Merry Christmas and all that." I smiled.

He did not answer. I turned and hurried down the path. I could hear the train coming now. The black and white dog joined me at the makeshift station as he ran from the store with the mail clerk.

He gave a quick lick at my hand and I stopped to run my hand to the top of his head. Such a nice dog! I boarded the train without a backward glance.

Ah, my poor lost little one, a grand warrior will soon come to rescue you from that insufferable losing cheat. I will show you what a true noble Anishinabe man is.

Back in Port Arthur, I opened my apartment door and went in. It was around ten o'clock at night when I hit the light switch and entered the kitchen with my suitcases. I stopped and looked around at the bare walls. The clean bare counter, the bare kitchen table - the bare everything. A rented furnished apartment. It was exactly what it looked like. Used. I decided that I was going to have a shower, get cleaned up and go to bed. I would go shopping early the next morning for Christmas decorations, perhaps a little fake tree, and some supper treats. Yes. I would have a lovely Christmas all by myself.

I had just finished unpacking and was getting ready for a long, hot shower when the telephone rang. After the initial heart jump, I recognized Linda's ring and quickly picked up the phone.

"Oh, Janine. I'm so glad you answered. I called last night about this time but there was no answer. I called again around half past eleven and there was still no answer. I just wanted to know if you were there or if you had gone home. So, you are there?"

I heaved a big sigh of relief and said, "Yeah, I'm still here. Who did you think you were talking to? My ghost? No, I'm sorry I said that. You must know I'm home or that I would be coming home, otherwise you wouldn't have called. I'm doing fine and I've decided to go downtown and do some shopping tomorrow, or maybe do some visiting, or whatever. So, you're at your mother's place?"

Her voice came back on the line saying, "Yes, I'm at her place in Hamilton. Look, I'm sorry if I made a mistake in giving your home number to Fred. I just thought that since he was from your community, you'd be safer with him or . . . what I mean is, that you would have a better idea what to expect from him . . . or that you'd have a good Christmas. Anyway, I'm glad you're home and to know you're safe. Have a great holiday. I'll call you when I get home."

I answered with as much enthusiasm as I could muster, "Yes. Happy Christmas wishes to your mother. Have a great Christmas and listen, I may not be here. In fact, I may be leaving tomorrow, so don't call back until after the holidays, okay? And don't worry about me. Have fun. Bye."

After a quick shower, I lay in bed flat on my back with my hands at my sides. I wondered what would it feel like to be dead? I wondered what I'd look like if I were dead and lying like this. No, I though, they'd have their hands crossed like this. I suddenly began to giggle. It was ridiculous! I didn't know what got me thinking about death. I turned to my recent acquisition in the corner of my bedroom. It was a twelve-inch black and white television that only had two channels but I got the local news or the odd show or old movie once in awhile. I rubbed my tummy as I felt another cramp. Every waking hour since that one thought which had occurred to me at the time Freddy nearly embedded his front teeth in the back of my scalp, I had been riddled with a guilty conscience and anxiety. What if I was pregnant? I thought I did not want a baby. I swore to and vowed to everything I could think of that could possibly aid in preventing such a thing from happening.

I was relieved when I discovered that my menstruation was right on time the next morning. I hummed our childhood version of "Dashing Through the Snow." As near as I could translate, our Ojibway version went something like this, "Dassing peenda moo." Which, by the way, translated to "there is poo in my pants" in English, and was followed by all the jollifications over the fields being in that condition. Hmph!

I headed downtown amidst outside sidewalk Christmas carols. I loaded up on decorations and some knitting yarn. I wanted to make myself a homey place to live. I came back rather tired after a whole day of bus rides and three shopping malls, and with nothing left of my spending money for the month.

I alternated knitting and crocheting with putting up Christmas decorations and picture frames, and sang many songs of thankfulness and promises never to do such a thing again. At night in my bed, Freddy was there in my mind. I imagined the sound of his voice. I visualized the way he walked and talked. I loved his gentleness with me. It would have been nice to have been with him. But when morning came, I also realized that I loved my freedom. I loved my independence. Yes, I loved being on my own to do what I liked, whenever I liked.

Then on New Year's Eve, the phone rang. I was watching a comedy on a local channel. I grabbed the phone.

"Hello."

"Hi, Jan. What are you doing tonight?"

It was Keith. He sounded very down.

"Keith? Well, I'm not doing anything actually. I've got my feet up. I have a pillow at my back and under my elbows, a bowl of chips and dip, and I'm just watching a comedy on TV. This guy is trying to juggle bowling balls. You should try that sometime. Why do you ask? What are you doing?"

I heard him heave a big sigh then he said, "Nothing. I am doing nothing at all. I thought maybe you'd want to go to the show with me?"

I dropped the phone back onto the hook. I didn't know why I talked to him at all.

On the television, I watched a person swinging his arms totally around and turning his body from backside to front. Oh, the world was full of strange people. I shut the television off and curled up in my warm blankets. Tomorrow was a brand new year. I wasn't looking forward to another year like this one. I took out my notebook and started writing about how I would like the next year to be. I imagined a cabin by the lake, close to the city and someone to . . . No, I thought, I'll just concentrate on me. But Freddy kept interrupting my thoughts and I had nowhere to fit him in my dreamland. He seemed so out of place there. I put my book away and shut off the light.

Well, this white man thing seems to have come to an end. So, I will be her handsome dashing Anishinabe who will be so undeniably wonderful and supporting and I will make her love me and be my own wife!

On New Year's Day, around suppertime, I had just pulled a roast out of the oven when there was a knock at my door. My heart thudded against my chest as I looked at the door. Who could that be? No one knew where I lived. I walked to the door and looked out the window. There was a Native man standing there with his head down. Thoroughly puzzled, I opened the door and asked what he wanted.

He said, "I am so sorry to bother you. My name is Nisha, from your community. My truck, there at the corner, broke down and I happened to glance at the street sign and I remembered your address. You see, I was the one who put the address on the envelope for your mother when she sent you the letter."

I nodded. I knew who he was. I remember people talking about him in the community. He just showed up one day. He comes and goes. He never actually says who he is or where he is from. Helps people out, stays awhile and then he's gone again. Heaven knows how long before he shows up again. From what I hear, he's quite reclusive and doesn't answer personal questions. Somehow, it just doesn't seem to matter once you start talking to him.

He continued, "I just wanted to know if I could use your phone. I need to call a tow truck or something."

I stood aside for him to enter. He glanced at me then stepped in. I showed him the phone and went back to the kitchen and became busy by the stove. I heard him talking on the phone and then he came in and sat down at the kitchen table.

I was taking out the yams from the oven when he said, "I was trying to decide what smelled so good. Ham, potatoes, carrots. . . right?"

I took two cups down saying, "Do you take your coffee black? Or with cream and sugar?"

"Anyway. Doesn't really matter what you put in it, it's still coffee," he smiled.

He was a really handsome man with eyes that were deep and dark. A perfect nose. The lips were full . . . those lips. His eyes were on me.

I said, "It's roast beef, potatoes, wild rice and yams."

He smiled and said, "That's an interesting combination of food."

"I know. I eat strange combinations of food. But, like you say, doesn't really matter how you mix it, it's still food."

He let out a laugh and I found myself laughing too. I heard myself say, "Would you like to stay for supper? I always make more than I can eat."

He looked at me and smiled, "Yes, I would really enjoy having a meal with you."

I noticed how his hands were so delicate looking. "What do you do for a living?" I asked.

He said, "Oh, bit of this and that."

He began talking as I dished out the food, telling me some of the funny things that went on in the community.

After another bite, he said, "One hot day last summer, I came upon Old Zacharias by the lake. He was lying on his back under his old overturned canvas canoe. One end was propped on top of a sawhorse and that's where he was under, reaching up to glue the frayed end of the canvas. I smelled the strong glue before I noticed a stream of it running from his temple into his hair like some bird crap. When he turned his head to get up I saw that a wad of it had already collected leaves and grass to the backside of his head. I didn't say anything about it and when I saw him again the next day, it looked like a big old grizzly had swiped the scalp down the side of his head. He had running bald spots and a big bald spot at the back where his wife must have cut out the glue!"

I managed to swallow before I laughed out loud.

He continued: "There was another time when Lazarus' wife was by the shore beside Joe's old canvas canoe and it looked like she was trying to fish something out of the water. She had a long pole with a string and a hook at the end of it. Her long pole began to bend and then I saw a long blade with a short broken wooden handle come up out of the water. She had managed to snag a broken ice chisel. Probably broke and got lost in the snow by the water hole. Anyway, she had this big grin on her face as she grabbed it to examine the long blade but when she stepped back, her foot turned on the rocky shore and she staggered backward over the canoe. Her hands came down to brace herself, with the chisel in her hand. Well, she stabbed a hole right through the old canvas canoe. But then, she quickly looked around and pulled an old rag hanging on a branch., She stuffed the rag into the hole. Then she turned and ran up the path."

Between the laughter, I managed to ask, "Where were you? Why didn't she see you?"

He answered, "Oh, I was sitting up on the rock ledge over by the rock cliff on her right. She never thought to look up, I guess."

After a sip of coffee he said, "I think the funniest thing I ever saw though, was that old couple who live by the little creek. You wouldn't believe it but that old man likes to kiss his wife a lot."

I started giggling. I could imagine the old lady kissing that bewhiskered old man who looked like a very porky walrus.

He continued: "You know he has the big belly and always wears those suspenders to keep his baggy pants up? Well his wife has a big belly too. So, there they are at their woodpile when he stops in front of her and puts his hands on her arms. They each lean forward after their bellies touch. His lips touch hers, then suddenly, his suspenders snap at the back and his pants plop straight down around his ankles."

I was laughing so hard I started coughing.

"Wait, that's not all. He has no shorts on. He is standing there with his hairy bare butt and the old lady laughing fit to burst when he leans over and slowly pulls up his pants. Oh, now that was a most horrible sight to see."

I was wiping tears from my eyes by this time. I asked, "Did they see you? Where were you?"

He glanced up from his cup of coffee. "I was coming along on the path when I saw them through the bushes. Well, after that sight, I turned around and went right back up the path."

I never knew that people back home were so funny. I guess it takes an outsider to get the inside scoop of a humourous situation.

We had just finished the last cup of coffee when he looked out the window and said, "There's the tow truck."

Grabbing his coat, he said, "You will never know how much I enjoyed this. I hope we get the chance to talk again soon. I haven't had so much fun in ages."

I, too, rather enjoyed his company, I thought as I walked him to the door. With another wave, he was running down the street toward the flashing lights of the tow truck. I came in and closed the door. Then the phone rang.

Chapter Eight

He had been so careful. He had done all he could to prevent anything from going on with him and Karen. He had really made an effort to be clean in heart and body for Charlie. He had called and called her number but could not get through. After another week, he finally got his animal pelts sold off and he waited for his calls to go through again. Finally, in exasperation, he found himself in Port Arthur. He had managed to get Charlie's mother to give him the address. He smiled now at her reluctance and then how she had quickly glanced at a letter lying on the table when she went off to get him a cup of tea.

He got to Port Arthur on a Thursday night and waited around the corner of the old church until he saw her come out of the office building. He had supper at the restaurant on Cumberland Street and an hour later had caught the bus up to Hill Street. He got off and walked down the hill toward her apartment building and waited at the corner store for a moment until he was sure that she was home. Just as he approached, a truck pulled up and a man got out and began to jog down the street, looking at the numbers on the houses. He stopped and watched him run up the stairs to Charlie's apartment. As he memorized the make of the truck and the license plate, he saw the young man go into the porch area and through to the main door.

Blind rage seized him as he walked back to the corner store, trying to rationalize what the man was doing visiting Charlie at her apartment. He waited around for what he considered timely for a social visit then went to the telephone booth on the other side of the building. He was about to dial the number, but hesitated then put the phone down. What was he supposed to say? Better calm down first.

Three times he went to the phone booth without making the call. He was not calming down. If anything, he was getting more and more angry as time went on. He saw a tow truck arrive and park in front of the truck. He walked back to the telephone again and dialed her number. One way or another, he was going to protect her. No man must touch her. Least of all, whoever that man was.

He took a deep breath on the third ring and was quite surprised to hear her answer quite calmly.

"Hello."

His heart bounced off his chest when he heard her voice. He managed to say, "Charlie, I miss you terribly and I'm coming to get you. Get your bags packed. You're coming home with me. I need you with me. Please, Charlie. You can't leave me now."

Her voice came again, "Where are you calling from?"

"Charlie, please don't be angry with me. Can I come to see you?"

"Are you calling from home?"

"I'm in town. I have your address. Got it from your mother's place. It was on the table with your return address on it. I think maybe she left it there on purpose. I went to see her when I came back from the trapline. I can't stay there by myself. I really want you there with me. Please, can I come over? I need to talk to you.

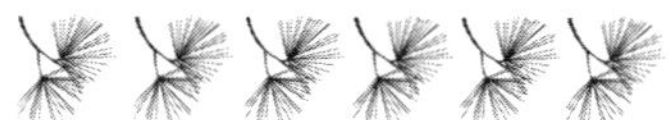

His voice was shaking. From the cold? He didn't sound drunk. I took a deep breath and leaned against the wall. I'd sent mother a note before Christmas to let her know that I was all right.

I heard him say, "Just for a little while."

I asked again, "Where are you?"

I felt a jolt of shock run through me when he said, "I'm at the corner store down the street. I'll be there in two minutes. Thanks, Charlie."

Two minutes!

He must have run because no sooner had I sat down at the table to catch my breath when there was a knock at the door. My eyes went to the two cups on the table and the two dishes still piled in the sink. He would see them! I grabbed the cups and threw a cloth over the dirty dishes as another knock came at the door. I opened the door and Freddy entered.

He seemed to fill the whole kitchen as he came in and sat down at the table. I could see his gaze sweeping the counter and the sink, and I instantly felt guilty.

"You just finished your supper?"

I stammered a bit as I said, "Yeah, but there's lots left if you'd like to have some."

I quickly did the dishes as he ate what was left of the meal. What would have happened if he had seen Nisha leave? I felt scared. Like he'd caught me doing something wrong. I was putting a pan away when I felt his arms come around me. I just stood there as he slowly turned me around, gently kissing my forehead. He held me in his arms for the longest time. I could hear his heart beating against my chest. So, now what do I do? I thought.

He did all the talking as I went about in a daze, packing my things. I had paid my rent for January; that should be enough notice for the landlord. The more Freddy's voice went on, the more I looked forward to his safe haven: the log cabin along the shoreline of the lake at his trapline. The cabin was apparently all ready for my arrival. After I'd left, he had gone there to prepare the cabin for my return. How had he know I'd come back?

I took all the Christmas decorations off the walls and he came and stood in front of me. He stood smiling down at me for a minute before he said, "I love you, Charlie. I have always loved you."

I looked into the deep brown eyes as his arms came around me. I heard myself say, "I love you too, Freddy.

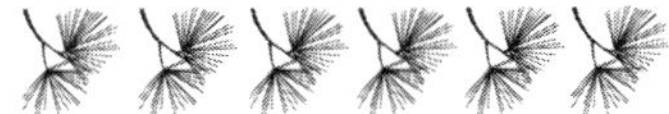

It had taken him no more than that to get her back in his arms. He relished his victory and claimed his virgin bride for the second time, all the while reminding himself that he was the only one who had ever touched her. He would keep it that way for as long as he lived. No other man would ever lay a hand on her.

When he had entered her apartment earlier, he immediately saw that the pipsqueak had had supper with Janine. The dishes were still at the sink. As he later checked out the place, he saw that the bed was neatly made and that satisfied him. He slept on the couch that night at her apartment. He vowed he would not touch her again until she was in his cabin at the trapline.

They managed to get a ride to Armstrong and then caught the train to the community. Janine barely had time to run and see her mother for a few minutes before he swung by with the snow machine, all loaded up for the trip to the trapline. He promised himself that he would take it easy with his drinking until she got used to him. Well, the way things were, it was pretty hard for him to face the community. He, the rogue, had claimed the princess of the community. He saw her as someone so . . . well, just so good, so beautiful, so . . . sinless, like an angel seemingly untouched by all the ugliness of life, poverty, and lawlessness.

He had watched her closely since she was a child. As soon as he was told that she would be his wife, he had begun to watch her. He had seen her haul water for the old man who was so sick with a hangover. He had watched her and Al fish the little animals in the sack out of the water at the edge of the dock. He had watched her shoot slingshots with Tom and Dave. She was a good shot. He had watched her cry by the stream when she had found so many small suckers, which the boys had left to rot on the shoreline. She was a strange girl indeed and he loved her all the more for it.

Only once had he found the nerve to approach her when she was crying. In answer to his question she had yelled, "I hit him! Many times! I hit him because he said bad things about his mother!"

He had laughed because she was feeling bad for beating up Al who had tried to hit her just like his father who always hit his mother. Suddenly, he was the bad guy because he had laughed. Oh, but girls were hard to understand. Now, she was a woman and a beautiful one at that.

How was he to keep her from getting mad at him? Love her. That was the answer! When she understood how much he loved her and to what pains he had gone through to make her comfortable, what more could she ask? He loved her and would treat her like a princess. He was going to make sure she would be a perfectly contented wife, living like a queen in their cabin in the woods. He would make her become a part of the land; part of his life. He would provide everything she had grown accustomed to. She would not go without. That was all she would need to know how much he loved her.

Chapter Nine

It was with such immense love that I watched Fred from the window, throwing the logs off the sleigh behind the snow machine. He turned and waved. I waved back. How did he know I was watching him? The cabin was very warm and cozy. I had just finished frying some fish. The rice and the bannock were already on the table. He'd be in soon. I stood by the table and smoothed down my apron. I heard his footsteps coming down the path to the doorstep and then he was in the room. The small cabin felt so empty when he was out. As always, he first hung up his coat then turned to the sink behind the door to wash up. Then he would come and gave me a big hug and a kiss. I loved the smell of him, the taste of him. He was all mine.

I found it hard to believe that we had been here for almost three months. It felt like such a very short time. We had not returned to the village yet and I had no wish to. I'd like it if we stayed here forever, all by ourselves. But I knew he wanted to go to town soon. If we were to stay here over spring break-up, we needed to stock up on food supplies. I didn't want to stay in the village while we waited for the ice to go; I wanted to stay there in our little cabin, but I had to go with him to get the groceries because I really didn't want to stay there alone.

"Now what put that expression on your face, my love?"

He brushed my forehead with a kiss as he sat down beside me on the bench. I kept my eyes on the beautiful view of the lake while he talked about the trip back to the community. We'd leave the day after tomorrow for a weekend trip. I hated the thought of that. What would happen while we were there? I wished I had my notepad.

"What are you doing this afternoon?" he asked.

He smiled and slowly chewed his food. I knew I was a good cook and he said he loved what I cooked. I had learned quickly to memorize recipes at the apartment after I got sick of bologna and macaroni in tomato sauce.

"Check my rabbit snares." I smiled back at him.

After all this time, I still felt shy. I just couldn't believe that this big hunk of a man was mine. My husband. Strange words.

He'd be at the woodpile all day. After hauling wood over, he'd get the power saw going and saw the logs into short pieces that would fit the stove. Then he'd split all the wood and stack them beside the cabin wall and bring some inside as well. I learned to just stay out of the way when he worked with the wood. He made me feel so inadequate, like a bumbling idiot when I was with him out there. I felt so embarrassed and my knees shook when I felt him looking at me.

The first week we were out here, I tried to figure out what he wanted me to do or what I was supposed to do. I soon found that every time I tried to do something he did not want me to do anyway, I always goofed up. Like the time I tripped on a branch and nearly fell on the power saw the first time I accompanied him to cut down trees. Another time, the axe head fell off the handle and just missed my head. And then there was the time I slipped on a piece of wood and landed close to the chopping block just as his axe came down. That was it; he declared the wood site out of bounds for me.

He made me feel like I was invading his territory if I was with him while he worked. I accompanied him to check the nearby traps and helped him with whatever else needed doing when he'd let me. He'd also tell me what needed to be done in the cabin, or suggested what I should be doing. I never objected or took offense to anything. I smiled and agreed. In that way, we had a lot of fun. I loved to hear him laugh. I didn't mind being left at the cabin for a short time. How else was I going to get any work done?

So, I got the bed made and tidied up as he came and went. At those times when he checked his traplines further out, I did the laundry or scrubbed the floor. I always rushed to get all my work done before he came home. He'd come home to see clothes and sheets hanging on the line. The next time, he'd come home to find them gone. The cabin was neat and tidy and there was always the smell of something delicious cooking. I made a point of never having him catch me doing anything. For some reason, I got very embarrassed if he saw me working. So, I made sure that I got all my work done before he came home.

One day, there was such a bad storm outside that he stayed inside the whole day. I felt uncomfortable and embarrassed as he watched every move while I washed the dishes and prepared our meals. That was all I could do that day. I even hated to go to the outhouse because he'd know where I'd been.

I was so embarrassed when I first went into the outhouse and realized that he had nailed on a brand new toilet seat just for me. A pink toilet seat! I felt ready to crawl into the hole. I'd smiled at the cabin when I first saw it. Everything was mismatched; but my heart melted at his attempts to make it nice and homey for me. I really didn't know how long I could do this . . . this house game he was playing. I knew he insisted on this by the way he talked and did things, that this was the way he wanted things to be. This was what he wanted me to be.

The problem was that the role I was playing was not really me.

"I guess this is one of your quiet days, eh? What are you thinking about?" He nudged me as he sipped the hot tea.

"I was just thinking about town. I hate to go but I don't want to stay here by myself either."

"You don't want to go because you don't know where we will stay. Is that it? Well, we're not going to your mother's so don't worry about that. I paid Sheila and Bob to fix up my family's old shack the last time I was down there, so we can stay there, if you like."

His family's old shack was the last one on the west shore. That might be nice. Suddenly, I felt a lot better as I picked up the dishes and began clearing the table. Fred was back outside again. Soon, the power saw would start. Compared to the normal peaceful silence, it was so noisy that you couldn't hear yourself think. I dressed warmly, grabbed my coat and left the cabin.

I took my time checking the rabbit snares I had set along the shore. Once in a while, I smelled the wood smoke from the cabin. I watched a woodpecker on an old poplar tree, so intent on banging his beak against the tree that he didn't even pause as I walked by. The chickadees and jays were quite indignant at my disturbing their business. I couldn't wait to see what this place looked like in the summer. He said there was a beach where he had his canoe hung up on the racks.

I was quietly walking along the shore in the shade of the trees when I first saw it. A lone black wolf seemed to materialize in front of me and then he was gone. I turned around. The sun was about to go down over the horizon. I soon noticed there was no sound of the power saw within hearing distance. I ran along the snare trail in my moccasins knowing that I should be able to hear it. I had the last time I'd gone this way when he was cutting wood. Maybe he was hurt! I ran as fast as I could back to the cabin.

I came running around the corner only to see Fred sitting on the woodpile. The power saw had broken down. I knew he didn't have enough money to buy another one until the next batch of furs was sold and he wasn't intending to do that until spring. I remembered the five hundred dollars I had in the bank in Sioux Lookout.

I watched the back of his head when I mentioned that I had some money in the bank. He would have none of it and seemed offended that I would suggest such a thing. He threw the axe on the woodpile and stomped into the cabin.

That night in my dream, the elder with the cloak was in front of me again. The lesson was progressing exactly where it had left off from last year. Was it last year? This person did not seem to know the passage of time. I understood the significance of each piece of bone and from which type of bird each piece came from but awoke in a thoroughly puzzled state.

What did the bones mean? What did they have to do with me? Why did I have to know these things? None of it made any sense to me. I would not dare ask Fred. He'd surely think I was going crazy.

We arrived in the community late at night and drove the snow machine right up to the door of the old shack. When a match was lit, I was surprised to see curtains at the windows and blankets on the bed. There was even a tablecloth on the square, rough, wooden table. I thought it was rather nice.

We had just got the fire going when we heard a snow machine

pull up. A woman's voice was laughing and a man's voice yelling over the noise of the machine. The machine stopped outside and when the door opened, Bob and Sheila walked in. She had a pot of stew while Bob carried in some pop and a whiskey bottle.

I glanced apprehensively at the bottle thinking: "here we go." A cup was shoved into my hand. It had pop mixed with the stuff from the bottle and didn't taste that bad. We laughed and talked into the night. Fred had us all laughing, talking about my escapades on the trapline. When the sun was tinting the horizon, the couple finally left and we crawled into bed. I fell asleep thinking that this was really nice.

The next morning, we got on the morning train to Savant Lake after a quick breakfast of scrambled eggs and bannock at Bob and Sheila's place next door. I didn't know Bob that well. Sheila was his second wife and had just moved in with him last year. I was relieved that they turned out to be a very nice couple.

Fred stayed beside me on the train and throughout the day in Savant Lake as we packed boxes of food and supplies. I couldn't resist buying newspapers and a few magazines. Just before the train came in, Fred ducked into the liquor store. With dismay, I watched him disappear inside. Maybe he wasn't buying it for himself. I had noticed that he was in the habit of buying liquor for others in the community. I'd known him to go and give a bottle to the old man at the end of the road down from his cabin. He came out with a bag under his arm and, with that, we got on the train back to the village.

This time, right after we gave our tickets to the conductor, he kissed my forehead as he got up and said, "I won't be long."

He went to the Club Car and I sat by myself all the way back home. I got a newspaper from a passenger several seats from me and I read every single article. Fred came along just as the train was slowing to a stop and we got off together.

Bob was there with the sleigh and snow machine. After they loaded the sleigh, Fred and I drove off to the cabin with Bob yelling that they'd be right over. We had just finished bringing in all the boxes when more people began arriving. One after the other, people from the community came and went, with each getting a swig from the bottle that Fred had bought. I noticed he had given two of the bottles to Bob. He'd had three in the box; now there was only one left.

Soon, the crowd began thinning out. Fred had been drinking and was beginning to show some effects when Mother and O arrived. I had already taken the cup from him several times for a sip and began to notice that I was feeling rather... well, just like the night before. After a few rough moments, O began to be a bit more civil when another cup was pressed into his hand. A few minutes later, Bob and Sheila arrived with the other bottles.

It was getting dark and I lit the lamp. After a while, I went to the outhouse with Sheila. I laughed out loud as she joked about a neighbour of theirs and laughed again as Sheila danced around, waiting for her turn at the toilet. She was such a good friend. I laughed as she told me things about Bob and the others in the community. It had taken me some time to realize that this was like a wedding celebration. That's why the people were coming over: To greet us and wish us well. My wedding. Hmph!

From the shivering cold, Sheila and I came into the cabin surrounded in a cloud of mist. Later, around eleven o'clock, I was right in the middle of laughing when I felt Bob's hand slide down my back. I caught Freddy's eye as I tried to brush past Bob and get to the other side of the room. But he pulled me down and I slid onto his lap. With both Bob's arms around me now, I saw the murderous gaze from Freddy across the room by the table. Sheila was babbling on about something and Mother was busy arguing with O. In all the chaos, I was struggling to get away from Bob when Freddy's chair crashed to the floor. He stood in the middle of the floor, yelling at everyone to get out. I watched Mother and O stagger out the door.

I muttered, "What are you doing?"

He yelled, "Get out! Get out!"

Bob and Sheila hurried out. Then silence filled the room. I had never seen Freddy this angry. I didn't know what to do or what to say.

I asked, "What's the matter Fred?"

Suddenly, I flew across the room and fell with a crash across the bed. I heard the door slam shut before a deep burning sting started across my face. He had hit me! Freddy had slapped me! In the silence of the cabin, I started to sob uncontrollably. I couldn't believe what had happened, and how quickly it had begun. I cried myself to sleep.

I woke up freezing cold. It was morning and the fire had gone out. Fred wasn't home. Where had he gone? I remembered that last night he had just turned and run out the door in a rage. Where could he have gone?

To that woman with the two kids!

Fuelled by anger, I got the fire going and made myself a strong cup of coffee. After drinking a second cup and still pacing the floor,

I decided to go look for him. I dressed warmly after I'd washed my face in the porcelain sink behind the door. I froze as I gazed into the little four-by-four inch square mirror hanging above the sink. There was a red mark across my cheek. I slowly sank to the floor thinking that this was had to end right now. I had to leave. Now! If I stayed, it would never end. But where would I go? I didn't have an apartment in the city anymore.

Oh, my darling Fred! Why have you done this? Fred, where are you?

I got up and rummaged through my cosmetics bag. Although some make-up hid the redness, there wasn't much I could do with my puffy eyes from all the crying last night. I grabbed the dark sunglasses I wore when checking traps in the bright sunshine, slammed the door and started down the path.

Where should I go?

I was close to Bob and Sheila's place when I heard a yell.

Chapter Ten

Boy, it had been a pretty rough couple of months. He had done his very best but it still wasn't enough. She was absolutely clumsy and unfit for bush life. He had to keep the fire going day and night for her. All she was willing to do was to keep the cabin tidy and smelling of home-cooked food. No, the problem wasn't that. Heaven knows how appreciative he was of her cooking. Now, here he had to give her credit. She could turn the most basic of ingredients into great gourmet dishes.

But even that was one of the things bothering him. It was like he was sitting down to a gourmet meal every evening. He wished for a more relaxed meal without steak knives, butter knives, forks and spoons. What did he have to buy the darned things for in the first place? Just once, he yearned for a big pot of rabbit stew where he could chomp through all the parts of the animal and damn the frozen veggies.

He was beginning to tire of the playhouse game they were into. Who did she think she was anyway? All he wanted was food to eat. He only used to light the stove when he was hungry or had anything to cook; now it was on full speed, day and night. He had to keep at it full time now, day and night, just getting the wood ready everyday for the next day.

Then there was her English. She spoke perfect English; the proper schoolmarm English. He often wondered if he'd ever get used to speaking English all the time. He had tried many times to speak to her in Ojibway only to have her answer in that unaccented proper English. There was that one evening in particular when she had grabbed a roll of toilet paper from the table and blew her nose hard. She suddenly leaned over going, "Oh, yuk!" and spit into the slop pail.

"What? Bleeding nose?" he asked.

"No," she had exclaimed, "I blew too hard and it bounced off the paper and went into my mouth!"

Why didn't she just say "snot" he wondered and turned to the wall saying, "Sorry that we ran out of tissues."

She had said nothing more and had begun tidying up.

Toilet paper and tissues were things that he never had to stock up on before. This was harder than he had thought. He just wanted to relax and be himself, but now he was stuck with the monster he had created. He wondered if she was like that all the time. How long would she stay like this?

Never once did she let her guard down. It was like he was watching her performing. She was so out of place. It was like he had plucked her out of her city apartment and plunked her into the trapper's shack but she went about her daily business as if nothing had changed. Wait a minute. Now wasn't that what he wanted her to be? Yes, but not like this. It was as if her spirit wasn't in it. She never let on what she was feeling. And, she never said anything about anything. The aprons looked good on her though. He was glad he'd thought to throw them into the shopping pile at the last minute. She always wore one when she cooked. She was so beautiful.

What had he done?

When they went into town, he swore to make a great effort to be civilized and vowed to do his best to please her. But when they got to Savant Lake, she made a beeline for a newspaper and picked out food that he never ate and supplies he didn't use. It was like she had no thought for him. She never even made a comment about the cabin. It felt like she was taking over his life while he got nothing back. On the spur of the moment, he had bought the liquor, feeling that he was entitled to a bit of fun and maybe to get part of his life back.

And so the drinking began. He had seen that Bob was getting a little too friendly but Janine only laughed. She had laughed to torment him. He loved her but evidently she had no love for him. So he'd drank and drank and now he did not remember the blind rage. He was in Karen's warm embrace on her kitchen floor. As always, when he drank, he immediately fell asleep. Karen always told him that whenever he was in town, she would make sure he fell asleep in her loving arms and not in the snow to freeze to death.

It was early morning when he awoke and decided to go talk to the Priest. He had to find a way to keep Janine beside him. He walked across the tracks and down to the Priest's cabin before he realized that he'd left his coat at Karen's. After a conversation with the Priest, of which he wasn't quite sure what they'd spoken of, he woke with his head on the Priest's table. He jumped up and then hurried back to Karen's to get his jacket. Karen was still fast asleep on the double bed, lying between her children. He decided not to awaken her and thank her for letting him sleep on her kitchen floor. It was as he crossed the railroad tracks and was coming over the hill when he saw Janine. Again, instant rage filled him. What was she doing by Bob's place so early in the morning? Was she coming from there?

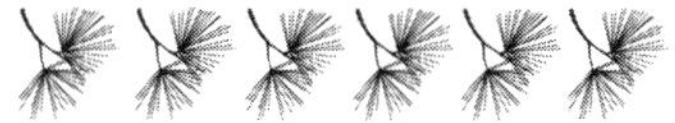

I glanced toward the sound of his voice and felt excruciating emotional pain well up to choke me. Fred was coming over the hill from that woman's place. He was coming from Karen's place. I turned and ran to him. How dare he! He still looked angry as I approached him.

He stopped and said, "So, you're on your way to Bob's for more?"

How dare he!

My arm shot out and took the glasses off his face. With my other hand, I punched him in the belly as hard as I could. He staggered back and then, grabbing his middle, bent over and promptly threw up all over his boots. I stood perfectly still as he retched. Vomit slid over his boots and onto the snow.

He gasped, "what did you do that for?"

Still angry, I said, "That was for thinking such an awful thing of me and that was for knowing where you are just coming from, and that was for . . . No I should hit you as hard as I can a couple more times for hitting me last night. Look at me! Don't you ever, ever hit me again! Do you hear me? Look what you did to me!"

Fred stood blinking for several seconds before whispering to me as if he was coming out from a deep shock. "I hit you. I hit you? Gosh! I really hit you, didn't I? Oh, love, I'm so sorry. I'm sorry, Charlie. I never meant to hurt you. I must never hurt you. Oh, God! I have never hit a woman in my whole life! I promise to never touch you in anger again. I'm so sorry! Please forgive me. Oh God. Janine, I'm so sorry."

He looked like a walking zombie with his arms stretched beseechingly and then he lunged toward me.

"I'm sorry, love. I'm so sorry, love"

His arms closed around me. We stood there, rocking from side to side, as his tears rained over my face. I turned us and we walked back to the cabin with our arms wrapped around each other. The hopelessness of it all overwhelmed me. I could not see any way out of this situation. I loved him dearly but I was choking to death in his suffocating grip.

We had just sat down at the table when I said, "You must tell me where you were last night or I'll keep wondering if. . . "

His hand stopped with a coffee cup in it.

After a few seconds, he smiled, took a sip and said, "I went to see the Priest. I woke up there this morning and came along the railroad tracks and across the hill. I guess I didn't want to walk by Bob's place."

I looked closely at him, trying to see if he was serious.

"Why would you want to see the Priest?"

"I guess I figured that you may not be so free to leave me if I married you. In the church, I mean," he said with a crooked smile.

I said nothing as this information registered in my brain. He was afraid of me leaving? He was willing to marry me just so I wouldn't leave him? I always thought that a man proposed to the woman when he loved her enough to want to marry her.

Nothing more was said as we began to repack the things we had bought. When I thought we were almost ready, I decided to go and visit my mother. I was about halfway there when Lenny and Benny came running up behind me. One was jabbering about last night, saying that he couldn't even get in the door to see me. They asked if I had I been drinking, saying they'd heard me laughing.

Then one of them said, "Later on, we came back and saw Fred at Karen's place. There was no light at your place."

I stopped and turned around.

"What did you say? When was Fred at Karen's place? What time was it?"

The tall one, Benny, answered, "Oh, I don't know. We were looking for Mom and Dad and heard noise at Karen's, so we went there. But they weren't there, just Fred and a few other people."

I turned around and headed down the path to the Priest's house and knocked on the door. The door opened before I could knock again. The Priest smiled as he bid me to enter.

I stopped just inside the door and asked, "Would you please tell me about what time Freddy left this morning?"

He stopped to think. "He came in around five. Such an early hour! Then he dozed off and left when he woke up at around eight o'clock."

So where was he the rest of the night?

"Thank you," I mumbled.

I turned to go when he said, "Wait. You didn't ask what he came to see me about."

I smiled, "If you remember Father, I am Anglican. Goodbye Father, and thank-you."

I turned and closed the door behind me. The Groundhogs were still standing by the door, waiting for me. I had no idea what time it was when Fred came over the hill. I had never thought to look at my watch when I decided to go look for him. I could ask around and sound like a ridiculous jealous wife. I would just have to forget it and hope that Karen and Fred weren't alone during the night.

I kicked at the snow as I walked to my mother's cabin thinking how much I hated this place and all the people in it. When I got back to the cabin, I found him dressed in his best clothes, all ready to go to town. And never mind his snowsuit, he had on his town coat.

"Where are you going all dressed like that?" I asked.

He smiled." Not alone. We are going to Sioux Lookout. I decided we could use your money to buy that power saw after all. I can't see us spending the next three months with just the axe and a handsaw. I'll be at the woodpile all day long, every single day just to keep you warm, if that's the case."

Although it was said with a smile, I did not like the sound of that. I was the cause of keeping the fire going? I was the cause of all his hard work? I thought that was what he normally did. Why was it my fault that he had to cut wood? Did he not keep the fire going when he was home? Well, if it was my fault, then I would pay for the damn power saw! But, then, there would go my ticket out money.

The eastbound train would be arriving soon so all I had time for was to grab my winter coat and change my boots. We ran to the station as the train was coming to a stop. After we paid for the tickets, Fred got up and left. I never saw him until hours later when he came and pushed me across to the window seat as the train stopped in Sioux Lookout. I didn't like this.

Later, we had no sooner checked into a room than he turned and went downstairs. I figured he'd be in the bar until closing time, around one o'clock in the morning. I went out for supper at the same restaurant, sitting at the same table when he'd come and sat down across from me last fall. Now, where was he? Probably in the bar with that woman.

I finished my meal and went back into the hotel, slowing down as I made my way up the stairs. Someone was in our room. As I approached the door, it was suddenly flung open and there was Fred, very drunk and very angry. I never even had time to say anything before he grabbed me by the coat and flung me onto the bed. I curled up, wondering what he was going to do. But he just kept pacing across the floor and yelling.

"Where the heck have you been? Eh? Where did you disappear to the minute I turned my back? Eh?"

He kept asking the same questions over and over again, getting angrier and angrier.

I finally yelled back, "I went to the restaurant for supper." Now he was standing over me with his face about a foot from mine. "Then why didn't you let me know, eh? Why didn't you invite me out to supper, eh? You always act like you are better than me, you know?"

I yanked off my coat and pulled the blanket over me saying, "Stop yelling at me and stop spitting into my face when you talk!"

He took a long hard look at me, dragged in a deep breath and then whirled around, stomped into the bathroom and slammed the door behind him. I lay still, wondering what he was doing in there.

After about half an hour, he came out and sank down on the bed beside me. He laid his head on my shoulder and I listened to the anguished sobs until he was able to speak. My brain numbly registered what he was saying. I was in unknown territory and had absolutely no idea what to do or say. I lay motionless, listening to him beg for forgiveness and try to explain what was happening to him, what he was feeling and what he had been feeling. He said he loved me more than anything or anyone else in the whole world. If only I would care, if only I could love him as much. He had his arm around me, begging me to let him know that I loved him as much as he loved me.

He could be right, I thought. I may not have shown him how much I loved him. I couldn't remember being able to hug him out of the blue like he could with me. I'd never known how to. I remembered Linda. She would understand. She would straighten out this mess and tell me exactly what I needed to do without actually telling me.

No. I had never actually shown him how much I loved him. I had actually told him just that once at the apartment, the time when he came and got me. I wasn't much good at such things. And maybe I did or said things that I might normally do or say in the city. That would make him think that I thought I was better than he was. But, I was only trying to be the person he thought I was or wanted me to be. Perhaps I hadn't changed as much as he had tried to do. I should work harder. Yes, I thought, I'll try harder.

I began to stroke his head and then bent to kiss the top of his head. I told him I loved him very much and that I would tell him how much I loved him every day. I would try to be a better wife to him. I assured him that I was only doing my best to be what he thought I was. Suddenly, I felt very nauseous.

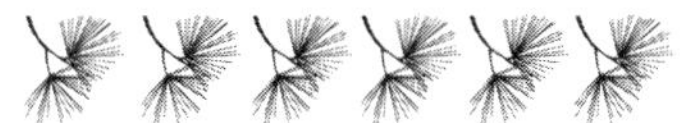

Begging for forgiveness, he thought, had been the best thing to do. He hadn't wanted to give her an excuse that would cause her to pack her things and walk out on him again. He was always in dread that she would just walk out. She had money stashed at the bank. But, at how many banks?

It was just getting daylight when he awoke with a splitting headache. He looked down at her shadowed face and heard her breathing softly. He slowly made his way to the bathroom and closed it quietly behind him. He was feeling utterly sick as he splashed water on his face. He looked terrible.

Yesterday, after realizing that he had slapped her, he had, in his own way, asked her to marry him. She had just looked at him as though wondering why he would say such a thing. Then she had just left the cabin without a word to go see her mother. She had been gone an awful long time and he had decided that if she spent some of her own money on the trapline, then maybe she'd have a bit more respect with the supplies. He would use her money to get the power saw. She took the news without comment, as if anything he did made a difference.

He spent the trip to Sioux Lookout in the Club Car to avoid any bad words with her. He felt it was better to stay away than risk saying something that would hurt her even more. When he was coming back to his seat just before the train reached Sioux Lookout, he saw her leaning over to talk to a red-haired man in the opposite seat across the aisle. The man had his head toward her and was waving his arms around to the conversation.

He'd stopped several seats back and was able to catch bits and pieces of their conversation above the click-clack of the train. They were in a discussion about world trade or some such thing. He had been swept with such rage that she would talk like that and not mind her place. He had felt such a wave of betrayal, embarrassment, and then fury; he didn't have a clue about what they were talking about. She was like them and would never be like him. He was excluded.

When they got to the hotel, he went downstairs for a drink and ran into Gladys. He was telling her not to come knocking on his door when she began to laugh. Gladys informed him that she had just seen his lady friend slipping out with a man. In fact, Gladys had seen her with the man several times before whenever she came to town. He rushed upstairs to find Janine gone. He became more furious as the minutes ticked by. By the time he heard her approaching the door, he was in a blind rage. But, had he not been drinking, he would have known that Janine would never do such a thing. Only women like Gladys did such things. Gladys. That bitch! She had done that on purpose. It was payback and he'd fallen for it. How she must have laughed!

Chapter Eleven

At the bank the next day, he stood behind me as I filled out the withdrawal form. Instinctively, I left one hundred dollars in the account. I never told him exactly how much I had in there. I also never told him that I had money in the bank in Port Arthur. It was my getting-out money and would stay there no matter what. I handed him the four hundred dollars.

I hadn't said much since I disentangled myself from his arms and legs earlier that morning. The train would be here soon. I went with him to buy the power saw and then we boarded the train for home. This time, he stayed beside me all the way to the village.

I sat looking out the window, wondering how long I would last in this situation. My hope was that we would get to the trapline before something else happened. I didn't even want to see my mother. I could just imagine what she would say. Maybe I could think of an excuse. Once out in the trapline, I'd have to decide how I was going to handle the next stage. I did not want a baby, but I hadn't had time to find a doctor to prescribe me birth control pills.

I wished I could get him to talk. But he just looked at me with that closed face of his. So, my mouth clamped shut and my tongue lay still. Only my brain reacted with silent comments, screams, questions, and hopeless suggestions as to what to do next. I glanced at him and shock went though me as a tear slowly made its way down his cheek while he stared out the window. I looked away. My heart continued to beat very hard and I still didn't have a clue what to do.

When we returned to the cabin, the emotional pain remained deep inside me for a good month before I could respond to Fred's loving attention. When the ice receded, we went hunting for ducks, tying the canoe on top of the sleigh behind the snow machine and loading up the canoe with camping supplies. We managed to take the snow machine as far as the mouth of the river where we decided to set up camp at a point. We shoveled snow off an area for the tent and the snow pile became my freezer.

Every time he killed a duck, I cleaned and prepared it and then dug out a little compartment in the snow, shoved the duck in and packed it closed with more snow. One morning as I shoved another duck into the snow pile, I heard him laughing softly behind me.

I whirled around, demanding, "What are you laughing at?"

He had just returned from a firewood trip and he stood there, swinging the axe back and forth.

"You're supposed to leave a stick in each spot so you don't lose the place where you bury them."

I looked apprehensively at the bank thinking, it wasn't like I had buried them all over the campsite. I'd put them between the end of the tent wall and that poplar tree. How could I possibly lose any?

A few weeks later when we moved to another site, he sat by the fire laughing when I could only find twelve of the fourteen ducks I had buried. I was still moving the snow all around the campsite, trying to find those two ducks when he finally persuaded me that I had miscounted. I thought of myself as a failure. It was about this time that I began to get very nauseous in the mornings.

My love for Fred deepened as he pampered me in the coming days and weeks. We knew I was pregnant. I was determined to forget the ugliness that had happened when we went into town. I treasured those days and weeks we spent together in peace and gentle kindness.

I got up very early one morning when we were no more than one hour's paddle away from the cabin down river from the spring hunting site. I had been so violently awakened with nausea that I had barely made it over to the woodpile to retch as quietly as I could. I thought he was still asleep inside the tent and was quite when I came back and saw him by the water.

I felt a shiver run clear down my back to my toes as I realized he was deliberately waving his arms to the left and right, in front of him and behind him. In his hand he held a pipe. I never even knew he had a pipe. I heard his voice in intonation but I couldn't hear any words. For some reason, fear and embarrassment came over me. I did not know this about him. I wasn't aware people even did things like that. I thought it was only when they were drunk that they would sing their wailing sad songs.

He was praying. I thought only the old Indians did that. I wasn't aware anyone still did. How? Why? What else did I not know about this man?

I was back in bed when he returned and got the stove going full blast. I waited for the tent to heat up while he made some coffee. He never said anything about the song or the pipe so I didn't ask any questions or make a comment either. Now, when I knew he was going off alone, I stayed well away from the area.

I got lost once. As lost as any idiot in the bush could get.

Fred had gone down the river in the canoe alone as I didn't relish the idea of barfing over the side of the canoe. I took the old .22 rifle and went in search of a partridge. I had no sooner cleared the woodpile than I saw one. I had the sight on him when a wave of nausea washed over me. The partridge was still there when I lifted my head again, so I lined up the sight and pulled the trigger. The partridge went down in a flutter of wings, beating them desperately against the mossy ground. It hobbled and flopped its way into the dense bush. I crept forward, but as soon as it became quiet long enough for me to put the sights of the gun on it again, the injured bird suddenly flapped and disappeared under another bush. In this way, I chased it deep into the swamp where every footprint popped out of the smooth fluffy absorbent moss. I'd left no tracks behind me.

After another missed shot, I crawled under an overhanging old tree and saw the partridge beneath a branch. I stopped and fired. This time it wasn't quite quick enough to lead me farther in. As I was standing in the middle of the swamp plucking the feathers off the partridge, I slowly turned around and came to a stop when I realized that I had absolutely no idea which direction I had come from.

How many times had Mom told us about the trickster? It could even be a partridge that would lead us to get lost in the swamp if we attempted to kill her or her babies. I had fallen for the old trick after being warned about it over and over again from the time I could remember. I had gone ahead and done it. I couldn't believe it. I stood in the middle of the swamp with my head hanging in shame when I heard the twelve-gauge shots echo around me.

My heart jumped.

Fred! I couldn't tell where the shots had come from because the noise echoed all around from the poplar and pine trees standing like sentries around the swamp. I had no idea whether it came from the left, right, front, or back.

Then another shot rang out in the distance, although it too bounced all around me. I went in the direction of the trees where I'd first heard it. I thanked those trees as I rushed forward, unceremoniously smashing the partridge against logs and moss-covered rocks to gain balance. I ran, skipping and hopping full speed through the swamp, climbing over and under fallen logs and tree trunks until I emerged well behind the last woodpile by the river. I saw no trace of Fred.

I hurried to the campfire and built it up. I threw up again behind the woodpile before putting the teapot on the fire and then another pot for the partridge. I was going to make partridge and dumpling stew that night.

I was lying back against a block of wood beside the campfire in total contentment when I heard the splash of his paddle. Against the quiet spring evening, with the sound of ducks settling down for the night, my mind kept drifting to that scene of Fred praying in the early morning light.

What was that ceremony that I had seen him do? I could remember no such thing being in our family. These things were done quietly and inconspicuously during the course of the day; affording respect to the birds, animals, and plants at all times without a big fanfare, recognizing their more predominant importance by respecting them without attracting attention to one's self.

I decided not to say anything. Did he think that I did not know? Or, was he hoping that I would chance to see him? Most likely though, it was that he didn't care whether I knew or not. What about my dreams? Were the ceremonies that I dreamed of anything like the ones that he knew? What did he know?

It was on nights spent out in the open that my spirit flights increased. I would soar through the night sky, swooping and swerving in absolute delight. On one night, I swooped down so fast that a sound escaped my lips and the screech of a nighthawk filled my ears. Immediately, I felt imminent danger at having revealed my presence. I came back down to my body and wiggled my toes, just to make sure that I was back.

After spring, we went into summer and I was quite content to float around in the water by the sand beach around the point from our boat landing. Fred was hauling logs for the tourist camp at the other end of the lake where they were going to build an icehouse or something like that. I was basking in love and happiness, deciding that no one or nothing was going to disrupt my little piece of heaven on earth. I listened to songs full blast on my small portable record player perched on a rock while I lay spread out with my growing belly floating to the sun. I smiled and closed my eyes. That was the best of my summer months.

It was on a very hot day in August that Fred suddenly decided he was going to take me to visit his favourite aunt who lived on a reserve up north. I was very excited about visiting her, as I had not met any of his relatives. I wanted to feel like a part of his family too. Fred ordered a plane from the tourist camp and we flew out directly from our cabin. After about an hour, we landed. We walked through two streets before he turned into one of the identically built houses.

"Hey, Gook!" he yelled as we entered.

From around the corner of the house, a woman wearing a long red- and blue-checkered dress and a blue sweater buttoned to the neck, appeared. The wrinkled face broke into a big smile as Fred swept her into his arms. Then she turned to me and touched my arm as her face again wrinkled into a big smile. Fred took our two boxes to a bedroom as he was directed.

I knew it was going to be a nice visit.

An hour later, I was quite surprised when Fred suddenly announced that he was flying back to town to do some shopping and that he'd be back in a week. With no more than just a pat on my arm, he was out the door and down the street.

Later, we heard the plane take off. He was gone. He had left me here all alone. Gull darn it! Why does he do that? I thought. In a few short minutes, he had undone all that we had built up in the past months.

The days came and went. One week went by and then another. I alternated between anger and worry. What had happened to him? Where was he? How could he just leave me like this? I took to taking Gook's canoe out alone whenever she wasn't up to accompanying me on one of my endless paddles along the shoreline. I couldn't stand the wait and anxiously looked down the street every time I heard a plane land.

I returned one evening and there was a little boy about five years old sitting on Gook's lap. I remembered that she had been expecting her grandchild. The mother had dropped him off and left on the same plane. He was a skinny little boy with deep, sparkling eyes. Apparently, Remy came to stay with her every summer.

"Gook" I discovered was short for Gookom or grandma.

Several days later, I heard her telling the boy, "Don't go out the window if you came in through the door. Go out the same way you came in!"

When the boy asked, "Why?" Gook heaved a sigh and said, "Because of the people in the room. You might tie their lives in knots when you do that."

I remembered that my mother had said that many times. As a child, I often thought about that, trying to figure out what it meant. The boy just shrugged and was gone again. I smiled to myself.

One night Remy and his buddy, who looked to be about seven years old, built a tent beside the house where they were going to sleep that night. The little tent was right under Gook's window.

I heard her saying in a hushed voice, "Don't look at the northern lights."

Remy's voice rang out. "Why not, Gook?"

Gook stuck her head out the window again and said, "Because they will come down and get you. And don't whistle to them either!"

"Why not, Gook?"

Gook said, "Those are ghosts dancing up there and they will start to dance faster and faster if you whistle to them, and then they will swoop down to get you. When they come for you, you will begin to hear a loud swishing sound that will get louder and louder until you won't be able to move, and then they will swoop you up."

I smiled as I sat thinking at the kitchen table. Yes, I had heard all about the northern lights too, and I wondered where I would be when I told my child such things? My heart was so heavy and although my morning sickness was gone, I now suffered from heartburn most of the time. What was I going to do? What now? Is this what he will do every time he wants to go to town and party with other women? Is this what it will be like for the rest of my life?

Will I have one baby after another while my husband just takes off any time he likes without explanation and expects me to stay exactly where he left me?

I felt used. I felt trapped. I felt very angry. I also felt helpless and victimized.

One day, just as the sun was setting, Remy came running into the kitchen where Gook was preparing fish for supper, yelling in English.

"Look, Gook! There's a cloud with a curly golden wig!"

I chuckled at that and glanced at Gook. I knew she was trying hard to get him to speak in Ojibway.

She looked out the window and spoke in Ojibway. "Oh, so it is. What once was normal, now looks kind of strange, doesn't it? Just an old cloud dressing up fancy."

The boy fixed his gaze on her face for a full minute without saying a word and then whirled around and dashed out of the house again. In my own mind, I had begun to repeat every Ojibway word that Gook used. She would smile every time I spoke to her. I no longer used English all the time as my Ojibway was definitely getting better.

It was exactly three weeks and two days when I happened to glance out the window and my knees became weak. Fred was coming down the street. I hadn't even heard the plane land. When he came in, he came toward me and gave me a quick hug. He smelled strange and he looked a lot thinner. There was no explanation other than it was just the length of time it took him to do what he needed to do. I didn't ask what that might have been. As far as I knew, we only needed some groceries, canvas, nails and paint for the old canvas canoe that he wanted to re-cover.

I deliberately kept my distance, moving away when he tried to reach for me in the single bed we shared that night. With their promises to come visit us, we said goodbye to Gook and Remy the next day, and flew back to our trapline.

Chapter Twelve

As I approached the cabin, everything seemed as we had left it. There was more grass around the wooden half step to the door, but nothing else was disturbed on the outside that I could see. The door creaked at the same middle hinge when I pushed it open. Inside, it smelled musty but otherwise, the water pots remained upside down where I had placed them on the left shelf beside the stove and the cot at the far wall was still laden with sheets and towels. The shelves with the radio, the clock and the bit of odds and ends beneath it, the double bed, still neatly made, and the kitchen table to the right, remained clean and tidy. He had not been here since we'd left. So, where had he gone? I did not ask.

When I unpacked the boxes he had set down inside the cabin, I found the clothesline I had asked for. It was one of those heavy-duty nylon coated wires with the long pulleys at each end. I put it aside. I'd have to wait until he put it up. Pain and anger lay deep and heavy within my breast. I would have to wait until something happened to let it out quick or let it heal on its own.

Weeks went by and the tension remained between us. I went about my own business. I still hung my wash on the nylon rope tied between two trees and lifted the middle with a pole I found that was long enough. After another afternoon of tough laundry, I had leaned against the tree gasping for breath when my eyes focused on a few strands of long dark curly black hair hanging from one of the lower branches.

I pulled them off. There were three strands. The person apparently got snagged in the thick lower branch. I stood running them through my fingers trying to figure out how they could have got there. His hair was short and mine was fine, long and straight.

These were definitely not my hair, nor were they his. So whose hair was it? Anger rose in my chest as I began to think. What did he do here while he left me stranded up at the reserve? Did he bring one of his women here?

I left the strands of hair hanging from a clothespin. Not that he'd ever notice them. I decided not to say one blessed thing about them.

Fred had taken to leaving for long periods of time. He'd be gone all day getting the wood, fishing or hunting for food. Even the trips to the neighbouring tourist camps soon became overnight affairs. He never asked if I wanted to come and I didn't ask to accompany him. He always returned from the tourist camp smelling like beer. I hated them for giving him the drinks.

Fred was gone all night again and returned early in the morning without a word and lay down to sleep. He slept into the afternoon. I tried to be very quiet around the cabin but decided to go out and look for some pine roots for a birchbark basket I wanted to make.

It was a cloudy day and the smell of the earth was very strong as I wandered deep into the swampland west of the cabin. After a while, I sat down and began to peel back thick mounds of deep moss, exposing the pine roots. I gently began to separate the long straight ones from the intermingling web. Soon my hands were black from coiling the roots as I removed each long strand. I had quite a few in my large apron pockets when I looked down at myself. I still wore an apron over my slacks.

From the very first day I had arrived here last winter, I'd worn an apron. I had four and I wore each in turn. This one was filthy with dirt now. I had a sudden strong urge to cry as my eyes settled on the mound of my belly. At that moment, I became aware of a sharp intrusion into my thoughts. I glanced around, and then surveyed the area to my right more closely.

I was being watched. I felt someone watching me, but couldn't see a thing. I calmly began rolling back the moss to cover the exposed roots while resisting the temptation to look around. Terror began to fill me as I pushed back the last chunk of moss and then, a fist-sized rock landed beside me and rolled against my knee. I looked around but saw no one and stood up as calmly as possible.

At first, I thought to take the rock but I could not touch what came from someone's evil hand. I walked away from the site, feeling eyes glued on my back. Then, in what seemed like a tremendous shot of pure animal survival instinct, I took off running at full speed, dodging to the left and right between the trees, avoiding a straight-line run. I jumped over fallen logs and crevices, staying on the rock covered ground as much as I could.

As I got closer to the long woodpile, my foot landed on a large branch and I felt my ankle give. A shot of pain made me stumble but I continued toward the cabin even though I no longer felt the presence behind me. I slowed down as I came behind the cabin, breathing hard and limping badly. I flopped down on a stump near the woodpile and held the stitch of pain in my abdomen.

The door opened quickly and Fred came rushing out. "What's the matter? What happened?"

He kept looking around while he waited for me to answer but all I could say was, "Nothing."

A wave of anger crossed his face and I put my head down, waiting for the onslaught. He quietly said, "Come inside. I'll look at your foot."

I stood up already seeing the swelling ankle beneath my sock. I gasped in pain and gingerly hopped to the doorway, saying under my breath, "It is not my foot. It's my ankle. I twisted my ankle."

He said no more about the incident until that night as he lay stretched out beside me. "What scared you today? Your face was white as a sheet and your whole body was shaking so badly. No wonder you twisted your ankle. You're lucky you did not trip and fall. Why were you running?"

I could hear the strain in his voice. He was trying very hard not to sound angry. What could I possibly say that would make sense? That I had ran and endangered the baby. That I could have fallen because I imagined someone was chasing me through the bush? That I got scared because I imagined someone was watching me when there could not possibly be anyone there?

I said, "I was picking pine roots for a basket when an invisible squirrel threw a fist-sized rock at me."

I expected him to make fun of me or to get angry if he thought I was making fun of his concern. Instead he said nothing for the longest time and then he asked, "Has this squirrel ever thrown a rock at you before?"

"No."

I didn't know where this line of questioning was going but I wasn't going to take any chances and give him the opportunity to change it into a metaphor that could be anybody's interpretation. I turned over and pulled the blanket closer around me.

My silences became longer as my belly became larger. What was I going to do? I had always asked myself, now what? Now I had no answer. There was nothing I could do. I started writing my future forecasts on sheets of grocery packaging that I had cut down to notepad size. I had my treasured four pencils in a cosmetic bag where I kept all my personal things.

One day, I had just finished writing down my notes of hope and blessings that I wished for my baby on a piece of paper at the kitchen table when I heard a rattling by the door. I wondered why he was home early today. It was just after lunch and I was not expecting him until late in the evening. I looked out the window to see a big black bear sniffing around the woodpile by the door.

I barred the door with the axe I always kept inside the cabin, a habit I'd picked up when I was at the trapline with my brother and sister-in-law. I waited but the bear would not go away. It hung around the door and then climbed to the top of the woodpile and decided to sit down, stretch his neck and look around. He gave himself a good ole' belly scratch. After a while, he climbed back down and came toward the cabin. I couldn't see it, but I knew he was just by the doorstep.

I sat down at the table and continued to write down what I was feeling at that moment. Loneliness, fear, feelings of total abandonment, and my hope that we would leave this place once my child was born. I would look after my own baby.

I put my head down and must have dozed off because it was dusk when I sat up. Oh, my back hurt! I thought I heard a noise. Yes, I heard the boat. The engine shut off at the dock and another ten minutes later, I heard Fred mumbling as he came up the path. I could tell he had been drinking. I jumped up to put a log in the fire that had almost gone out.

I put the kettle on and pulled the axe out of the doorframe in time to hear Fred exclaim, "What the heck! Get away from me, you! Shoo! Go away! Go away! Janine! Charlie!"

I pulled the door open to see Fred scrambling to the top of the woodpile as the black bear came out from around the corner of the cabin. I grabbed a block of wood from a pile outside the door and banged it on the washtub that hung there. Bang! Bang! The bear turned, took one look at me and lumbered off into the bush.

I could tell Fred was mighty peeved off as he stepped off the woodpile and lunged for the door. I lit the lamp as he came in and dropped down on the bench beside the table. I was busy at the stove trying to get the fire going enough to heat the supper that I had cooked for him when I heard him swear and then he was in front of me, shoving papers at my face.

My notes! He had read them!

He threw the papers into the stove, grabbed the stew pot and crashed it onto the floor and then stomped out of the cabin. The contents of the pot had splashed everywhere and the smell of it filled the room. With tearful eyes, I whirled around from the stove to see where he had gone and slipped and fell, banging my head on the corner of the bed. The sting merged with the sudden ache in my belly before hissing darkness engulfed me.

I became aware of the smell of blood. Oh, how I hated the smell of blood. After that first time I was with Freddy when he killed the moose right outside our boat landing, I would never again forget the smell of blood. Now, I lifted my head to see that I was on the floor of the cabin. It wasn't moose blood I smelled; it was my own blood. Fred was nowhere in the cabin. I felt along the top of my head and found a blood-congealed lump on the side of my head.

There was the mess of the stew all over the floor as I crawled over to the sink and began washing the blood off me. As I pulled myself up to reach the water pail, I felt a kick deep inside my body.

My baby! Oh, my baby!

I broke down and wailed and sobbed against the counter. I cried, as I had not done since I was a child. Daddy! Mom! Help me!

I was assailed with dizzy spells followed by nausea. I crawled to the bed and curled up on top. I gradually became aware of Freddy sponging my face with a coldwater cloth. Then he began kissing my eyes, my face, my lips and talking to our baby inside me. I heard promises, words of love and affection.

But, I was dead . . . dead inside. I couldn't respond. The next afternoon, I thought I heard a plane land outside at our dock. Then I heard Gook's voice and she was there beside me.

I found out later that Fred had gone to the tourist camp and asked Gook to come and stay, as I was ill with the baby. I learned from Gook that I was out for at least two days from having lost so much blood. She stated emphatically that I should not be climbing to the top of the woodpile where I could fall and hurt myself. She flitted around trying to make me comfortable.

As she was fixing my pillow, I asked, "What was his wife like?"

She stopped for a moment before shoving another pillow under my head and said, "Well, she was a nice-looking girl. Very gentle."

She bristled under my stare and pushed the hot water bottle closer to my feet.

"It was a few years before she married Fred when I first saw her. She was married to Fred's friend at that time. You must have known him. I believe he was from your community too. Oh, what a tragic accident that was. Poor Remy was not even a year old then . . ."

What did she say? Who was she talking about?

But, she had gone out the door. I waited patiently for her to come back inside the cabin. When she finally sat down beside me, I asked, "Gook, who was Remy's father?"

She wiped my face with a mint-smelling cloth before responding softly, "Jeremiah. You remember."

Jere! That was Jere's son? Jere was the first love of my life. He was my first teenage love. Why didn't they tell me? Why didn't she tell me? Why didn't anybody tell me? Then again, why would they?

My chest ached as it dawned on me that Remy was one half of Jeremy. I remembered now that Gook had said that was what the little boy called himself. Remy's baby talk. And I'd thought that was his full name.

I began to moan as another stream of tears ran down my face.

"Now, now. Don't upset yourself. He loves you, you know, He'll take care of you. He's just so upset that he might lose another wife and baby, like that first time... well, you know."

I managed to get the words out. "He hates me, Gook! He is very mean to me! He threw the pot of stew I made for him on to the floor. That's what I slipped on, Gook! I would not go climbing around on top of a stupid woodpile!"

She froze and then abruptly stood up and poured liquid from a cup that she had been heating on top of the stove. She explained to me earlier that it was to speed up my recovery without hurting the child inside me. I drank all the contents in the cup and sank back down against the pillow in a dreadful weariness. She hugged my head to her breast and I knew she was crying in that silent anguish that old women cry. I felt the deep shudder of her chest against my head as I drifted off to sleep once more.

A few minutes later, I thought I heard her giving a thundering lecture to Freddy but I was never sure whether I was dreaming or not. I awoke to find Freddy stroking my forehead. It was early morning and I was in his arms. I felt love and warmth once again. He kissed my head, my nose, and then my lips as he stroked my belly. Then he stooped to kiss my belly and went to get the fire going.

It was a beautiful morning, crisp and clear. Ice had formed along the shoreline and Gook was told to be ready for the last plane out of the tourist camp, one that was willing to taxi to our end of the lake. Gook accompanied me to the outhouse and back. When I stopped to breathe in the fresh cold air and rest against the woodpile, she said, "Look, there! It's Remy's cloud with the golden wig!"

As we stood there Gook made me promise that all my mornings must be this way. If not, I must not think twice about leaving. I was shocked to hear her say that. I couldn't just leave. Not right now. It would be like admitting that I couldn't keep a relationship right; that I couldn't keep my man; that I had failed as a wife; that I couldn't keep the man I loved happy.

All the things I'd heard in the community rushed through my mind. I wasn't ready to do that yet. Not right now. When would it be the right time? When the baby was born? What then?

As if reading my thoughts, Gook looked me right in the eyes

and said, "Your love and spirit comes from deep within you. If it is not right from deep down inside you, then nothing will live outside of it. If you do not find it inside you, it will rot and fester and eventually will kill the spirit within you. If that happens, you will be nothing. You will care about nothing. Your spirit will be broken and cease to exist."

I nodded. Part of that I could understand; the other part, I wasn't quite sure of. I watched her sort out the roots and herbs she had gathered during her short stay with us. She laid them all out in equal doses, which I was to take until I got back to the community. This would be in late November when the ice was thick enough to travel to a hospital.

That night, I dreamt again of the elder with the bones. I did not seem to be aware or know that I was pregnant. I listened as the bones were rearranged in different locations. I repeated the ancient words that slipped from my lips as the ceremony began.

Chapter Thirteen

There were times when Fred was assailed with tremendous fear and apprehension about the coming baby and what it might do to Janine. At other times he felt such guilt that he hadn't made sure that she wouldn't get pregnant. He figured that since she had not gotten pregnant before, there was no reason why she would. She never told him anything.

So, in August, he decided he would have to make sure the baby would be well taken care of when it was born. That had meant that he would have to go see Jere's sister in Winnipeg and ask if she would be willing to defray some of the money he was sending for Remy's keep into an account he wanted to set up for the baby. What else could he do? He was doing the best he could with the little money he had coming in.

In the times of total frustration, his mind would wander to the time at the spring camp by the river when he had stopped cutting wood to watch Janine at the campfire singeing the feathers off the ducks. His eyes had followed her to the snow pile that she had shoveled out with her snowshoes. She had dug holes into the snow into which she shoved the ducks. One by one she had gone across, row after row, sealing them with a wad of snow. He wondered if she remembered anything she had learned in the bush with her family, or whether she had just totally forgotten everything.

He chuckled when she turned to look at him. "You forgot something, Charlie."

"What?"

"You're supposed to mark each spot with a stick sticking out of it, otherwise you won't know where you buried the ducks."

She giggled saying, "I know where I buried them. I don't need a stick to mark the spot."

"How many do you have buried right now?"

"In total, fourteen."

When they were ready to move, he laughed as he watched her poking at the snow with a stick looking for more ducks. She had come up two ducks short. He loved her so much at that moment that his chest hurt.

At the end of July, he stood by the shoreline thinking of her. What was he going to do? Things had remained much as before, with perhaps a bit more love and play until August when he thought to take her to Gook. There was no way he was going to see Jere's sister with her along. Jere's sister was hard enough to deal with at the best of times without having Janine to complicate things. Janine would never have believed that Remy wasn't his son. He just couldn't saddle Janine with a five-year old child in the condition she was in now. He could just imagine her thinking to herself, "So, how many of these do you have scattered around that you are still paying for?"

She had a way of speaking her mind without even opening her mouth. She could be so nasty with a glance that would leave him shaking with rage. How dare she. But how could he respond when she never actually said anything. Oh, she could be so frustrating.

Then there was Jere's sister. The woman was always screaming at him, saying that he was the one who had saddled her with Remy when he was the one responsible for the boy. As he had told her, as far as he was concerned, if it wasn't for him, Jere would still be alive today.

But he never explained. There was no need. He remembered

that night clearly when he and Mary decided to cozy up by the train station with the baby between them. After all, Mary had been his girlfriend long before Jere showed up. As usual, Jere had moved in on him and now there was his baby between them.

They had not even been aware that Jere was in the truck that had come to a stop across from the railway crossing when the bars came down. It was not until they saw him running toward them in the train's headlights. He never knew whether Jere had tripped or what but he hadn't made it.

And then there was Mary and the baby. He had done his duty, married Mary and took the boy as his own. Then she was gone, leaving the boy behind. He paid Jere's sister to look after Remy, and Gook was there to look after him in the summer when Jere's sister went off on vacation with her family.

She was convinced that Remy was his son, not Jere's. Well, he knew the child was Jere's son. He had not gone near Mary in that year when Remy had been conceived.

This time, he caught Jere's sister before she left. When he saw her in Winnipeg, they argued and he had won the battle with the promise that he would take Remy off her hands forever and look after him when he was married to Janine. He decided not to tell her that there was another baby on the way.

He was quite happy when he left their apartment and headed for downtown Winnipeg when, who should come yelling and screaming at him from one of the hotels but Big Al, Karen's husband. He was in a snot of a temper.

Fred didn't have time to find out what the problem was before he saw the blow coming. He'd ducked enough so that it missed his face but the big fist landed squarely on the side of his head. He went down spinning, fell flat on his back and heard the sharp crack of his head hitting the pavement. Bright stars spun inside his eyes. Anticipating a kick across his middle, he quickly rolled away, kicking sideways as hard as he could.

Sure enough, he made contact with one of the big man's legs and Al came down hard, right on the edge of the cement steps of the hotel bar that he had just emerged from. People came running. Fred pushed himself to his feet and stood there swaying as he stooped to check Big Al, who had a pool of blood beside his head. Then the police and an ambulance came.

At the police station, he found out that Big Al was in the hospital. Well, to make a long story short, he spent time in jail until a witness verified that he had not even fought back at all and that the big man had tripped. Fight back? Heck, nothing could have stopped Big Al. Fred might have tried to fight back but he was just lucky to be able to trip him. He knew that Big Al would have beat him to a pulp once he had got his hands on him.

When he was released from jail, he headed straight to Armstrong to pick up the supplies they needed and flew them back to the trapper's shack. From there, he made straight to the Reserve, relieved to find that she was still there. But in truth, she was there in body only. She had put a huge distance between them and try as he might he couldn't do a darned thing about it. There was no way she would believe anything he said, so he didn't bother trying to explain. What did she want from him anyway? What did she want?

Another thing that bothered him immensely was the tourist guide Jason. He was always hanging around the site when Fred wasn't home. He had seen the man several times but before he could get out to check, he was gone. Of course, when he had asked why he didn't hang around, Jason said he didn't know what he was talking about.

Another time, he had come roaring full speed on his twenty-five horsepower Johnson motor to find Jason inside the cabin. Jason's excuse was that he had seen him in a canoe coming into the landing and he'd come across only to find that he wasn't even home. So, who the heck was in the canoe? He had the boat and the canoe was turned over at the boat landing. Janine just looked at him with a blank expression as if she didn't know what was going on.

There was also the time when a lightning storm hit very badly and the wind was threatening to knock the tree down in front of the cabin. He had glanced out in time to see the head and shoulders of a man behind the woodpile. By the time he went out there, there was no one in sight.

Several days later he came across the boot print beside his canoe and dashed up to the cabin in such a hurry that he did not see the bear until he stumbled upon it by the door. Oh, man, now that had him scrambling up the woodpile pretty fast. He was embarrassed that Janine had saved him from the black bear. Or so, she thought.

That was when . . . He hated to think of that time and had stopped trying to rationalize what possessed him to treat her like that. Gook had been so angry she actually hit him across the face with her medicine bag. He'd seen how immediately sorry she was as big tears welled in her eyes and he'd pulled her into his arms. Oh, how sorry he was for the stupid things he had done in his life!

There was only one other single human being in his entire life that he would never hurt for any reason and that was his Gook. To be the cause of those tears in her eyes had wrenched his soul. How he loved the people he seemed to be hurting the most.

He was reacting to situations now and felt that he was no longer in control of anything. He would wait to see what would happen next and the result was that he did nothing at all. But these things that were happening . . . there was nothing he could do about them. He had absolutely no control over anything these days.

He wished Janine would talk to him, tell him who had been and was still visiting her while he was away working, getting wood, checking his traps, fishing or hunting for food. But, no, she said nothing at all. She just looked at him with those bewildered, questioning looks, or worse still and more often of late, the silent accusations, the snide comment looks, and her actions and expressions all condemned him, without her even opening her mouth. If he ever dared to mention the strange footprints or the man he'd seen around the cabin, she just turned her head away without comment.

In her own way, she was always telling him that he was nuts; that she was innocent of all accusations; and how dare he question her. What was he to think?

So, without a word to Janine he helped Jason with the construction of a new icehouse at the tourist camp. She wouldn't care anyway. It was one more thing to argue over because he promised that he'd build a woodshed and instead he was building an icehouse at the tourist camp.

The days came and went as Janine got bigger and bigger. Would she leave when the baby was born? That was what she had written on that piece of paper. That had hurt! But then, maybe the baby wasn't even his anyway. Who was this guy hanging around the camp? The one he had yet to catch. When he did, he had no doubt as to what he would do.

Ha, ha, ha! I am thoroughly enjoying this! Why didn't I think of this before? Well, perhaps it has been too long since I walked among the people. As you can see, I am very, very good at this. Do you want to see how quickly a man can go crazy? I had to go away for a while. It seems that I was getting some birds and animals a bit ticked off at my liberal use of their forms. They held a Council and I had to try to explain some things.

Anyway, I am back and I see that I need to do something very quickly.

There were times that Fred would try to trick Jason into confessing he'd been to the trapper's shack when Fred wasn't there. Instead, he got many accounts of the times when Jason would drive down there only to find that Fred's boat and motor were gone from the dock. There was never any trace of anything, or a glimpse of anyone, other than those on the lake. Fred felt that after all the time he had spent with Jason, that if he was any judge of character, he knew Jason was not the man hanging around the cabin.

So, who was it then? No one saw anything. That was what was making him so furious. Well, he had come to the end of his rope. This had to stop and he was going to make sure that it did not go on to another year.

He could pinpoint the moment when things began to get screwy. It was around the time Janine came to the trapline. Was it someone trying to keep her out? Who could it be? He doubted that it was someone from the community, otherwise people would know. Someone would know if one of the men was up to no good. He'd know if someone had been gone when he got back. But everyone was where they were supposed to be and nothing seemed unusual when he got back.

After that first time when he had nearly stepped into one of the connibear traps, he had been more careful and watchful. He found the trap right below the tree where he had hung the whole bunch. He knew she hadn't done it. There was no way Charlie would be able to pull and set a large trap like that. Why would she do such a thing like that anyway? They had been happy then.

Then who was hanging around the trapline?

Maybe it was a parasite that had attached itself to her, following her from Port Arthur. Would someone follow her? He doubted that a city person would be able to elude him in his own territory so he discounted that idea.

As he listened to the snap and crackle of the last flare of birch logs he'd thrown into the stove, he carefully placed his arm around Janine's middle, cradling the baby within her. His baby. He would protect his wife and their baby with his life. No one would ever take them away from him. They were his. They were home with him, safe and sound.

Chapter Fourteen

It was around the second week of October that I stood outside feeling slightly exasperated. Fred had gone off early. It was around mid-morning when Jason stopped to say goodbye. He said he was going out on the last plane from the tourist camp. He waited around for about half an hour but Fred didn't come home so I put the two boxes of food that Jason had brought over inside the cabin. The food had been left by the last tourists in the cabins. Jason said he'd boarded all the buildings and locked up everything for the winter. He wished me luck with the baby and then he was gone. It was now late afternoon — cold and overcast — and still no sign of Fred.

We'd had snow several times in the last three weeks but it always melted the next day. Winter would soon be here and the new clothesline was still not up. Fred still hadn't put the boat and canoe away either. I hoped that the washed clothes had softened somewhat in the breeze before they froze into stiff boards since the bit of snow this morning had left them soaking wet again. The little nylon line could only hold up a few sheets at a time but I had a lot more to do now. I couldn't wash two or three loads a week as I had done before.

Also, I was still smarting from yesterday's incident. After I had hung up the washing, I saw that the pole I had used to prop up the line and keep the clothes off the ground was leaning against the green wood log pile. I tugged at the pole but soon found that it was pinned at the top by a long pine log. I pulled hard and in a thundering roar the top logs cascaded down. I barely had time to get out of the way when one of the logs swung off and landed end first where I had been standing.

Shaken, I went in for a cup of tea. Why did he do that? He had

had no need to move the logs, since he had not cut any firewood in about a week. When he got back, he had made no comment. I watched him pile the logs back into a neat pile.

I noticed that I was getting skinnier and thinner than ever. This made my belly look even larger than it was. I just didn't have any energy. At this moment, Fred came from around the corner of the cabin looking furious. I turned from the clothesline and took two blocks of dry wood into the cabin. He stood aside as I went in and took a seat at the table.

Fred stopped beside me and pulled my blue shirt out from under his coat. The shirt was my favourite. It had flowers embroidered around the collar. I had been wondering where it had gone. I had searched for it everywhere at the last washing. When was that? Four days ago.

Jason had just laughed when I asked him what day it was. Although I had a calendar hanging on the wall, I never made much of an effort to mark off each day and I had soon lost track of which day it was. It basically did not matter one bit which day it was anyway.

Suddenly Fred barked, "Look at this. Isn't this the shirt I bought you?"

I looked up and said, "Yes. It's the one you bought me at Savant Lake."

He took a big breath and threw it on the table in front of me. He gritted out each syllable between his teeth, "I found it on top the last woodpile deep in the bush. How did it get there?"

I looked at the shirt, wondering how on earth it would have gotten there, unless Fred was just making this up to get mad at me for something. He was still standing there glaring at me. I didn't know what I was supposed to say? So, I shrugged and said, "I don't know."

He still had not moved so I waited. Finally he said, "He was here again wasn't he?"

I wondered whom he was talking about. I wouldn't consider Jason's visit to see Fred an "again."

"No one has been here except Jason. He came to say goodbye to you this morning just before lunch. He brought two boxes of left-over food, right there beside the door. He said to tell you that he had boarded up the tourist camp and that the key was where he always left it, in case the boss wanted it. He was leaving on the last plane out, which must have been the one I heard taking off around mid-afternoon. Oh, and he wished us luck with the baby. He waited for a little while for you before he left. But, that was all."

That was the longest string of words I had uttered in many months. He took one exasperated look around at the cabin and then focused his attention on me for a full minute before stomping out of the cabin. I heard his footsteps recede with no idea when he would return. I really didn't care anymore.

After I had a cup of tea, I went back outside and looked at the pine tree. With new determination, I dug out the box from under the table and pulled out the huge roll of clothesline with the two pulleys and hauled it all outside. I lugged one end of the coil over my shoulder up the woodpile and placed my foot on top of the first branch of the tree. I climbed that tree until I was sure that no amount of slack would drag the clothes down. Then I set about wrapping the wire around the tree and got the pulley positioned. As

I tugged the bottom wire through the pulley, my foot slipped off the lower branch. I was slammed against the tree so hard that I lost my breath. Gasping, I hung with both hands around the branch until the pain receded from my side.

Then I heard Freddy screaming his head off at the bottom of the tree. I knew I was in trouble so I climbed down slowly and carefully. Not because I was afraid to fall, but because there were continuous stabs of pain in my left side. I stepped down to the ground with Fred still stomping around and yelling that I was deliberately trying to kill his baby. When it registered in my brain what he was yelling about, I reacted.

My strangely unfamiliar voice yelled, "What did you say? That I am trying to kill our baby? Do you honestly believe that I would intentionally hurt someone growing inside me? It is you who is trying to kill us. The baby and me! You don't want us, do you? Why don't you just kill us right now instead of torturing me to death."

I could have said a lot more as I'd stored enough awful things in my head to keep my mouth going for a long time. But then he was gone. As usual, he just whirled around and left for who knows where. I didn't much care at that point. He could have another trapper's shack with his other women housed in it for all I knew.

On a sudden impulse, I hobbled down to the lake and saw that his boat was pulled up on shore. I turned the canoe over and pushed it out into the water. Holding a paddle, I stepped in and pushed the canoe off and began paddling out into the open steel-grey lake. I thought that perhaps a bit of paddling would calm me. The pain in my side had receded to a dull ache when I heard the motor behind me. Fred coming at me full speed! I dropped my paddle and grabbed the sides of the canoe to steady myself as waves crashed against the side of the canoe.

I screamed at him, "You stinking rotten muskrat! You flea-bitten mangy dog!"

He lunged forward and grabbed my arm. "Get into the boat right now! The canoe is sinking!"

I stopped to look down and lo and behold, the canoe had a good two inches of water in it. With an old pair of rubber boots on my feet, I hadn't noticed. I shut up and got into the boat and we towed the water-laden canoe to shore without another word between us. As I headed up the path, I heard him grumble under his breath as he pulled the half-filled canoe to shore.

"Why the heck she did this, I'll never know."

I stomped into the cabin. Yes, blame me. Always blame me. Half the time, I hadn't a clue about what he blamed me for or why he got so mad.

That must have been quite a big hole in the canoe for it to fill up like that. I took a swig of Gook's medicine and lay down on the bed.

I awoke, still lying in the same position on the bed and noticed right away that it was very quiet with only the sound of the flickering fire in the stove. I got up and went to the window. There in the full moonlight I saw that all the clothes were on the new clothesline. I turned and saw Freddy sprawled out with all his clothes on the spare bunk we had set up beside the stove.

I went to him, knelt down and slowly brushed back the hair from his forehead. I was so totally emotionally exhausted from the tension between us and wanted desperately just to hold him, to concentrate on him and to love him freely and openly.

His eyes flickered open when I kissed his lips and I whispered, "I love you Fred. Thank you for putting up the clothesline."

He didn't say a thing, just looked at me until I grew uncomfortable and pulled away. I got into bed under the goose down comforter that we had filled with feathers collected from our hunting camp last spring. He did not join me in bed. I had tried to reach out to him but now I was kicking myself for trying. He might as well have pushed me away. I lay alone in the warm comfort of the feathers that we'd had so much fun picking together and felt an intense pain across my chest. I could have cried for a whole week. But, I lay dry eyed and looked into the blackness of the night.

Things went relatively well for the rest of the month. I never did find out what caused the hole in the canoe. Fred had to patch an inch and a half gash on its bottom. After my outburst, I felt ashamed at what I had called him but could find no way to apologize. I could never take back what I had said. And, at times, it revisited me.

One evening, I heard Fred coming in on the boat and went down to see him. He was at the lean-to that he had built to either clean fish or skin the smaller animals. This time, he had a muskrat on the table. He smiled as I approached. Then casting a side-glance at me, a grin traveled across his face and he said, "It's just a stinking rotten muskrat."

I reacted like he had just slapped me in the face. He was throwing my words back in my face. The pain spread across my chest as I blinked back the tears, veered away and headed to the shoreline.

I heard him coming after me but then he stopped. I felt him

standing there as though wondering what to do. I took a deep breath and looked at the sky. I must not cry. I turned and saw that he was back at the lean-to. I walked back to the cabin and set the teapot on the stove.

Come to think of it, I never did find out what my blue shirt had been doing at the woodpile either. But, I was careful not to disturb the new tentative openness that had developed between us and really hoped nothing else would happen.

When the snowstorms came, quietness descended. The outboard motor was now housed in the corner under the kitchen table. Wood was piled under layers of canvas just outside the door. There was no need for the power saw anymore. What hunting he did was along the shoreline or in the bay about a mile from the cabin. Most of the time though, he was in the woods. We were on a point of land and could travel from one side to the other in half a day. He knew where the moose were but had to wait until it was cold enough so we could freeze the meat.

We had a few funny moments and some light-hearted fun, but nothing of the happiness when we had first come here. I realized it was partly to do with my big belly and the cramps that suddenly assailed me. On the whole, it was nice. I had a new sense of safety and comfort with the onset of the snow. I still dreaded the coming Christmas season and wondered what would happen.

I often had a strong urge to run to my notepads and write down what I'd like to see happen. But, there was one thing that Fred had said that got me to thinking. It was the only mention to the notes that he had found on the table that evening when the bear had kept me indoors. I was sharpening a pencil to sketch the outdoor evening scene when Freddy had paused by me.

"You jinx the things you wish for when you write them down you know?" he said and then went out with the water pail.

I rolled the pencil between my fingers wondering if maybe he was right. Did any of the things I wrote down ever come true? No. I can't honestly say that they ever had. I must destroy all my notes about the baby, I thought. I scrambled around in all the nooks and crannies, and shoved every page into the stove before I heard his footsteps coming up the path.

From then on, I sketched outdoor scenes: clouds with golden wigs, the trees, and the islands. Most of the time though, I sketched Fred at work: stretching animal hides, hauling wood, cutting wood, splitting wood, hauling water and building a cradle that looked much like a huge snowshoe without a front or bottom. It was a meshed-in structure with the sides and bottom laced with woven rawhide. I sewed beadwork patterns of flowers on leather and attached them to the head and foot pieces. We worked on this cradle together from beginning to end. It was the one thing we did together and it was really quite beautiful.

Preparations for our baby were finished by the end of the third week in December. I had made it clear that I was not interested in going into the community for Christmas. Freddy, on the other hand was insistent that he get us Christmas presents and some grocery treats. I was partial to that idea, as I had developed an insatiable desire for peanut butter. I made him promise to bring back at least a dozen jars for me.

He needed to replace some connibear traps and we needed more rice, flour, baking powder, oats, lard and perhaps some face cream for my stretched belly. My face felt so dry at times that I must have looked as bad as I felt. I was still very much concerned that I was losing weight when I should have been gaining it. And then there was the other thing I really longed for since I had noticed wolf tracks near the farthest woodpile the last time I'd gone for a walk. I mentioned them to Fred and added, "If we had a dog, it would bark and chase any wolves away."

Fred had been lying down with his hands behind his head as he always did, but now he came up on one elbow. "You want a dog? Why didn't you say so?" He knelt down beside me and cupped my face in his hands and said, "I promise I will not bring home a flea-bitten mangy one."

I recognized the words but his gentle eyes held mine, and his hands stayed firmly around my face. This time I understood. I was forgiven. Tears flowed down my cheeks and his thumbs wiped them aside. He held me close and lightly kissed me, then bent down to kiss my belly.

Chapter Fifteen

He left on the twenty-third of December. Christmas came and went. And then, New Year's Day was gone and I knew he had goofed up again. He always had good intentions but was easily distracted before he'd suddenly remember what he was supposed to do or where he was supposed to be. He'd just better concentrate on what he was supposed to be doing, I thought, or I would be in big trouble.

I had the rabbit snares and regularly caught one a day. If I did not feel like having a rabbit for supper, I always had a partridge in the box on top the roof. The only other things that got on my nerves were the martins. Man, you couldn't hide anything from those guys.

There was Josiah, Peter, Terry, that rascal Oscar Martin and the lady Lucy. I absolutely had no liking whatsoever for Oscar. He was the meanest martin I had ever come across in my entire life. I would have clamped a trap around that old rascal with my own bare hands if it weren't for the thought of catching Lucy instead. She was a sweet girl, that Lucy. Oh, well, never mind, that old raven was back at my fish freezer box again. Between the ravens, the martins and the blue jays, I wondered if I still had fish left to eat.

I had made some jam with the frozen blueberries that we kept in the box on the roof when I felt the first searing pain. Chalking it down to gas pain, I endured the regular cramps into the evening. It was now the eleventh of January and I still had another three weeks to go before the baby was due. What were these pains? I was still alone. It was then that I realized that with all my worrying and waiting for Fred, I had not felt the baby move in a long time. When was the last time I felt the baby move? Last week. No, it was four, maybe five days ago?

I experienced the spasms of intense sharp pains, which diminished into an acute ache before being assailed with another searing pain. I endured the pains all through the night and now it was the twelfth of January. What was I going to do? I was terrified at having the baby alone. Didn't I ask him to not leave me alone for more than three days? No more than three days, I had begged.

"What if something goes wrong? Please do not leave me for no more than three days, please!" I had begged him. But now, he'd been gone for two and a half weeks.

As the pains continued, I knew I was in trouble but I still didn't know what to do. I didn't know a thing about babies. I was supposed to go to the Sioux Lookout hospital at the end of January and wait until the baby came. That was the plan. Now, what was I to do?

I cursed Fred and swore that I would never forgive him for this. In desperation, I packed some things into a packsack. In went four baby blankets, still in the packages, baby socks, several baby gowns, a bottle, matches, baby diapers, raisins, a can of milk, a knife and a chunk of bannock. Next went my personal cosmetic bag. I couldn't think of anything else because I didn't know what I'd need.

I tied a flannel blanket around my middle and folded a quilt over the seat of the old snow machine, praying to God that it would take me the whole seventy miles back to the community. Freddy got so fed up with this old machine stalling that he had finally bargained for the newer machine, which he'd taken. I had used the old one once to get some wood. It still ran but had a tendency to stall. Sometimes, it would sit for several weeks before it would start again after Fred had taken it apart for the zillionth time.

"Why are you doing this to me? I thought. You didn't just left me alone for no reason. Why? What's happened? Has something happened to you Fred? Are you still alive? What's happened? You wouldn't just leave me like this, would you? Would you?"

No amount of questions would halt the spasms of pain that ripped through my back and across my belly. I knew labour was supposed to take a long time and hoped to goodness I had enough time to make it back to the village.

I put the lights and the stove out in the cabin. I thought of leaving a note but after that incident about the notes, I decided to forget about the idea. I had to have a deeper faith that things would be all right and we would be together again — Fred, the baby and me.

The old snow machine started like clockwork. I estimated the time to be about eight o'clock in the evening. My watch had long ago died and since we didn't have a clock in the cabin, I had no idea of the exact time I left. As I pressed on the throttle and the machine sped across the lake, I hoped and prayed that I would meet Fred along the winter trail. Without slowing down, I roared over the creek and into the dense swamp bush, up and down the hills, over Devil's Gorge (a jump of over ten feet) at full speed with only two skinny pine poles bridging the deep gorge. I didn't even hold a breath. I'd been through there before. My only thought was to line up the machine, close my eyes, hold my breath and press the throttle at full speed.

Soon, I was out into clear bright moonlight on Whitewater Lake. The machine roared at a constant rhythm beneath me as another cramp seized me across the middle. I moaned as I hit a deep snowdrift and then I was on hard packed snow. I crossed the lake and was eventually at the marsh area in the middle of Best Island. It was somewhere in the middle of the centre pond that I hit a drift that threw me in such a sharp jerk to the right that pain shot like a huge boulder had gone right through my belly and straight out of my back. The machine continued on at full speed while I gasped to catch my breath.

My mind screamed, “I do not want to have a baby in the middle of nowhere on the ice!”

I knew that no one was on this lake at this time of the year. My hands clamped on to the speed clutch as I went at break-neck speed across the island and straight on to the narrows. I eased off a bit as the machine climbed up the bank and into the portage. Applying more speed as I came out the other end of the portage, another spasm invaded my abdomen. I kept my hands around the throttle and went at full speed across the short bay and into another portage, sending sheets of snow spraying at each snowdrift. I came out careening into a solid snowcap that sent me sailing back on to the path. I was still on at full speed when another pain doubled me over.

It was another half hour before I emerged at Loon Narrows, a place from my childhood. “Dad, help me!” I moaned out loud. Screaming and crying, I barreled through the narrows and out onto the open but frost-hazed Smoothrock Lake. Another sweat-drenching pain enveloped me as I passed between the two islands. It was still a long way to the other end where the other portage was. Somewhere in the middle of the lake, the machine started to sputter. There was no other soul around for the next thirty miles.

I screamed out loud. "No, No! Please don't do this to me!"

But, the machine stopped dead. I stood leaning over the handlebars as another sharp, insistent pain passed over me. I couldn't stop now. I had to keep going. I pulled the starting cord just as another pain shot across my middle. I screamed again. I tried to time the next pull to when I felt the pain recede. In this way, I pulled and pulled to get the machine started. It finally sputtered to life and I managed to go for another mile or so. On and on it went. Stop and go, stop and go until I crossed the portage out of Smoothrock Lake and headed toward the channel. Finally, I made it to the small lakes that led to the last lake before one last portage into the community. It was a long three-mile portage to where I expected Fred to be and where I hoped my mother was.

I maneuvered the machine across the dense bush and had just emerged into the last clearing when the machine stopped again. As I pulled again to get the machine going, I felt a gush of something beneath me. I looked down at my feet and saw the snow was coloured red.

If my water had broken, why was it red? Was it supposed to be red? Why would they call it water if it were red? Thank God there had been neither hide nor hair of wolves throughout the whole crazy night. Otherwise, I would have been scared out of my wits.

I had but two miles to go when my water had broken. The machine was going again, and there was no sign of wolves . . . yet. I eased off the throttle as I crept slowly up the hill and into the bushes. When another pain seized me with a ferocious force, I involuntarily clamped on the throttle that put it at full speed down the bush road's left and right turns, up and down the gullies and swamp log trails. I came shooting out of the portage trail so fast that it apparently caught the attention of the old man who lived in the very last cabin.

I would hear later that the old man had been bringing the morning firewood into his cabin when he heard a snow machine come to a sudden stop in the bushes by the graveyard. As we all knew, when someone's machine ran out of gas, they were always appreciative of someone showing up with gas. When he found me, I was drenched in blood and straining to have a baby that wasn't coming out.

Mother came with me to the hospital in Sioux Lookout. I felt the bandages at my belly where they had taken out my dead baby. Later in the day, I woke to find Freddy sitting beside me. I heard myself scream, "Get out! Get out!"

The doctor told me that I was lucky to be alive and that my husband had been there all day waiting to see me. I told the nurses that I did not have a husband and they were not to let anyone except my mother come near.

I grieved for my baby and was extremely angry the whole time I spent at the hospital. On top of that, an infection set in and I had to stay in the hospital for another week. They had buried the baby without me there. If I had seen him at that time, I probably would have punched Fred from here to kingdom come, along with whatever woman he had been with.

I blamed everyone for the hell I had just gone through. Why hadn't someone come to check up on me when I was in the bush? I did a lot of screaming and crying at that hospital in those several weeks. The unfortunate thing was that it was all done silently inside my head.

When I finally arrived back at the village, I got more bad news when I stopped in at the post office on the way to my mother's place. The postman informed me that my good friend Linda had been killed in a car accident after the New Year. In my mind, somehow, there was no separation between the pain I felt with the loss of my baby, Linda and Fred. They all rolled into one horrible gigantic pain that invaded every space in my heart, mind and soul.

I lay curled up into a ball on the single cot beside the window in my mother's cabin. For the very first time, I felt unreasonable fear. Every footstep coming to the door sent my heart racing against my ribs. I was terrified that Fred would show up yelling and screaming that I had killed our baby.

I couldn't cry. I had not cried at all. As the days came and went, the Groundhogs kept me well fed. In fact, they would not leave until I'd eaten. I became stronger.

About a week later, I heard an airplane land. A snow machine was coming toward the cabin. My heart raced as I backed up against the wall by the bed in fear. I heard voices and then the Groundhogs burst in.

"Someone to see you, Janine."

Oh, no! I thought. I grabbed my jacket, but then saw that it was Gook. She made a beeline across the floor to me and held me for a long time as she shed silent tears. At one point, I lifted my head to see my mother at the table watching us. I could not understand the look on her face until I realized that she probably wished she could do that too. Hug me, I mean. It most likely never occurred to her to do that.

Gook stayed for several days. After a long conversation with

Mother, we decided on what I should do. With the help of the Groundhogs and armed with an axe and a hammer, we headed over to Fred's cabin. The boys had the padlock brackets off the door in no time. The snow machine was in the middle of the floor. Fred always brought it inside when he was going on the train. I guessed he had not returned. My suitcases were where I had left them. Everything that was to go to the trapline was packed in wooden crates and paper boxes. All my town clothes were still in the suitcases. I was never one to leave any of my things scattered around, but I watched Gook shove a sweater into the suitcase.

I stood and looked around, feeling the urge to cry.

Gook said, "Let it all go, Channie. Let it go. Leave it all here within these cabin walls. Logs are very good at that you know; they take out the pain and sorrow from you. They absorb it all. Leave it all with them. If you take any of the bad feelings with you, they will fester within you like a huge sore. Let them all go. Leave the hurt and ugliness within these walls. They will take it all from you and it won't hurt you again...so bad."

I took a deep breath and calmly walked out the door. The boys nailed the padlock brackets back on the door then we all walked to the train station. Gook and I got on the train with no more than a wave from Mother and the Groundhogs.

We were halfway to Sioux Lookout when Gook said "I want to tell you that I put some money in the suitcase when I put the sweater in. It is not mine so don't feel bad. Fred sent me money over the years. That was the only way I knew where he was. From the time his mother died, he decided that he would take care of me. He never told me to keep it for him; he just sent me the money.

What am I going to do with the money? I am an old woman. I don't need the money. I have enough to live on. Remy has his own money too. So, what you find in the suitcase is yours. It is yours. Don't argue with me. Take it and use it to get started again."

I looked out the window and said nothing. Part of me had died last month. My problem was that I didn't know which part. How could I even begin to heal myself when I wasn't quite certain where the exact spot of injury lay? I just seemed to hurt all over. I was in agonizing pain, mentally and spiritually, although the physical pain had long gone. I would wake up in the middle of the night dreaming that the baby had kicked. Oh, that tore me apart! It was at those times when I stared into the darkness until the sun came up.

Gook took my hand and we sat like that until the train rolled into Sioux Lookout. She was going on to Winnipeg to see a cousin and where she expected to find Fred. I never even knew they had relatives there. At Sioux Lookout, I gave her a hug and got off the train. When I got to the hotel room, I unpacked for a hot bath and found the money. I unrolled the sweater and what I thought to be around fifty one-dollar bills. It came to one thousand and twenty-five dollars in money orders, hundreds, fifties and fives. I was totally shocked. Tears came gushing out in a torrent of emotion. I finally released the tears I had kept bottled up for so long.

Chapter Sixteen

I took my time finding a job in Port Arthur. I sat in a motel room for about four days just looking at myself in the dresser mirror when it occurred to me that I no longer knew the person I saw there. I had been through so much and most of it had been on my own. I had no one to share those experiences with. In the whole time I had been away, I had not seen myself in a mirror or had anyone to balance my thoughts and feelings with. I mean someone with whom to talk, someone who would set my sights straight and help me find a balanced perspective. "An even-keeled point of view" as Linda would have described it. Oh, how I missed her. I thought that maybe I had sunk too low.

A week later when I felt I'd found some semblance of myself, I got up and went looking for a furnished apartment. About three days later, I found a cozy little place close to downtown Port Arthur. I got a job a short time after that at the Indian Affairs Counseling Unit and began to rebuild my life. Slowly, one day at a time.

Around eight months later, Nisha suddenly walked into the office and stood leaning against the counter, looking at me with a slight smile on his face. He had come to pick me up for lunch he said. At a total loss for what to say, I got up and we went for lunch in the restaurant downstairs at Eaton's. I wasn't saying much, so he did all the talking.

Before I realized it, he had me laughing at the endless tales of comical situations. We sat in the shade of the trees outside the office before I went back in. I smiled when he replied, "Nisha-bego," to my question as to why he had come into town. That meant "just for nothing".

I've got her now! She's mine! You see, I took care of Fred. I took that baby too. I want her all to myself. All to myself. All to myself. All to myself... Wait, I feel the sense of someone. Someone knows me. I feel him searching for me. I must see who it is. Distract. That's it!

As the days went by, Nisha showed up for lunch at least three times a week. He had a job at a warehouse and was driving the same truck that had broke down when I'd first met him. One warm evening in October when we walked up to Hillcrest Park, he put his arm around me. Then quite unexpectedly, he leaned over and kissed me. I, like an old partridge, froze and couldn't move.

I knew that this wasn't going anywhere and pushed him away. I explained that I was not ready for another relationship and that all he would ever have from me was friendship. He looked quite shocked as if that was the last thing in the world he expected to hear. He said nothing about it on the walk home and we chatted along the way as if nothing had happened. What was he doing? Pretending that it never happened?

Then Nisha disappeared. Christmas came and went and I didn't see him. I went to work and came home. I always stayed home on weekends and I never went anywhere, or felt the need to.

One evening in January, as I walked past my living-room window, I saw a man leaning against the lamppost across the street. I pulled the curtain shut and glanced out once more before it closed. He was gone. I had no idea who it might have been. It suddenly occurred to me that most evenings when I came home, a man would materialize somewhere on the street. Each time I tried to get a closer look, he would melt into the shadows. I never thought that he might have anything to do with me, until now. I always thought it was just someone out for a walk. Now it got me to thinking. Could it be Fred? I wasn't certain because he always stood in the shadows or had a big parka on with the hood pulled low.

I was coming home one evening and it was about the fifth time that I saw him there. This time he had a snowsuit jacket on. I turned around at the door in time to see him move into the light. I recognized him. It was Fred!

Shock and anger shot through me. How dare he! Furious, I ran toward him as fast as I could. I was going to make sure he never dared hang around my door again. I ran flat out right across the street, yelling his name as he started to turn. He stopped when he saw me coming. When I was within arm's-length, he grabbed me and pulled me into his arms. I was catching my breath and starting to push myself away when he crushed me so hard to his chest that I couldn't move.

At that moment, I saw a truck slow down outside my apartment and then the screech of tires as it sped away down the street. It was Nisha! What was he doing here? I thought he had gone out of town again. Maybe it wasn't him. It could have been another truck.

I started hitting Fred on the chest until he released me. I shoved him away and stood back gasping.

"Don't you ever touch me again. Go away and stay out of my life!"

He threw his head back and laughed, a menacing, idiotic laugh. His face was gaunt, full of lines and badly in need of a shave. When he turned and quickly walked away, I ran blindly back to my apartment.

Why was he doing this to me? How long had he been stalking me? Had he gone mad? He hadn't sounded sane. A shudder went up my back.

Toward the end of January, my phone rang. It was the postmaster from my home community. My mother was sick and asking for me to come home. I put the phone down and cried bitterly for about an hour before I started packing. I had to go back. I would call work from there.

I hoped Mother wasn't seriously ill. I hated the thought of having to give up my place and my own sense of security, or whatever was left of it. I would pay for an extra month so that I didn't lose it, but I figured I was going to lose my job.

I caught a bus to Nakina and took the evening train west, getting off at around eleven o'clock. Amongst the hissing steam, I could hardly see the little step that the conductor had placed on the ice-covered gravel beside the railway tracks. His hand on my arm kept me balanced as I stepped off the train. Still quite distracted with worry, I automatically nodded to him.

"Thank you very much, sir. Good night."

There was a noticeable pause of a few seconds before he responded. "And good night to you too, Miss."

The people who were getting on the train stood aside as I stepped down. I got my suitcase, which another conductor was handing down to the conductor standing beside me. I whispered another "thank you" and then left the station. I made my way along the path that ran parallel to the railway tracks and across the creek toward Mother's place. The train was gone and the path was deserted. All I heard was snow crunching under my feet.

Oh, my! Was it ever cold!

I had gone about halfway when I heard footsteps coming at a run behind me. I paused and put my suitcase down thinking that whoever was coming up behind me in such a hurry could very well go around me. It was Ron. He came to a stop beside me and after a brief silence, picked up my suitcase. I walked ahead and he followed without a word until we got to the top of the hill. I stopped and turned around. He put the suitcase down and faced me. The moon was full and I saw the frost forming on the loose curly hair around his cheek.

"Thanks," I said.

Then his teeth flashed bright in the moonlight and he started to giggle.

"What?" I said hesitantly, not quite sure what he found so funny.

He started laughing outright. "Oh, that was priceless! The way you got off the train! Girl, you had everyone so shocked they nearly froze in their snow machine boots!"

My smile slowly disappeared. "What do you mean?" I asked. "Are you making fun of me? What did I do that was so funny?"

He shrugged and waved his arms. "Oh, no. It wasn't so much what you said but how you said it. Absent-minded — the proper, prissy type. Well, you know, 'Thank you.' No wonder you drove Fred crazy."

I did what? Feeling rather offended, I continued walking. I drove Fred crazy? What on earth did he mean by that?

I heard him coming up behind me almost on a run before I

realized that I had been walking fast. I slowed down. We were nearing the cabin when I stopped and turned around again.

He put the suitcase down and I said, "I'm sorry, Ron. I'm just not myself. What did you mean crazy? Has Fred gone crazy?"

He said, "Janine, don't you ever say you're sorry to me. I don't ever want you to be sorry about me. Understand? Let's keep it the same now as it has always been between us; just open honesty, trust, and love. Don't ever be afraid to talk to me. Tell me how you feel. I'll understand, and you know that I'll always be here to help you if I can. I always have."

What a grand speech! I watched him swipe the long jet-black curls back off his forehead with both hands. He used to call them his "Elvis locks."

I smiled and whispered, "Thanks. Is Mother that sick and is Fred really crazy?"

He giggled again, "No, your mother isn't that sick. Just got a touch of pneumonia, that's all. But, there was no one to look after her, to get water, wood and such. As for Fred . . . Well, it's hard to tell what's going on in his head. Won't talk to anyone anymore. I heard he was in a hospital in Toronto for an awful long time though. But I don't know what happened."

I was puzzled. "So where's O?"

Ron answered, "Well, his first wife died and now he has to take care of things. The boys went with him but they came back alone this morning. Your mother couldn't go with O when he left. That was the day she got sick."

I started walking when he asked, "Did you get on at Armstrong?"

"No," I said, "Why?"

I heard him take a deep breath. "Oh, my wife left last week and hasn't been back since. I thought maybe you might have seen her."

I kept walking and said, "I got on at Nakina and, no, I didn't see her. Did you ever marry her?"

"Oh, no. No way she'd ever marry me!"

We stepped on to Mother's porch. As we neared the door, he whispered from behind me, "Janine, wait!"

I stopped and turned.

With a hand cradling my chin, he said, "Be really careful. Old Henry says there's evilness about. A strange spirit or something."

I froze but didn't have a chance to say anything. He pushed the door open in front of me. Just what on earth did he mean by that? I felt a smile touch my lips as I stepped in. Silly guy! The heat nearly knocked me back. Was it ever hot in there! Mother had a fever, along with a very bad cold. She was laying on the double bed in the corner of the room. It was a good ten minutes before I got her more comfortable. I didn't even notice Ron leave. It was really strange what he'd said. Evilness. Why would he say that? I'd never known Ron to be superstitious.

In-between coughing fits, Mother informed me that O, the rotten scoundrel, had taken off and sent the kids back for her to look after. Well, where were they? I no sooner had that thought when the door burst open and they were all over me, both yapping at the same time.

When things got down to normal, I began to take more notice of them. Benny, the taller one, was almost as tall as I was. Lenny was stocky rather than tall. Funny about those twins; you could not tell them apart before but now their bodies certainly left no doubt now. I no longer had to guess which one I was addressing when I asked Benny why his father decided not to come home.

We were outside splitting and bringing in wood for the stove. He was certain his father had not gone back to the town where their house was. He thought O had to go somewhere else, something to do with a will, and something about a bank. That was why O's explanation meant nothing to Mother; she wouldn't have had a clue as to what that was about.

Later, as I was chiseling the ice to widen the water hole, Lenny came down with the water pail. I asked him if he had heard where his father was and why he had not come back. He said O told him that he was going to Savant Lake about a will and then to a bank in Fort William somewhere and that he'd be back as soon as he fixed things up. I decided that I'd to go to the store and call Savant Lake in the morning.

The black and white dog met me as I was halfway to the store the next day with Lenny and Benny behind me. It was so good to see him. His tail wagged as he licked the "skin off my gloves" as the boys said. I petted his head and told him how wonderful it was to be back and how glad I was to see him. The boys laughed and snickered behind me.

I called the store's owner in Savant Lake where O did his shopping and kept a mailbox. The telephone rang. The Groundhogs were standing there anticipating my words as I pretended to be a secretary of some kind.

At the fourth ring, a man answered and I said, "Good afternoon, Sir. I am inquiring as to the whereabouts of a certain Mr.

Hugh Sigmondson. Has he been to see you recently?" I flipped an imaginary scarf over my shoulder that got the boys clamping their hands over their mouths.

After a brief pause, the voice at the other end replied, "Yeah, he was here. I give the envelope to him like she said... his wife, I mean. Who's this?"

I ignored the question and said, "Thank you very much, Sir."

I hung up the phone.

The Groundhogs broke into a sputter and soon they were rolling with imitations of my voice, "Thank you very much, Sir."

I laughed with them as they doubled over in laughter behind the potato storage counter. The boys were still howling with laughter all the way home at their imitations of me. I thought that maybe O had some legal business to attend to, and I would have to stall Mother with all kinds of explanations. So, in the days to come, as we waited for his return, I made Mother's favourite meals and told her wonderful stories about the city.

As I smoothed her forehead, brushing the hair away from her face, I noticed the black hair now laying a solid dark grey across her forehead and temples. Her dark brown eyes looked into mine. With a jolt, I felt like I was looking down into my own eyes. To cover up my reaction, I immediately bent forward to kiss her on the forehead and give her a hug. Her arms closed around me and for the very first time in my entire life, I actually felt her hug me. I gave her a quick kiss on her cheek and was out the door with the two boys right behind me.

I stood by the water hole, listening to the noise of the community and thinking how nothing was fair in this world. You never get what you feel you deserve. There wasn't a thing you could do to prevent bad things from happening to you. You paid a horrific price for some ghastly outcomes. You lost immensely precious things without having anything to do with it or having any say whatsoever.

Mother was sent away to a sanatorium for tuberculosis treatment when I was about six. She was gone for about five years, and came back (with one lung) to a child who didn't know her. I was raised by my two older sisters and never knew a mother's love when I was a child. But, my mother was still here. I still had time. I'd take it one hug at a time. I had been doing a lot of thinking lately, thinking back, taking a good look, and trying to understand myself.

O finally came home in such great spirits that none of the tongue-lashing he got from Mother seemed to dim his happiness. He sat the boys down beside Mother and told them about the stocks and bonds which he had accumulated over the years and had given to his wife. And lo and behold, she had willed it all back to him for the boys.

The boys yelled, "We are rich! We are rich!"

After that, O was treated like royalty. He settled down on the bed beside Mother and the boys ran around doing his bidding.

The next day, just before I went out the door to return to Port Arthur, I bent close to O's ear as he was being handed another cup of tea in bed and whispered for only him to hear.

"If I see you still in bed being waited on hand and foot when I come back in the spring, I will personally launch you out onto a chunk of ice straight out to the middle of the lake. Do you hear me?"

For the first time in all the years since he had been with Mother, he grabbed my hand and pulled me forward. I heard him say, “If I had ever had a daughter of my own, Janine, I could not have wished for a better daughter than you.”

Generous mood, eh!

Making a face at him, I pulled away. But I met his eyes for a moment before I stood up. I had always thought that he didn’t like me, that he’d always been hell-bent to get rid of me and then he says that? I smiled to myself and without comment, turned and walked out. Of course, the Groundhogs were behind me taking turns carrying my suitcase. Yeah, there he was to meet us and walk us to the train station — the old dog.

You were lucky. I felt sorry for you. I was going to take your mother too, you know? But, now is not the time. A time will come when you will want me, my lost little one. You will want only me... only me... only me...

Chapter Seventeen

When I got off the train at Sioux Lookout, I headed straight to the hotel. The woman at the desk didn't even glance at me as I paid for the room and walked up the stairs. As I stepped into the hallway, my heart suddenly flipped, for the door in front of me opened and out came Fred! His eyes widened when he saw me. I could feel my body moving and then I was on the floor kneeling and he was pushing my head down, getting the blood to rush back into my head. With one arm through my elbow, he led me to my room. I sat down on the bed. Without a word, he pulled off my boots and took my coat off.

Then he was there with a wet cloth. I froze as he sat down beside me and began wiping the warm cloth across my face. I had clamped my jaw shut so hard it began to ache. I remained like that with just my eyes following him around the room. Then he was pulling the woolen blanket over me from the foot of the bed.

Suddenly, I came to life, throwing back the blanket, I jumped up, yelling, "What the hell are you doing? Just what do you think you're doing? Get out! Get out!"

He took one look at me and then turned to the door and went out. The door clicked behind him and I heard his footsteps going down the stairs. I lay back down and swore I could see my heart beating against the blanket tucked so close around my chest. My thoughts alternated between panic and excitement, and then nothing but plain white searing anger. Still, I waited.

I waited until I got so drowsy that I found myself trying to blink away the weight from my eyelids. A stupid thought settled into my brain that the sandman had planted his solid butt on top my eyelids. I never for the life of me ever imagined seeing Fred again.

Oh heavens! I 'd known I still loved him the split second I saw him. I felt the tears rolling down my face as I realized the situation I was in.

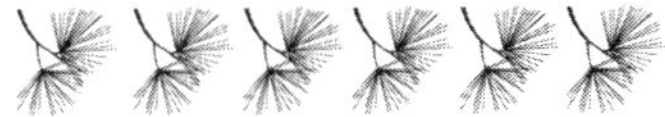

Fred sat in the restaurant. He hadn't just left her out there. He had been chasing a man whom he thought was the man sneaking around their cabin. Someone had been at the trapper's shack.

The man used to come around once in awhile but he could never catch him. He'd been sure Charlie knew someone was around too. Anyway, he'd been trying to find out about a puppy when he'd heard a guy saying that the worst part for mosquitoes was the swamp by Clay River. That had got him started wondering how that guy knew about that place. Nobody went there without first passing his place. He'd gone to see and found out that it was that strange guy who popped up once in awhile at the village. Nisha. Or whatever they called him.

When Nisha got up and left, he'd gone after him. All of a sudden, a bunch of men had popped up around him and beat the heck out of him. He'd been sick a long time with broken ribs, a punctured lung and other injuries but eventually, he got out of the hospital in Toronto. Charlie was in Port Arthur by then, so he went there.

That's where he saw him again. He thought it was Nisha but the man took off before he could catch him or see his face. Then he flew out to the trapline again. When he finished putting his traps away, he went back to Port Arthur where he saw the same guy again, so he followed him. He knew the man would find Charlie and sure enough, there she was.

The man didn't hang around because Fred had seen him. The next day, he'd stood across the street from Charlie's place and waited for the man just to see what he did when Charlie came home. A couple of times, he watched the man watching Charlie. But the man never did a thing. He just watched her come home.

Fred didn't think the man would hurt her but he was sure that the man was the one causing him all the grief and pain. He sure had been having some close calls. The guy was smart, real smart. Nobody had ever come near his place without him knowing, but this guy, maybe he'd even helped himself to a cup of tea while Fred was right there. In the winter, the spook had gone away. Didn't leave any tracks. But, then that didn't account for the weird attraction Fred had been getting from wolves, bears, ravens and such.

Fred sighed, maybe he ought to go talk to her and tell her his side of things. Would she listen? Maybe. Maybe not. He was just plain going crazy.

Talk about crazy, Ol' Henry was at the store in the community recently when he'd gone in. His glassy eyes had settled on Fred from where he sat on the bench beside the door. Damn crazy old Indian! He really gave him the spooks! Did it on purpose too, the old coot!

After he got a few groceries and was heading out the door, the old coot stuck out his cane to block his way. "See that old dog that always hangs around you? That's him! That's him, I tell you!"

Fred saw the old black and white dog outside the window. He just stood there. Man, he didn't know who was crazier, him or Ol' Henry.

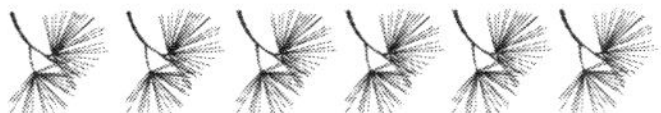

I heard footsteps coming up the stairs followed by a knock at the door. I jumped up to open it and there stood Fred.

"You know we have to talk. If you don't want to talk to me, then please hear me out because I need to tell you a few things."

I backed away from the door, determined not to open my mouth again. I sat down by the table, indicating the other chair for him.

He sat there fidgeting for a long time before he finally blurted out, "I don't know if you will believe me or not, but it doesn't matter now. I never told you things because I thought you wouldn't believe me anyway. Maybe I should have just told you. Anyway, I have made mistakes one after the other. I guess I don't need to tell you that, but I have nothing left now but to tell you the truth."

I kept my eyes down on my clasped hands on my lap. He cleared his throat several more times before he took a deep breath and rushed out a bizarre tale, that . . . no, I probably would not have believed if he had told me then.

Fred had apparently been hunting for "our invisible man" and had got very close when he was suddenly beaten and put out of commission for quite a long time. That was when I had my crazy snow machine ride in the middle of the night. This meant that no one would ever know who the person was until Fred himself caught him. I shuddered. So, there was someone out there at the trapline. Why hadn't Fred ever said anything? When did he find out that there was someone out there with us? Questions were starting to race around in my head again. It was at those times when I became totally oblivious to anyone and everyone around me.

I was remembering one night at the trapline late in October

when winter finally set in. Fred and I were lying in bed watching the flickering lights against the ceiling from the fire in the wood stove when he had asked, "Did your parents ever talk about the legends of long ago?"

I repeated, "Legends?"

I could feel him turn to look at me and I smiled in the dark saying, "I don't know, but when we were kids we used to hear all about Weesquachak's exploits and all the tricks he would pull on the birds and animals, all the things he would do to the people. He was really funny at times."

There was silence for quite awhile after my voice faded. Then he asked, "What would you think if we had Weesquachak pestering us here in the summer?"

I remember I'd laughed and said, "There are no young ladies here to lure or some hapless little animal to trick."

I thought he had just been teasing me. Had he actually thought back then that there was someone sneaking around our cabin? What about the shirt? The canoe? The woodpile? The long black strands of hair?

No, that was ridiculous.

I became aware of Fred's voice in a conversational tone. "... and the dog danced in shoes with shiny silver twinkle toes and the moon laughed as a ladybug glued itself to the dog's nose."

He stopped as he turned from the window to see that I was watching him.

In a serious tone I said, "Don't you go crazy on me, please."

He laughed. "I just wanted to know if you were even listening to me. You didn't answer me. I asked you if you still feel like you are my wife?"

I felt anger creeping up my throat again and I swallowed hard.

"That is not what we are here to talk about. I want you to tell me why you piled the wood on the top of my clothesline pole, knowing that when I pulled it, it would come crashing down on me. I want to know why you accused me of so many things? Like the shirt I lost and whose hair was caught on the branch. It was not yours and it was not mine. I want to know . . ."

His voice cut in, "Who planted that huge connibear trap right where I would step? Who put the big hole in the canoe? Who . . ."

His voice died.

I looked at him in disbelief as all that registered in my brain. What? He was looking at me like he was witnessing the most fascinating and totally horrifying thing on earth.

He shook his head, saying in a whisper, "You didn't?"

I heard my voice saying, "So, it wasn't you?"

We both shook our heads. This was absolutely crazy. Maybe I had gone just as crazy as him and didn't know it. This was too much to take. I couldn't deal with all this information right now. He stood up and looked as though the walls were closing in on him.

He walked to the door and paused. "You didn't answer my question."

What was his question? Do I still feel like his wife?

I looked at him, then down at my hands again and said in a voice that was just above a whisper, "Yes, I will always be your wife, Fred."

With that, he went out and closed the door behind him. I spent the rest of the night going over every single painful episode of our time together in the bush. I just could not . . . no, would not, accept the explanation that a Weesquachak figure was responsible for it. That was like someone telling me that I was, after all, one of the three little pigs.

Wait. What was Ron's warning? What had he said?

"There is an evilness afoot" or, something like that. If there was an evil presence about, I firmly believed that if it could leave a footprint, it could also be caught.The next morning, after a fretful night, I left the hotel and boarded the train to the city without another word from Fred. A week later, right after work, I had no sooner arrived home to my old apartment in Port Arthur than I noticed that a man was there again.

He wore the same long dark brown overcoat that Fred used to have. He called it his "city coat." He said he had lost it and I knew now that it could not have possibly been Fred all those times out there. A new fear came over me. I had not been that scared thinking that it was Fred out there. Now, I knew that there was a strange man out there watching me. I didn't know what to think. I went about my daily business trying not to think about consequences.

Had I misjudged Fred all that time? Why had he not said anything? Why hadn't he told me about the footprints at the time? Why had I not told him about the things that I'd seen? Why had I not asked him about the things that he was accusing me of?

I wish we had learned to talk to each other. I wished that I could have shown more love and affection. I wished that I could have found it in me to tell Fred that I did love him. Worst of all, I knew that had I been able to do all those things, my baby might have lived.

The man stood out on the street watching my window. I could never get a clear view of him, which soon drove me to distraction. I sat in my living room knowing he was out there. I made my supper knowing he was out there. I was getting very paranoid and jumpy.

When my work contract ran out, I paid another month's rent and decided to go home to see how Mother was doing before I looked for another job.

Hah! He thinks he knows me, then? But, my sweet lovely one, I will hand you your lost one on a cedar bed platter, but only when I feel you are ready. That old man Henry, in the community, he's one smart old man. I think he figured me out but nobody will believe him. He's harmless to me. But, wait. I have to take care of someone else first.

Chapter Eighteen

That night in Sioux Lookout, I kept having nightmares about the dark shadow of the man materializing in front of me every time I turned. It was close to train departure time when I awoke the next morning to discover that I was not well. I must have caught the flu or something. I definitely had a fever. I got to the station on time and sat in the waiting room gasping quick short breaths until the train came. There was pain in my chest. It did occur to me that since I was there, perhaps I ought to go to the hospital, but all I wanted to do was to curl up somewhere to sleep forever and never wake up.

I slept most of the way home and was light-headed when I stepped off the train. I walked on rather shaky legs to the store and into the post office.

The postmaster had just dumped the morning mail on to the counter and said, "Janine, are you alright?"

"I have the flu or something. I feel terrible right now, but I'll probably be fine after a nap. Is Mother home?"

He paused a moment and said, "Oh, you're losing your voice. You sound bad. No, your mother's not home. They left for the bush. She said they wouldn't be back until after break-up. But, she left a key in your mailbox, in case someone came back."

I took the house key from the envelope, thanked the man and slowly made my way through the store. Two of the older men from the community were leaning on the counter, smoking and talking about spring hunting spots. With a thin smile, I nodded at their glances of welcome and pushed the door open.

Stepping out of the store, I realized there was no way I was going to be able to carry my suitcases all the way to the other end of the community to Mother's place. My chest was aching, my throat hurt and I had a huge splitting headache. There were six kids fooling around and wrestling on the hill at the corner of the store. To the side of the path was a small sleigh with a wooden box nailed on top. My suitcases would fit into the box perfectly.

I yelled to the kids, "Hey, whose sleigh is that?"

Johnny came running. He was Ron's nephew, quite a big boy about ten or twelve years old.

"I'm not feeling very well, do you think you can pull my suitcases on your sleigh? I'll pay you."

His face broke into a big grin, "Yeah, sure."

He ran to get the sleigh and heaved my suitcases onto it. I followed him down the path along the railroad tracks and listened to him prattle on about everything that had happened to every single person in the community since I had left. Why did I have to pick someone who talked so much? He quieted down when he had to pant with the effort of getting the sleigh up the hill and over the path by the railroad tracks. Then he ran as the little sleigh bounced along behind him, down the hill to the creek. I followed in long strides behind, trying to keep up and gasping for breath.

It was as I was finally catching up with him when he slowed to get up the hill that I heard him saying, "And he was going to kill somebody!"

I paused a moment before I asked, "Who was going to kill someone?"

He waited for me on the top of the hill before he answered, "Your Freddy!"

Oh, I was feeling awful. I wasn't even going to ask whom he'd want to kill. At that point, I really didn't care. We were nearing the cabin when my brain spat out the word that had stuck. My Freddy? There it was again. Why was he always "my Freddy"? I looked to the side at the long wide bay where the village lay. Yes, from now until forever, according to "them" I would always be Freddy's and he would always be mine. That is, until one of us married someone else.

I unlocked the door and Johnny brought the suitcases in. Our breath seemed to hang in the cold air of the room. I walked to Mother's bed in the corner and threw myself down thinking that I would start the fire later. I reached into my pocket for some money when I heard Johnny at the stove. He quickly located Mother's fire-starter box where she kept paper, birchbark, wood shavings and splints. Next, in went the smaller pieces of chopped up wood. O always left the wood ready for lighting. Johnny soon had a good fire going. When he came and stood beside me, I reached into my pocket and gave him a bill.

"I can get you some water too." he said.

I looked up at his rosy cheeks and said, "If Mom left last week, that water hole would be frozen over solid. I doubt they'd leave the chisel out there and I'll have to look around for the old axe."

"Oh, I'll get water."

He turned and went out the door with the water pail. I could hear the pail rattling inside the wooden box on his sleigh. The room was beginning to warm up so I made one more effort to make myself a bit more comfortable. I hauled up one suitcase to the bed and took out two chocolate bars that I had in there and left them on the table for Johnny, along with another two dollars in change I found in my pocket. I think I'd given him a dollar already. I pulled a comforter from the corner and threw it over me.

I must have dozed off. It was some time later when I heard Johnny coming back in. I looked at my watch. He had been gone for about an hour. I had to swallow several times before I managed to say, "Where did you go? To Armstrong for water."

He was struggling with the water pail, trying not to bump the bottom as he put it on the shelf against the wall beside the door. He came towards me beaming. "No! I had to take the path around the point and into the little bay to my grandmother's water hole. Ron isn't home either, you know. So, Grandma and Grandpa are you're closest neighbours. Everybody's gone spring hunting."

He had gone all that way for the water. No wonder he was gone so long.

I pointed to the chocolate bars and the change on the table.

"Take those. How much did I give you earlier?"

He grabbed the chocolate bars and stuffed the change into his pocket and mumbled through the dark chocolate that was now gushing out between his teeth.

"Five. You gave me five the first time, and now I've got seven. Thanks, Janine. I'll bring in some more wood too before I go, okay?"

I smiled. The little rascal! I had been feeling bad thinking that I had only given him three dollars for his efforts. I let him bring in several more loads of wood before he got set to go home. I asked him to bring me a glass of water and he threw several more logs into the fire before the door closed behind him. Then I was alone.

I woke up late in the evening to find that the room had cooled down quite a bit. My head spun as I sat up. I had to keep the fire going or I'd never be able to start it again. I kept the quilt around me as I slowly made my way across the floor to the stove. There were still some glowing embers at the vent so I threw in some paper and twigs before I put the split wood, with several round pieces on top, into the stove. The fire started again almost immediately so I crawled back into bed.

It was totally dark when I next awoke. I found the matches on the table but I was shaking so badly, I nearly dropped the glass lamp chimney as I lit the coal-oil lamp. The water cup was empty and I could see that there was only a small glow of embers through the stove vent. I sat on the bench by the table for quite awhile before I could muster enough energy to cross the floor. I put the last log into the stove and fell against it. I became frightened. What if the stove had been hot? I could have burnt myself! I turned to the water pail. I had to get back into bed. With concentrated effort, I carried the cup of water back to the bed and lay down like I weighed a ton.

Fire! The house was burning down! I was burning! I threw off my blankets and the cold air jolted me awake.

I had been dreaming. I was very hot. I knew I had a high fever. I could see that it was almost dawn. I decided to look for some headache tablets later and rolled over, hugging the pillow to me.

I fought my way through another thick nightmare and opened my eyes. The light was coming from the front window. It must have been midday. I thought should get up and make the fire, but I only took a sip of water and lay back down. I could see my breath in the cold air. When I next awoke, I was suffocating from the heat inside the quilt and having trouble breathing. Somewhere within me was fear. I needed to get up and get the fire going. I needed some headache medication too. I didn't have any more water left in the cup, but I couldn't get my body to obey my order to get out of bed.

Out of the darkness of my dreams, I heard a snow machine come to a stop outside the door. The door opened and a light went across my closed eyes. I rolled into a ball to escape the noise, the searing light and the oppressive heat.

In the clutches of unforgiving nightmares, I struggled with thick hot animals at my throat and chest, and the smell of cedar was almost overwhelming as the animals continually dragged me into their dark hot caves. Then, there was a smell like someone was burning grass fires around me, and the sound of a soothing chanting voice, and then at times, there was cold, blessed cold water on my face. I was so thirsty that I wished I could just catch some of that rain into my mouth.

I felt someone's hair under my hand. The hair flowed softly between my fingers. My eyes opened and my hand became still. I stared at the wooden ceiling beams above me as I slowly removed my hand from the head. I looked down. It was Fred. He was asleep, leaning against the bed with his head down beside me on the mattress.

Oh, my love!

I was overcome, wracked with uncontrollable sobbing. I hugged my knees to my chest, and strong arms held me tightly as my body threatened to break into pieces before the blackness came again. When I awoke, it was daylight. I smelled chicken noodle soup and realized how hungry I was. I opened my eyes to see Fred in front of the stove with his back to me. I watched his slumped shoulders roll as he stirred a pot.

His hair was neatly combed. He looked all muscle, not all skinny like he did the last time I saw him. I closed my eyes when he turned. I heard him come to the table. Then he was beside me again. He lifted the quilt and my eyes flew open as sharp cold air hit my skin. He removed a hot pad off my chest that I hadn't even known was there. I did not move but he was so intent on what he was doing that I could watch his face as he replaced the hot cedar poultice on my chest. As his hand was coming up to my forehead, his eyes locked to mine. His hand paused before he touched my forehead and brushed my hair back.

I made several attempts before I could get my voice to work. "I was dreaming that hot animals kept pasting themselves to my chest and I couldn't pull them off. Then there was smoke and a grass fire that was going to burn me alive."

He leaned over and kissed me on the forehead and whispered, "Your fever's gone. Are you hungry?"

I nodded. My head felt light but I pulled myself up in bed as he shoved pillows behind me. I looked down to see that I was wearing Mother's nightgown.

He saw my gaze and he said, "You were sweating buckets so I had to change your gowns several times."

He dished out the soup at the table and continued. "I thought the other night that I should take you to the hospital, but then I figured it would do more damage dragging you outside and into the train for a five-hour trip to the hospital. So, it was right that I didn't take you anywhere, eh? Now, you're going to be fine."

He smiled and put a bowl on my lap.

"The other night? How long have you been here?"

"Let's see. I left the trapline Monday, stopped to repair the old machine at Whitewater Lake. I got in on Tuesday night. I stopped at the store and they told me that you had come in on the Monday morning train. Then Johnny was hanging around my machine when I came out and he told me that you were sick. So, I came over after I dumped the pelts and traps at the cabin. Eat your soup before it gets cold."

I slowly sipped the first tablespoon before I asked, "What day is it?"

He smiled. "Thursday morning."

My spoon stopped halfway to my mouth as I blinked in shocked silence. Two days! I had lost two days. I looked at his flashing brown eyes and saw that they looked tired.

"You mean I spent two days fighting those hot furry animals off my chest?"

He smiled, nodding as he ate his soup, "They made you well."

I said, "And the smoke. What was the grass fire that was threatening to burn me?"

He smiled, "That was cedar branches on the stove."

Suddenly, feeling uncomfortable, I put my head down and began, "I'm sorry I put you to so much trouble. You didn't have to."

Suddenly, he was kneeling beside me saying, "Don't. Don't let us start that again, okay? Leave things be. Everything is fine. You are well. I am here. I will be here until you tell me to go, all right?"

I nodded.

I ate another bowl of soup while he brought in more wood. He told stories as he went about the inside chores. I watched, listened, and periodically dozed during the day. But by evening, I insisted on going to the outhouse. He walked with me and stood outside. Strangely, I felt no embarrassment at the sudden turn of events. He seemed totally at ease. I too felt strangely comfortable now. We had reached somewhere I did not understand at all. But, it was okay.

By Sunday, I felt stronger although he continued to stay with me in the cabin. He slept on my old single bed by the window while I remained on Mother's double bed in the main room. We played cards in the afternoons and some evenings he went to his cabin to pack for the spring. He informed me that he had only come to town to do his spring shopping and sell some furs.

On Monday night after we had gone to bed, we talked to each other across the dark room.

I said, "The days are getting very warm. You have to leave soon. Don't worry about me, I'll be all right. I've been thinking of going to Winnipeg."

There was no response in the darkness and I soon fell asleep.

He got on the train early Tuesday morning to get supplies. I was quite surprised when he came back on the evening train.

When he came in with a big smile on his face, I said, "What are you doing here? I didn't expect you back until..."

That wasn't coming out the way I wanted it to.

He came and sat down beside me at the table. "I only went to Savant Lake. That's where I do my business now. I don't know anybody there, no old drinking buddies to bother me. I've quit drinking."

Maybe that was the change I'd noticed in him. Or, did the

change have to do with me getting sick. He was comforted knowing that he had been there when I needed someone, this time. I watched him, thinking that it was going to be very painful when I had to leave. And this time, it would be me who would leave. Did I really want to go?

Fred asked softly, "Why are you looking at me like that?"

I shook my head and said, "I know you too well now. You are up to something. What is it?"

He threw his head back and laughed. I felt my heart skip. It had been such a long time since I had heard Fred laugh like that. This was the Fred I used to know as a kid. This was the Fred I loved.

I continued to look at him as he turned and faced me.

"I bought something for you."

I took a slow deep breath and said, "Fred, I don't want anything from you. I don't need anything."

He shook my shoulders as he said, "No, listen. I bought you a gun. Your own .22."

I looked at him stupidly before I whispered, "A gun? What for?"

Again, the grin spread over his face, "So, we can go hunting. Come with me to the trapline. We'll go hunting and fishing. I'll show you how to shoot down the ducks in mid-flight. I'll teach you a thing or two about fishing. And you can have all the peace and quiet that you need right now."

"Wait!" I interrupted, "What do you know about what I need? I probably know more about catching fish than you do and, as for shooting ducks, I'm probably a better shot than you are. You just never gave me the chance."

His face was about a foot from mine as he said, "Yeah?"

I answered, "Yeah. You never knew that because you never gave me the chance and besides I was too busy playing housewife. But, I could never do that again, Fred. I couldn't do it again."

He smiled and stuck out his hand. "It's a deal. Come with me to the trapline as a friend, a hunting and fishing buddy. That's all."

Was that possible?

I smiled, shaking my head. I didn't know. But, what else was there for me to do? I had nowhere to go. Right now, I just wanted to disappear somewhere for a while. I guess the trapline was the best place for that.

I looked at him and said, "If you can keep your distance, I can keep mine."

He smiled and said, "It's a deal."

I knew that this arrangement would become a battle of stubborn wills but that would be my strongest assurance. Neither of us would admit to being weaker; neither of us would give in. It was the best guarantee possible.

I smiled and asked, "When?"

"Right now! Just bring your bag, leave your suitcases here and we'll go to my cabin. I still have your snow machine suit and your bush clothes there."

I looked around the cabin feeling quite dazed by the turn of events but this time determined that I was going to live. I looked straight at him. I felt no tension or apprehension, just an old friend standing there in front of me, giving me a chance to breathe, giving me a place to recover. Huh! Life was strange.

He returned my gaze and I nodded. I could do this.

Now, now. Wait! This is not supposed to happen! Oh, these humans are unpredictable creatures! Fred is no problem. He's easy to manipulate, but the girl... can't reach that girl. She is too far away. Her... her spirit... no, her intuition... no, her knowledge... no, her acknowledgment is lacking. That's it! She is too far away from her culture but, strangely too strong in some aspects that I can't reach her! If she does not know I'm here, how can I reach her? Hmm, I must use that stupid man as a bridge... I can trick her into... Yes, Yes, that's the plan. I am just so smart and cunning. I am so smart, so smart, so smart... Hey, wait! I notice I am having some kind of difficulty here. Why are my words going into replay as I'm changing form? It's like my brain is bumping along with my burping body... body... body...

Chapter Nineteen

I rode behind him on the snow machine with the loaded sleigh behind us down the path, across the railroad tracks and onto the portage road. Strangely, this road was well used by people getting wood, people out setting traps, snares, or just out ice fishing on the lakes along the road. I cried when I came to the spot where I had lost the baby's water. I tightened my grip around Fred's middle. I wondered if he ever thought of the things that went through my mind.

We stopped for a meal on an island at Smoothrock Lake. It was quite dark as we built a fire, warmed up a bit and made a pot of tea. After a hurried midnight lunch of bologna sandwiches and hot tea we were back on the snow machine. I was unusually quiet but he had made no comment. Perhaps he knew what I was going through, retracing my steps along this route. As we entered Whitewater Lake, I remembered the excitement of my first trip to there. I had been so naive and hopeful of a bright and happy future; so full of love and life. I wondered now how I would be the next time I came back this way.

It was dawn when we entered Clay Lake. We were just coming to the point where the cabin was when the sun came up over the horizon. Fred slowed to a stop and shut the engine off. We sat still, watching the big orange sun rise up. For some reason, I had a strong urge to cry and covered up my sudden emotional reaction by swinging my leg off the seat and stomping around behind the sleigh. I was trying to get some circulation back into my feet. When I turned, Fred was spread-eagled in the snow beside the machine making a snow angel.

He smiled and said nothing as I flopped down in the snow a

good two arm's-length away from him. I swung my arms and legs into a wide arch and started laughing. How ridiculous we must have looked.

We were back on the machine and headed to the cabin when we came across a trail in the snow. It was from a wolf.

The cabin was the same as I had left it. It seemed like I had been gone a very long time, but there it stood, looking so familiar. When Fred pushed the door open, I entered behind him. I saw the single bed in the corner of the room beside the stove. There was bedding on the bed and a small shelf had been nailed to one of the logs above it. Someone had been here with him. He saw me looking at the bed while he was getting the fire going and threw his head back to let out a deep belly laugh.

Indicating the bed, he said, "A high-school drop-out. One of the boys decided to quit school and become a trapper like his dad had been. Well, the mother asked me to bring him here with me, teach him the ropes. The very first day... no, the first half-hour after we got here, I asked him to split some wood while I got the water hole opened up. I was coming up the path with the water pail, when I saw him swing the axe down on a block of wood that was propped up like a see-saw. Well, it was too late. Before I could shout, he hit the block of wood a little too far out to the edge. The wood spun upward and hit him square on the forehead and knocked him out cold. He just fell over like a log. The tea wasn't even hot on the stove when I decided right then and there to take him back home. I was just scared of what he would do to himself next. Oh, you should have seen the huge hockey puck that was popping out from between his eyes. By morning he had two huge black eyes and swelling, besides the huge lump on his forehead."

I found that I was laughing along with him as he gestured, imitating the poor kid. When I stopped to pull off my snow boots, he continued.

"He tried to help out here and there, but he was so clumsy. I gave him some rabbits and a few muskrats to skin, but he just wasn't interested. He basically just waited until the bruises were gone before he let me take him home. When I went back to the community later on, I found out he'd gone back to school after all."

I glanced at him and smiled, "So, one day when he becomes a doctor, a lawyer or a veterinarian, he has you to thank?"

Fred laughed. "I doubt it. I don't think he liked me very much after the month and a half he stayed here."

That was the longest conversation that I had ever had with Fred inside those four walls. I grabbed the chisel and went out to get some water. From now on, I would do as I pleased. I didn't owe him anything.

As I stood there gradually widening the water hole, I saw in the distance a small dot making its way across the lake. It was the wolf. By the time, I got back with the water Fred had the fire roaring full blast. He made the tea while I went to bring in more wood.

Next came the ongoing setting and checking of traps and then the preparations for the spring hunt. I didn't think it was important but Fred insisted that I keep track of what I caught so that I could get my share of the money when he went to sell them.

I came in from bringing a couple loads of logs with the snow machine and threw my jacket on the bed. The stew pot was slowly bubbling on the stove. Fred sure made delicious stew. I still had a few pelts to stretch so I got up on the stump that we used for a chair and peered over the wooden shelves strung along the ceiling. As I was pushing aside muskrat boards to get at some smaller beaver stretching racks, I saw a roll of moose hide. Fred came in with some frozen fish, which he threw into the sink beside the stove.

I pulled the moose hide off the nail and asked, "When did you kill this one?"

He looked up from the table where he had begun stretching some mink skins and said, "Oh, in the fall. I cut off the hair, scraped off the flesh and stretched it just before Christmas. That was all I did with it. I brought it in and kind of just let it dry like that."

We had long since stopped talking in English. Now, our conversations were mostly in Ojibway.

I looked at the roll of hide and said, "Tell you what. Let's work on this together and when it's done, I'll make us some new mitts, mukluks and moccasins. Providing you help me with all the pulling when it comes to the softening process."

He laughed and said, "I remember my father and mother doing that. They used to sit foot to foot on the floor and they would rotate the hide as they pulled around and around. Each time my mother pulled, we would watch to see how far Father's butt would rise off the floor."

I laughed. It was so nice to talk and laugh with him.

Then I said, "Remember the story of Weesquachak when he was a woman and became the third wife of a hunter? The two women were pulling the hide like that and Weesquachak lost his grip and he fell backwards, his spread legs flying up in the air and the women across from him saw his male genitals."

My smile disappeared and Fred's straight face looked back at me. We both remembered our crazy discussion in Sioux Lookout.

A month later, we had the leather all made and we even smoked it into an even beige shade. Then, some of the fur we trapped went into the cuffs of the mitts, moccasins and mukluks. I loved the layers of muskrat skins on my feet. They were a lot better than socks. I made all his things first and by the time I had finished my pair of mitts, I was running out of beads. I had only what I had left after that cradle we had made for the baby. It still hung in the corner by the double bed. I remembered that when he was bending the bottom curve of the wood, it had slipped from his hand and slapped him on the cheek. Smack! I had told him that it had a particularly soothing sound to it. I smiled at the memory.

I slept on that bed and Fred slept on the single bed beside the stove. He had asked if he should remove the cradle and put it elsewhere, but I shook my head. It looked like it belonged there. Someone coming to visit might think that it was just a decoration, but I liked opening my eyes every morning and seeing it hanging there. It had become a reminder of what would happen if I dared to let myself get too physically close to Fred again. It pained me that we immediately pulled away if we happened to come into contact during the course of our everyday activities. But, I knew that there could be no other way. I had said that if he could do it, then so could I. No way was I going to be the one to give in first.

Spring came with the leaves coming out in one giant growing spree and the songs of the frogs filled the swamp and the shoreline around the cabin. If there was ever a time when I would have loved to have snuggled up in bed and listened to the frogs it was then. I found this to be the hardest: being in one corner of the cabin with Fred in the other. The wolf that we had spotted when we first arrived had kept a very curious eye on us. He never wandered far from our cabin. We kept an eye on the tracks.

Once, I even dragged a half-dozen suckers in a tub to the place he always come out of the bush and to the lake. I dumped the fish there and went back to the cabin before Fred came home. He only used the suckers for bait anyway.

When June came, we went swimming. That caused another problem not so much on my part but on his. I could not help having my shirt and pants sticking to my body when I stepped out of the water.

There were some funny times too. Like the time, he got out of the water and put his arms up over his head to dry his underarms, and I saw something flapping around under one arm. It was a huge bloodsucker. How I laughed at the sight of him trying to shake it off and trying to pull it off. I ended up prying it off with my fingernail. He could peel off his shirt at the hottest time of the day in the boat but I did not dare take off mine. After the first couple of times, we soon found that these were things we could do only when we were alone. We had to give each other a lot of space and time alone.

Then, the day came when we finally admitted that we just had to get back to the village. I needed supplies. We needed food. Fred needed things of his own. I had found that he went through a lot of tobacco but I never saw him smoke. Only that one time when we first went spring hunting, was when I had seen him with the pipe. I never saw it again. I did not know where he kept those things. It was none of my business. I too had my own bag of necessities that he did not poke around into.

It was in the second week of June that we set out for the village in our canoe. We had asked Jason to keep an eye on our place and left. We took our time crossing Whitewater Lake, camping overnight at the point on Best Island. The mosquitoes were just horrible. After choking on black flies as we tried to get the fire going, we dove into the tent and sprayed the last of the repellent to kill the giant blood-sucking mosquitoes that followed us in. I knew this place was bad at this time of year because of the swamp directly behind us, but oh, the beach was just gorgeous.

We left early the next morning and had lunch at the mouth of Loon Narrows. I told Fred stories about this place and in return, I heard stories about his family at the same location. I had known nothing about that.

I mentioned that when I was a child, I had seen a pair of dark, shriveled, leather pieces that looked to have been a small pair of moccasins tied together high up in a tree. He said that those had been the moccasins of his oldest brother who had died in this area at the age of five when Fred was only a baby. The moccasins would have been hung up in a tree branch shoulder high. That would have been before I was born. We sat for a long time in silence. Our families had crisscrossed this region for many generations, yet we did not know each other's history.

We spent the rest of the time talking and reminiscing as we paddled the length of Smoothrock Lake. We pulled in late and slept at the big portage. The roaring river seemed so loud after the quiet solitude of the last several days. We had a visitor during the early hours – a bear cub. To my relief, there was no sign of the mother around our campsite.

We left early in the morning and paddled through the lakes and channels, rivers and portages pretty much in silence until we came to the last rock cut. Around the bend was the last portage and up the path about two and a half miles was the village. Fred stopped paddling and the canoe drifted for half the length of the bay. I waited. I did not move my paddle. I just waited. Then, I felt the dip and pull of his paddle away from the portage and into the channel. That would take us through two more small portages along the railroad tracks, then over it and into the lake at the village. He decided we should come up to the community by canoe on the lake, rather than by portage with packsacks on our backs crossing the clearing in front of the store and down past the church to get to his cabin by the bay.

Yes, I liked that better. I had not relished the idea of having a packsack on my back, of having to sweat and pant across the railroad tracks and through the community. We'd have to go across the front of the store where people would come to the window and stare, down by the church, accompanied by children and barking dogs then down to the bay where we would finally reach Fred's cabin. This way was a lot more private, and a lot more dignified.

When we arrived at the portage that crossed the railroad tracks, Fred pulled out the tent. No, he was not going to arrive late at night. We were going to camp one more night. We set up the tent and the smell from the tar of the railway ties was very strong. When the next train went by, the ground shook and the air was thick with train exhaust and tar smell. I took deep breaths and relished the smell of home. A dampening effect seemed to descent upon us. I watched and waited. Fred had become very quiet since we had set up the tent.

Finally, as we sat by the fire sipping the last of our coffee, he took a deep breath and said, "I'm sorry if I seem almost dead. I'm just so . . . scared. I'm afraid."

This was new. He was actually telling me what he was feeling.

I asked hesitantly, "Why?"

He took a deep breath then, leaning against a tree and looking at the sky, he said, "Because I'm afraid of what might happen, that we may not come back down here together again."

I did not know what to say. I had been apprehensive too. I did not know if I was prepared to face Mother and pretend that everything was all right. I would be embarrassed if people found out that the only way we could get along was when we lived like brother and sister. I didn't think I could face them if they knew.

I kicked the heel of his boot that I could reach and said, "Hey. People can't hurt us unless we let them. If we stick close together and not let anybody come between us we'll be okay. We'll come back down this portage together again."

He turned and smiled at me. Then we had to dive into the tent to get away from the mosquitoes. This portage too, was in a swamp and hummed with huge mosquitoes at night.

Chapter Twenty

Early the next morning, we paddled out into the bay of the lake toward our village. Big white water lilies bobbed in the waves of our canoe, sending out a fragrance that was better than the expensive perfumes that I had smelled in the department stores. I put my head back, closed my eyes and took a long deep breath.

I heard Fred chuckling behind me, so I said, "There isn't a perfume better than this. You can't even buy this!"

We paddled in silence to the community. As soon as we came around the channel, we could see the white cross of the Catholic Church in the clearing. Then we heard the dogs barking. The train went by like a long black and white garter snake all along the bay. It did not stop this morning. Then silence descended with seagulls overhead, screeching at our paddles. Soon, we were past the island, past the dock, and into the bay beside his cabin.

We got out, pulled the canoe up and unloaded the canoe. Together we went up to see if the cabin was still in good shape. Fred whistled at how high the weeds were around the cabin and said he'd have to cut them back. The cabin was as we had left it. When Fred swung the door open, the smell brought back a lot of memories. I set the outside campfire going.

I had the teapot steaming when Bob and Sheila came down the path. Sheila said that they had seen the smoke from the campfire. Being a Saturday, Bob was home. She had a new baby in her arms. The bad memories of the last time I saw her disappeared when I looked down on the peaceful, beautiful face of her baby girl.

Bob went inside the cabin where Fred was rummaging around looking for a larger frying pan. Sheila sat down beside me. I poured the tea out for the men and handed Sheila a cup. Quite naturally, to free her hands, I took the baby into my arms. The weight of the baby in my arms and her natural tilt to my chest brought out such an overwhelming emotion of intense pain that I found myself blinking back tears.

When Sheila had settled back kneeling on the ground, she asked in English, “Are you expectin’ again?”

Quite taken aback and without warning, I answered, “Oh, no. We haven’t got to there yet. We... we’re living like brother and sister.”

I was feeling the warmth of the beautiful child in my arms when I realized what I had just said.

Then Sheila said, “I am just so glad our baby girl is still here. I was so afraid in the spring when she came down with such an awful cold. She couldn’t breathe and then her fever went up so high. Oh, I was in panic and tears, an’ Bill was in Sioux Lookout. But then Nisha shows up. Remember the guy I was tellin’ you about last year? He says Bill told him he had tools for the motor and he’d just come by to fix that motor of Bill’s that’s always broken down. Well, I invites him in while I go rummagin’ in the shed he’s got back there, and worryin’ about the clothes if they are going to be dry in time for the train to the hospital. I mean my dress and the baby’s diapers . . . I mean, I had been tendin’ the baby day and night and never got time to do the washing . . . anyway, this Nisha, he just knocks on the door saying he needs the tools and then, he would watch her while I looked for them . . . and wouldn’t you believe it? I come rushin’ in, and there he was, standin’ over the baby’s crib. He had his hand on her head and I swear he was saying something . . . anyway he turns around . . . and, and, you know, I just can’t explain it to this day. But, anyway, he just looks at me and says, 'She'll be fine now. She doesn't need anything. She'll just sleep all night and she'll be right as rain, maybe even before the train comes in! Got the tools?' I walks to the baby and him standin' there and I give him the tools and then, he goes out whistling a tune. An' you know? Her fever was gone and just like he said, she was gigglin' and kickin' up her feet by the time the train went by! Go figure! Eh, go figure! How do some people know them things? I am always so amazed that people can know them things."

Just then Fred and Bob came out and sat down beside the fire. I did not say anything. What was she saying? Did she think that Nisha healed her baby? That sounded a bit too weird to me.

After plans were discussed about having supper together, Fred walked back to their cabin with them to get the axe that Bob had apparently borrowed last month. I found that English sounded so foreign now, after all this time of speaking in Ojibway. But, Bob and Sheila only spoke in English.

I had just cleared up the teacups and pot from the campfire when Fred came back with the axe in his hand. I saw immediately that Fred had a furious look on his face. With a sense of total disappointment and betrayal, I took a deep breath and waited to hear what the problem was but he said not a thing. He walked right past me and down to the lake to get the rest of the things. I watched his back until he disappeared from view. I sighed, thinking that it was back to the old silent treatment again. The plan to keep communication open sure hadn't lasted very long.

I yanked out a clean shirt and pair of pants and got a clean towel from the box. I dug out from my bag a bar of soap and a bottle of shampoo that I had left in the cabin and headed out to the point of land by the high rock cliff. I knew that no one hung around there.

When I got to the rock point, the gentle waves were lapping at the rocks much the same as they did early this morning. The sun shone overhead and the seagulls circled around on their endless search for food. I kept my clothes on and dove into the deepest part of the bay. The water gurgled against my ears as I dove deeper into the water. I stayed down there to the count of thirty before I came up for air. I used to do that when I was a child. This summer I was able to count to over forty. I dove in several more times before I just floated around staring at the sky.

I left the shampoo and soap on a rock close to the shore and helped myself to them until I felt it was close to supper. I had pulled myself up on the rock and stretched my arms to the sky, relishing the feel of the breeze against the wet clothes plastered to my body when I felt eyes watching me. I had been enjoying the luxury of washing with soap and shampoo so much that I'd been unaware that someone was watching. Now my eyes fell on Fred. He was sitting beside my clothes in the rock shade.

I went up the rock toward him. When I got near, he got up and walked past me and without a word, stripped off his shirt, pants, and dove into the water. I smiled as I settled down on the rock to dry my hair. When I had combed out my hair, I watched him pull himself up onto a rock and stand up. I knew exactly how he felt as he turned his face to the sun and combed back his hair with his fingers. Something else touched me deep inside as I watched him coming up the sloping rock toward me. But, I distracted myself by running the brush through my hair once more. I had gotten so good at distracting myself.

He sat down beside me and I noticed that the goose pimples from the cold water were still on his thighs as he sat back. He had never come this close to me before, dressed as he was with only his under shorts on. What was he doing?

I took a deep breath and asked, "So, what got you angry? After only half an hour here, you got angry at me about something. If we are going to get through this trip, we have got to be open and honest, isn't that what we agreed? You have to tell me why you got angry."

Fred put his head down and hung his arms over his knees as he said, "Bob told me that Sheila had told him about what you had told her."

I turned around and faced him, knee to knee and asked him, keeping my eyes to his, "Just what exactly did Sheila tell Bob?"

Fred fidgeted somewhat under my gaze until I whispered, "Tell me, Freddy."

Then he blurted out, "Why did you have to tell them for? It is none of their business!"

I had known it was a mistake the second I had said that to Sheila. I put my head down and said, "She put the baby in my arms and I was just so torn inside . . . and then she asked if I was expecting again . . . the next thing I knew I was giving the baby back to her as quick as I could and telling her that we have only been like brother and sister and that it would take time."

In English, I added, "I'm so sorry."

He suddenly focused his eyes on me and said, "You know, that is the first time since I have known you that you actually said 'I'm sorry.' But, you don't need to be sorry about anything. The rule is to think before you speak or act. That way there's no need to say I'm sorry. Has it ever occurred to you why we don't have the words 'I'm sorry' in our language? There are no such words in Ojibway."

I kept my head down. I didn't know what else to say. Deep inside, resentment began to build. He didn't need to lecture me; I knew these things as well as he did. I also had his share of "I'm sorry!" How dare he lecture me on who says I'm sorry!

As the silence lengthened, I asked, "Why did you find my comment so upsetting? Why were you so mad that they found out?"

He turned and glared at me, then softly said, "No, I am not the cause of the problem here; you are the one with the problem."

I looked down and thought that perhaps he was right. Maybe I was indeed the one with the problem. Wasn't I the one who always made sure that things were always at the proper distance? The one that always remembered things had got close enough? It was almost a daily challenge that, if he could keep his distance, then so would I. But, it wasn't really that. My problem lay plainly in the fact that I did not want to have another baby. I did not want to get pregnant again while things were the way they were.

His hand moved and it closed over mine. He held my hand as he looked at me and whispered, "Why? Why did you have to tell them that?"

I looked up into Freddy's eyes and said, "Because I didn't want to feel like I was the failure . . . that I couldn't have another child."

I watched his eyes travel all along the shoreline before he said, "That comment from Bob made me feel like I was less of a man because I couldn't even give you another child."

I couldn't meet his eyes even though I knew he was looking right at me. Oh, how sorry I was for opening my mouth to that woman. I looked at the lake and on a sudden impulse, got up and dove into the water. Its silence and intense pressure held me in the murky depths. I held my breath for the longest time ever. When I came up for air, I felt Fred's arms close around me in the water. He held me so tight that I could barely turn around to look at him. Then I felt his urgent lips on mine. There was a sudden overwhelming pressure that seemed to engulf us both as we got out of the water and gauged each other wearily. There were no tricks here. No one was going to back down at the last minute. We got back to the cabin and no sooner had the door closed that I heard the lock click into place and felt Fred's arms around me. Supper would wait. That night, I discovered a depth of love that I had never experienced in my whole life.

At the store the next day, I was walking behind Fred. He had gone in ahead when I heard a high whistle and there I saw Ron sitting on the platform by the storage shed. I turned from the door and walked toward him. He sat there with his head a bit to the side. I felt his eyes travel up and down my whole body. I could not ever remember noticing this about him before. When did he start doing this to me? I became rather uncomfortable and embarrassed by the time I reached him.

I came to a stop in front of him and asked, "What? Why are you looking at me like that?"

He smiled and answered rather softly, "You are so beautiful. No, you are gorgeous. You can't tell me that you are not aware of what you look like!"

My mouth flew open, trying to think of something to say when I noticed his eyes focusing on someone behind me. I turned to see Fred standing in the store doorway as though he was waiting for me.

Ron whispered loud enough for me to hear, "See, he's not even going to let you out of his sight for a second now."

I smiled slightly. I couldn't think of a thing to say, so I turned around quickly and headed back to the store. I could not figure out what had come over Ron. Never had he done that before. Was he just trying to aggravate Fred? We went into the store and Fred went right through and into the back mailroom. I stood around in the open store area when I started to feel my skin crawl. From what source? Then I turned and saw Ted sitting there in the corner of the storeroom. An old battered green cap sat on top his dirty long unkempt hair that trailed over his grey, leathery looking face. From among the strands of hair, I saw the beady eyes glaring at me. A pink tongue shot out several times, sweeping the length of his thin lips before I heard him say in a rasping voice, "My good Charlie, watch for those . . . you think . . . who care."

I smiled and nodded in his direction. Oh, he looked bad. He looked like someone from a horror movie. He couldn't be much older than the rest of us here, we all played together as children. I looked back at Ted one more time then joined Fred in the mailroom.

We sorted through the mail then Fred found out how much the sales of the fur were and how much we owed. We came out in the financial shape we thought we would. There was several hundred dollars that I could not account for when I glanced at the balance sheet, but I didn't question him. I knew he did not know how much I could discern with a glance. It was none of my business and I had no doubt he knew exactly what he was doing.

I ran to Mother's cabin before the train came, to find the Groundhogs lying sprawled out on the floor, up on their elbows, head to head. I looked over Lenny's shoulder to see a whole bunch of wingless houseflies frantically circling in a deep ceramic bowl set between the two boys.

I gasped, whispering, "Oh, my gosh! You are not supposed to do that! Better kill them quick! Better pray they don't get back at you because that is exactly what you or your loved ones will become."

Something in my voice got Lenny quickly on his feet and he began a weird dance as he stomped on the flies, just missing his brother's hands as Benny scrambled up.

Mother and O had gone fishing. Flies forgotten, the boys scrambled up and followed me back to the station where Fred was waiting. In that time, they talked nonstop.

Between my lapses of tuning out, Benny caught my attention as he was saying, ". . . the cabin was dark, but we saw someone sneaking around behind the cabin and then Lenny tripped and the man saw us, I think. Then we thought he was chasing us so we ran into the bushes toward the swamp and then . . ."

I interrupted, "Where? Who was sneaking around?"

Lenny answered, "Fred's place. We heard you came back so we went to visit you but the cabin was dark. That's when we saw this guy sneaking around behind your cabin."

A shock went through me as the information sank in, but

Benny was babbling on again, "Anyway, Lenny tripped over a huge stump and suddenly, it popped up shining bright. I screamed and crashed into it, a chunk fell on my pants and I grabbed some. Did you know old stumps shine in the night, Janine? Huh? When we got home, we looked at the shining piece in my hand and it was dark bluish-green rotten wood."

I answered, "Yes. Yes, I remember seeing one when I was a kid. But, they don't shine long do they?"

I wondered if it had been the Weesquachak sneaking around again. Who was this Weesquachak anyway? Fred's invisible man. I wondered whom it would turn out to be if or when Fred caught him. But then, how on earth would he know we were here? The boys must be mistaken. They could have seen a dog.

Fred did not drink and he never left my side during the entire time we were in the village and on the shopping trip to Savant Lake. I mentioned the man the boys had said they'd seen. He thought for a moment then shrugged. We said nothing more about it.

When I told him the story about Sheila, her baby and Nisha, he just threw his head back and laughed out loud. We talked of other things on the way to Savant Lake on the train and back again. At Savant Lake, we stopped at a store. Fred stood in front of the newspaper and magazine rack and, with a glance, indicated that I shouldn't forget to get them. I shook my head. I felt no need to try to keep track of what was happening around the world. I was only interested in what was happening with my life and those around me. As for magazines, I didn't care much for make-up or fashion any more. My jeans and checkered shirt were good enough for me now.

I laughed at the stories Fred told me on the train. He talked of many things he had seen and done in the communities along the railroad tracks. It reminded me of Nisha. I still could not believe that the spying man could have been Nisha. Where was he? No one had seen him since the spring following the Sheila and baby incident.

Fred also told me stories of how his buddies got their nicknames. There was one about a guy named Tom who had come around the corner of a deck they were replacing. Tom was about to tell Bill there was a phone call for him just when Bill hit the last board off the frame. The board came flying off, whacked Tom right across the face and broke his nose. Tom's new name became Board Nose.

There was another time when they were replacing the roof at Ed's. Ed was below, reaching down to pick his tool belt up off the ground when Andy, on the roof, knocked a can of roofing nails over and they rained down on top of Ed's head. He ended up with little bloody specks all over his neck and back. Now, the guys sang "Nails keep falling on my head" whenever they saw him.

Then there was Jerry and the wet cement mixed inside a wheelbarrow, all ready for the fence posts they were putting in. Jerry tripped on a board and staggered backwards and slowly sank into the wheelbarrow – sat right down into the wet cement. He got out to howls of laughter and went inside the house to change. Later, when his wife got home she found his jeans sitting straight upright on top of the laundry basket. He became known as Hard Ass.

Fred had stories about each of the train stops as we watched people getting on and off. He pointed out buildings and land sites, telling me what had happened here and there. I began to understand a side of Fred that I'd had no idea existed until now. There were a lot of people who stopped to say hello, shake his hand and wish us well. It felt good to be with him.

I found to my dismay that I had only one month's supply of birth control pills left. They had been stuck in the corner of my suitcase. After I had lost the baby, I'd made sure I had them with me at all times. What had happened in the cabin would be all right since I was only a day away from my period, but then I couldn't be sure either. The few pills I had left, I took back to the bush. There had been no way to get to a drug store. Fred only shopped in Savant Lake and there wasn't a drug store there. I wanted to go to Sioux Lookout where there was one, but Fred insisted we could get what we needed in Savant Lake. I could not bring myself to tell him why I wanted to go to Sioux Lookout. Knowing that I had at least one month of worry-free days, I followed Fred back to our cabin at Clay Lake.

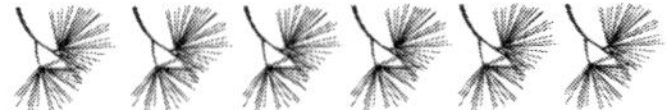

Fred's mind wandered as he paddled along the long stretch of Smoothrock Lake. It wasn't that he was unfeeling. He understood the pain she'd gone through last year when, alone on a snow machine ride, she had struggled to get to the village as her body strained to push the dead baby out. How could he not feel that! It was only when the sun had come up that the tension lessened and he was able to disentangle her hands from his jacket. He stretched himself out on the snow in an effort to show that life could begin anew between them in the dawn of this coming new day. He'd had such a strong urge to bury his face into her arms, to hug her close and tell her how much he loved her. But, the deal remained that she would be in her corner of the cabin and he in his. Even with that arrangement, he felt satisfied. It was better than none.

He had hoped with time she would change her mind and they could renegotiate. But she was one stubborn person. Not once did she waiver. It got to a point where he was calling himself every name under the sun and kicking himself until he could not even face his shaving mirror. From the moment they had walked into the cabin that afternoon, he'd known things were going to be different. She'd snatched her aprons from the kitchen table and thrown them into a box. Then she grabbed the chisel. Oh, he'd loved her more than he ever had. Then came the painful weeks, one after the other.

Now, at the last portage, he watched as she stooped down to splash water on her face. He remembered her comment about the white water lilies and was tempted to comment that she was pure nature, wonderfully natural and that nature could never be duplicated. He looked to her as a source of oxygen for his lungs and blood for his heart. He loved her wholly and utterly and knew he would have to adjust to the influence of those who came between them. He saw his love for her as a sort of self-preservation that he would protect at all costs. That was the extent of his love for Charlie.

Looking back, he was grateful that the anger that sparked between them over the comments from Bob and Sheila seemed to light an incredible flame which had finally engulfed them that one night in the cabin at the village. But Weesquachak had also been there.

When they got off the train that evening, he found himself

scanning faces, trying to figure out which of them was Weesquachak. He was not absolutely sure that it was Nisha. Nisha was not in the community at the moment and it had to be someone from the community, if that had been a person last night. He saw Ted, Ron and about four other guys at the storage shack beside the store. There was no way it was any of them. He knew them too well.

Chapter Twenty-One

There was such a release of tension between us. We were both more spontaneous with loving gestures and gentle touches and revelled in near abandonment for the entire month. I had to break the news to Fred after July since I would be out of birth control pills by then. I knew this was not fair to him but I continued to prepare myself for the separation required for the days I would not have pills.

During the second week of August, Jason had started coming by to visit every once in a while. One time, Fred had gone to check the fish net when Jason arrived, so I asked him when the next plane was coming in. I made no bones about my present situation. I needed to go to a drug store for pills. Jason promised to come by and pick me up in the morning before the plane came.

Then he told me about the tourist who got a hook caught on the seat of his pants. They had to cut his pants out around the hook and found the hook firmly imbedded in his left buttock. This image got me laughing out loud. I could just imagine this bald-headed top executive of some company from America in that state. At that point, Fred came around the cabin. Jason was inside the cabin and we were both doubled over in laughter. Fred reacted in a way that reflected a man being made a fool of and was being laughed at by his wife and her lover. He turned around and walked out, consumed with rage.

I was embarrassed. Jason left after awhile and I went about getting ready for bed. I was furious that Fred would do that. When was he going to learn to be civil when other people were around? I hated his jealousy. It was quite late at night and I was beginning to worry when I heard him come in and he went straight to bed. I got up, lit the lamp and sat down beside the single bed where he was.

He gave no response so I pulled his arm and demanded, "We have to talk! Fred we can't go on like this. We must talk because we're going to go back to exactly what we were doing the first time."

Fred sat up then moved to the bench. But before long, he stood and paced the floor before he flopped back down on the bench.

"Talk? Why don't you ever tell me what you're thinking about? I can see what you're feeling but I don't know what you're thinking. Every day, you tell me that you love me but you don't love me. I find you wanting me but you won't let me near you. You tell me you don't want me, yet you say you love me. At other times, you don't love me. Gull darn it, woman! Tell me what is going on with you?"

I took a deep breath to gather the nerve to begin. "I only had one month's supply of birth control pills. Then I saw you with the cradle board we had made for Baby . . ." I swallowed to keep my voice even as I fought the tears that rolled down my cheeks. "I was terrified that I would get pregnant again. I still feel the pain so bad. That day when I saw you with that cradle in the storage shed I ran because I had to have a good cry. I'm sorry. I didn't want you to see me like that. I'm not ready yet for another baby."

I went to him to put my arms around him, as I desperately needed a hug. But he pushed me away. I sat down, stunned and quiet, on the bench for what seemed a long time. Fred lay back down on the single bed and turned his back to me so I got up and went back to bed. There was only one way I could see to get out of this situation. I had to get those pills, come back, and then everything would be all right again.

The next morning, I heard the boat taking off from the dock. It was the same thing he would do that first year we were together. I got up to wait for Jason. Soon, he arrived to get me and when the plane came in a short while later, I left. In Sioux Lookout that night, I went to bed early and the next morning made a visit to the bank and then to the drug store. I caught the afternoon train back to Armstrong and was back on the dock the very next day.

When I got off the plane at Clay Lake, Jason came up to me in a very sheepish manner, like he had done something wrong

I asked, “What’s wrong?”

Jason pointed at Fred’s boat on the beach. I knew that Jason was telling me that Fred had left. I nodded, got into the boat and headed back to the cabin. I found the cabin empty, much as I had left it. I knew it would be another week before the plane came back with a new load of tourists so I decided to take the canoe back to the village. I had to find Fred quickly. I did not trust him alone out there. It would be a three-day trip at the most. As soon as I got over the rapids between Clay Lake and Whitewater Lake, I’d be on my way.

As it happened, it was two days later when I came out of the Whitewater Lake channel, paddling slowly and softly for I had discovered that there were people ahead of me. I’d stopped to put out a campfire at the Clay River portage. Someone had doused the fire but the underground moss was still smoldering. As I paddled out of the channel into the open of Whitewater Lake, I discovered six canoes in front of me. As soon as they saw me, they stopped. Their canoes drifted as they waited for me to come abreast of them.

In the evening stillness, I heard one of the women say, “Who do you think that could be? Oh, it's a man for sure."

Someone snickered. "What would a woman be doing around here in the middle of nowhere?"

"No, wait, I see a ponytail behind that baseball cap. Must be an Indian, no white woman would be around here by herself," said one of the women.

Another voice piped up. "Hey look, the canoe is coming in one straight line, no left or right swerve with those strokes. A professional!"

"Hey, got that cream for blisters handy?" I heard one ask.

Someone laughed and in high-pitched voice said, "Oh, just to hear his voice at this moment. One more word and I'll shower embers over your sleeping bag. You hear me?"

It seemed to me that they were playing out scenes from a movie. As I got close, I lay my paddle across the canoe and leaned back. "It's such a quiet evening, I'd be able to carry on a conversation with you from clear across the lake."

The canoe carried me right between them, with three canoes on each side. As they looked me over, I examined them and decided they were in no worse shape than I'd be in before I got to the village. I had guessed that they had started from Nakina and found I was right. One of the women wanted to know what a white woman was doing in this area since I had no Indian accent.

I pulled up my sleeve and said, "I'm afraid this is as light as I get."

The others laughed when they realized that my skin was only a few shades lighter than my early spring and summer tan.

I wondered just what they expected an Indian accent to sound like so I said, "Well, I doon'no. Watch'yu'wanna'see? Looks to me, I cun' teech yu more, if yu cun cutch up wi' me."

In one stroke of my paddle I shot away from them. Shouts and hoots of laughter sounded out. They followed me, stroke for stroke, down the length of Whitewater Lake to Best Island. As I pulled up to a stop at the long finger of sand, a deep sorrow fell over me. How many times had I ran along this beach screeching, howling, and screaming with excitement and happiness. Just last month, I'd laughed so hard when Fred discovered a bloodsucker stuck between his toes when we were lying in bed. Good thing he was wrapped inside his own blanket. Now, I was coming upon this stretch of sand with heaviness in my chest and a half dozen strangers behind me. Sighing mightily, I continued past the island, through the channel into the quiet bay and onward to the portage.

Oh those ladies! I found that they were a motley crew: full of energy, confidence, and a good bit of strange camping habits. I named them all in my mind as I observed them. The quiet, stone-faced one I named the Sentry. The one who had her legs over the front of the canoe wiggling her toes, now sat before the fire wiggling her toes, became Mrs. Wiggles. There was Ms. Winks, who would wink to indicate that she knew something the others didn't. There was the Sergeant, who liked to bellow authoritative commands on where each tent was to be pitched. There was Corrinna. C-o-r-r-i-n-n-a. She had spelled it out during introductions as if it made a difference what she was called out here amongst the mosquitoes and the frogs. As for the one I named Trapper, one glance told me that she was comfortable in the bush. She didn't hesitate to do what needed to be done and did it quickly and efficiently. I remember thinking at one point that I would like to spend some time with her at the trapline. We'd probably catch more animals, the two of us. I let the thought go.

All the younger women seemed to take their orders meekly. It reminded me of office procedures. As we went through portage number three, past Whitewater Lake into Smoothrock Lake, one of the young women, who I'd named Miss Mouse, lost a shoe in the mud. She whimpered softly, gasping in distaste and hesitantly dipping her toes into the submerged sucked-up-in-the-mud shoe to pull it out.

I walked by and said, "Make sure there are no slugs sticking to your sock when you put that shoe back on," and continued along with the canoe on my shoulders.

When we came out into Smoothrock Lake, the women wanted to take a dip. They dropped their packs, hurriedly stripped and took off running along the beach with just their panties on.

"Hey!" I yelled, "Watch out for broken glass!"

The Sentry asked from behind me, "What glass? We're in the middle of nowhere."

I turned and smiled, "You see that campsite. It's a good place for a shore lunch for the tourists. I'd bet my life that there are broken bottles all along the shoreline."

Suddenly there was a shout, "There! There's another one!"

The Trapper had disappeared in the opposite direction of the sand beach. I walked along the shore until I had left them all behind me. Near an overhanging tree with its branches scraping the surface of water, I came across two more ladies out in the water. I lay down on the soft sand and watched the clouds overhead drift by.

Soon, Wiggles came out of the water and sat down beside me, saying, "Gee, I'm glad there is such a thing as tampons."

I heard the newly named Ms. Simpleton come up right behind Wiggles saying that she was all for trying to catch a loon in case it had a fish in it. Simpleton came and lay down rather close beside me. I stretched out and yawned widely.

"You know, my mother used to tell us that since bloodsuckers are naturally attracted to blood, they can wriggle their way into your vagina to suck up the blood. That's why we were never allowed to go swimming if we were on our periods."

Ms. Simpleton sat bolt upright and ran like the dickens, spraying sand into our faces. I lifted my head and looked at Wiggles.

"What's with her?"

Wiggles giggled. "She doesn't wear tampons. She wears pads and puts nothing on when she goes swimming."

I too was seized by a case of the giggles but had brought them under control by the time the Sentry came by, collecting as many broken pieces of beer bottles she could find. The clouds coming up above the treetops looked menacing. A hurried conference ensued at the beach as I pushed my canoe out. I was a good way out before I heard the ladies thumping their canoes, coming up behind me. They had decided to come with me.

I did not relish getting stuck at this end of the lake if the waves got too high. We were about halfway across the lake when the storm hit. We hugged the inside shores of the islands as rain came down in sheets. After being blown pretty much the rest of the way, we finally entered the narrow channel to the portage at the other end of the lake. I was totally drenched even though I wore a raincoat. My traveling companions were in much the same shape as I led them to the portage campsite.

After I set up my tent, I stood beside the lake near the overturned canoes and watched a white mist come up like smoke over the lake. Thick drizzle continued to come down in sheets, creating a sound like sizzling bacon in a frying pan. From out of the mist, a seagull, gliding on the rain-swept winds, came right toward me. It suddenly swerved upward and disappeared over the treetops. I turned to see Miss Mouse behind me, with her face turned toward where the seagull had disappeared. She had a big smile.

The next morning, we all dressed and I waited to see how they were going to start the fire. In a rather loud voice, Simpleton demanded that the Indian show the group how to start a fire on this damp and miserable morning. I figured she was trying to pay me back for the panic on the beach the evening before. They had all turned to me with smiles so, I went to my canoe and got out my little bleach container filled with gas and pulled out a plastic bag with dry pine branches and twigs then headed back to them.

I saw that the whole crew had come to see how this Indian woman was going to start a fire after the storm we'd just had. I went over to a small dry poplar tree, pushed it down and quickly chopped it into three-foot lengths. I shoved the contents of the plastic bag underneath the pile of limbs and chunks from the tree, poured some of the gasoline on and threw a match to the wood. A big roaring fire was going within minutes. All the ladies laughed and clapped. The Trapper, with her blond hair plastered to her head, looked like she had been struck with lightning. She stood to the side with a grin on her face. I smiled.

When you live in the bush, you learn to find the most practical and efficient means of getting things done as it could mean the difference between life and death.

We entered the lake to the village late in the evening. The women paddled toward the vacant field site beside the dock and got out. After hauling in the canoes, the Sentry and Mrs. Wiggles went to call the train dispatcher to notify him that they, and their half-dozen canoes, had arrived on schedule.

The Groundhogs arrived on the women's second trip back from the station. My arms absently went around them, but they felt stiff and unresponsive. I realized they were beyond the age for hugs, especially in front of strange ladies.

I asked, "How's Mom?"

They both answered, "She's fine. She's with Dad at home."

I noticed they were almost the same height as me. I waited until we were well away from the others before hugging them both to me. When we got to my canoe, Lenny got in at the front with the paddle and Benny got in the middle without a paddle. I pushed the canoe off and we headed out into the dark waters.

The sun had gone down and it was quickly getting dark. Like seasoned hunters, the boys insisted we sneak up to the cabin. We got the canoe to the landing without any noise but as we pulled it up over the rocky shore, we knocked Lenny over. He landed with a splash into the water and followed that up with some loud curses. After that much racket, O appeared at the door. He stood shadowed with the lamplight around him. He looked so miserable I wished I hadn't come here first. I should have gone to Fred's cabin. I left the packsack and everything else in the canoe and followed the boys into the cabin. Mother was in bed, propped up on pillows and O was now sitting at the table.

He asked, "So, how did you get into town?"

"With the women in the canoes," I answered.

I sat down at the foot of their double bed and began rubbing Mom's toes, massaging them and trying to make an effort to connect with her. O's voice came again.

"They all got on the train then?"

This time, Mom answered. "Oh, shucks! You just missed a whole bunch of white women. Oooo, how they would have loved to have gotten their hands on you."

A quick action from the table sent a dishcloth across Mother's face but she just smiled and made a face at him. O indicated a pot on the stove so I dished out a bowl of meat and macaroni soup. With O now lying on the bed with Mom, I sat down at the table and told them about The Sentry, Simpleton, Miss Mouse, Winks, the Trapper and Mrs. Wiggles. They laughed at my descriptions of each.

I finished eating, washed the bowl and spoon then sat there watching them. They seemed very happy. O was actually smiling and laughing quite a bit.

After a moment, I turned to the boys and asked, "Is Fred here?"

There was an awful silence for nearly a minute before Lenny answered. "Yeah. He got off the train this morning but was still drunk this afternoon."

That was it. We were over!

I sat there looking down at my feet and decided then and there that I would go to the cabin and get my suitcases. If I didn't go get them now, he might show up here once he heard I was back. Without another word, I stood and went outside. I pushed the canoe back into the water and paddled out into the open lake. It felt safe out here. In the darkness, I listened to the sounds of life coming from the community. Everything was loud and clear. I heard the door close at Mother's cabin and the boys laughing. They were probably wrestling on the way to the outhouse.

I reached the other end of the shore and slowly maneuvered the canoe past the solid black point where Fred and I had first gone swimming together. In the dark current of the creek, I barely made out the outline of the rocks in the small channel but I finally reached the little bay where the landing was. I pulled the canoe up, heaved the packsack over my shoulder and pulled my sleeping bag up on top. I also threw the light tent over top of everything else.

I smiled as I made my way to Fred's cabin thinking that I must look like a real trapper returning home. I wondered if he was home. I doubted it. He was probably at Karen's place. I paused to check the door to see if it was locked from the inside but it opened at my push. Fred was not here. What did I expect anyway? He had probably gone back to drinking and back to Karen.

I entered and deposited my packsack and bags behind the door then lit a match. I found the table and lit the coal-oil lamp. At that instant, I saw someone turn over on the bed. Fred's face registered shock and surprise. Then I saw Karen fast asleep beside him. I stood there stock-still before I whirled around and ran back down the path toward the lake with my face awash with tears. I pushed the canoe back into the water and headed onto the lake as fast as I could.

How could he do this to me? Why? Oh, I loved him so much!

Why, did he do this? I really thought he loved me.

I stopped paddling and drifted for a good five minutes as my mind swirled in disbelief. Then with quick strokes, I made for the east shoreline toward Mother's place. I was just coming around the corner of the island when I heard a shout coming from the shore.

"Charlie! Charlie! Come over here!"

It was Fred. He had followed the path along the shore.

I ignored him and drifted along until I reached the point across from Mother's place. I couldn't go to Mother's. He'd make a big scene and upset everyone. Instead, I steered the canoe to the point and got out. As I pulled the canoe up, sure enough, I heard him coming up over the rocks and through the stand of trees behind me. I sat there, elbows on my knees, waiting for the onslaught. He was drunk but not staggering. He must have slept some of it off.

He rasped out, "How did you get here? Who do you think you are anyway? Walking into my cabin like that! You think you're so darn high and mighty, don't you? Hey. Say something!"

I stood up and in a low voice said, "You might want to remember that everybody in the whole community can hear you."

I tried to whisper but ended up nearly shouting. "You are asking me what *I* was doing there? What were *you* doing in bed with that woman?"

Spit sprayed my face when he hissed at me, "You asked for that. You are the one who's always pushing me away. I'm only human you know. You've always turned your back on me like I'm not good enough for you. Is that it?"

Barely above a whisper, I said, "I went to get some birth control pills because I don't want to get pregnant. I don't want a baby right now. Don't you understand? You'd only take off on me again, wouldn't you? Wouldn't you? That's why I left. But I came back again like I said I would. But you were the one gone. Why did you leave? Huh? Why did you leave?"

He turned toward the lake. "I didn't think you were coming back. I thought maybe you left with Jason. He wasn't there either. Did you consider having his baby instead of mine?"

"What? Jason? Why on earth would I leave with Jason? Listen to yourself will you? I love you and only you! But, what about you? Eh? What about you and that woman? Why did you go and do that to me for? Just how many of your children does Karen have? Eh?"

"Two! The two young ones are mine!"

His words hit me with a jolt that nearly doubled me over in pain. A moan escaped from my throat as I pushed him away from me so hard he splashed into the water. He was swearing a blue streak and I could hear water dripping off him as my shaking legs got me back into the canoe. I pushed out and paddled toward the middle of the lake with hot tears streaming down my face. I heard a motor starting and then a boat was coming toward me at full speed.

Could he even see me?

I paddled faster, trying to get to the island. I could tell he was in a big aluminum boat with a twenty horsepower motor. The boat came straight at me, very close as I swung my canoe around. As it roared past the driver turned. It was Fred all right. He must have just jumped into the first boat he saw.

He slowed down beside me and yelled, "Get in the boat! You hear me? Nobody! Nobody else will ever have you. Do you hear me? Get in the boat!"

I yelled back. “No! Go away! Get away from me,” and paddled as hard as I could.

The boat roared to full speed, came straight at me and with a bang, hit the front of the canoe. The paddle flew out of my hands and the canoe spun around so quickly, I almost overturned. He was still screaming at me to get into the boat when the noise of a motor and the sound of another boat approached, at full speed too.

The boat intercepted Fred and soon there was a lot of shouting and banging between the boats. A large bright flashlight swung back and forth as I saw a man jump into Fred’s boat. It was John, Ron’s neighbour. It must have been John’s boat that Fred had taken. All of a sudden, there was Ron, steadying my canoe alongside his boat. He quickly pulled me in then tied the canoe behind. John’s motor started and we took off for shore. Ron kept his arm around me as we headed for Mother’s landing.

I sat there shaking as pain slowly rose in my chest. I could barely breathe when we arrived at Mother’s place. I lurched up to the cabin, bent over and gasped for breath. I was moaning from the pain that had clamped itself around me. Mother opened the door and ushered me to the single bed beside the window. I sat in silence as she busied herself in the kitchen. Silently, she pressed a hot cup of tea into my hands as O and Ron entered the cabin. I was embarrassed that Ron was involved in this.

Then O was saying, “So, you sure created a bit of entertainment for the community, did you?”

Mother pushed him aside. “I’ll give them a bit more entertainment with you at the end of my walking stick if you don’t keep your mouth shut!”

I was aware that Ron was still in the room. When I felt the pressure clamp of tension begin to release my chest, I looked up to find him standing beside the stove. His eyes met mine as he stood unmoving. I couldn't tell what was going on in his mind as a slow smile spread over his face and a twinkle came into his eyes.

I was seized with an incredible urge to laugh and did, bent over with my arms around my waist. I realized that no one else was laughing. Later, my mother made me lay down on the bed and began wiping my face with a wet cloth. I fell into a deep sleep.

When I woke up, Ron was gone. I could hear the boys breathing as they slept on the double bed in the corner. O snored slightly in the next room. I could never hear Mother's soft breathing in her sleep. I lay there crying and wondered how I was going to deal with this mess.

Although I had been aware of the possibility of him doing something like that, I never believed he would actually do it. What did he see in that married woman? In fact, until I saw them in bed with my own eyes, I would have never thought it possible. I knew he loved me but why would he do this if he loved me. I felt betrayed and angry. After all we had gone through to get past our communication barrier, shared our beliefs and had real expectations, we were right back where we started. There was no more room in my heart to go on. I wanted it to stop. I would leave and never come back.

Oh, being a woman can have its perks too. Especially when this stupid man didn't even know I was there! Ha, ha,ha,ha...

Oh, my poor little lost one! Hah, I found out my shifting

form didn't take to moving from man to raven too often. Kind of skidded my brain on the surface too much. That's why my echo...
There is someone else though, that I still need to take care of.

Chapter Twenty-Two

The next morning, Mother and O decided to set the fish net and left right after breakfast. Although the sun was shining and the sky was clear, I felt a wrench in my heart. I wished Fred and I could go back in time to July when we stood by the shore beside the boat deciding how we were going to spend such a beautiful day.

At this point, I began to think the birth control pills weren't even worth it. I'd lost everything I'd worked so hard on to make this relationship work, just because I did not want to get pregnant. All Fred wanted was for me to show I loved him by having his baby. Now, there was no turning back.

As I went about numbly washing the dishes and sweeping the floor, I realized that I was constantly glancing out the window and pausing at the doorway to look down the path. I was expecting Fred to come by. I heard the train arrive and pull out again before the silence descended on me.

After I cleaned up the cabin, I went down to the lake and sat down on a rock to watch tiny minnows swim by. A little later, I heard footsteps coming up behind me and steeled myself for the encounter. Would he be angry? Or sorry?

I turned, but it was only Ron. He sat down on a rock next to me and said nothing for the longest time. I waited patiently until he decided to talk.

After about five minutes he said, "He got on the train this morning."

I looked across the bay to where I had pushed Fred into the water last night. How could he have just left me like this? He couldn't even be bothered to come over to talk to me and tell me to my face that he wanted nothing more to do with me. I heaved a big sigh. So, it was up to me. As usual.

I turned to Ron and said, "Thanks for helping me out last night."

He threw a twig into the water and we watched it float away before he answered. "I've told you many times, I'm always here for you."

I smiled as I looked down into the water. Yes, he always said that.

He reached out to brush a strand of hair away from my face and said, "So, what are you going to do now? Fred won't be back for a long time. Why don't you stay here for the rest of the summer?"

I shook my head 'no'. "I can't stay here. He'll be back and it will start all over again. I have to leave."

"I could make sure he never bothers you again," he said softly.

My head came up and his eyes held mine. Shock went through me for I saw no trace of my friend Ron in those deep brown eyes. I looked away, shaking my head. "This is crazy. I'm just exhausted," I thought.

He was staring at the shimmering lake.

I asked, "What do you mean you could make sure he never bothers me again?" My voice rose as I continued. "I don't want you getting involved. This is our problem… my problem. Stay away from him."

Instantly, he turned to me. "I didn't mean to upset you. I wouldn't hurt him. Huh! Me, hurt him? He'd probably wrap my hide around his fists. I was only saying that if, maybe if you were with me or made it look like that, he wouldn't bother you."

I smiled. That was nice of him to say. He was always so nice, always trying to be helpful.

A thought occurred to me then. "Why are you always saying those things to me? You do have a wife, don't you? I always thought you were being a gentleman to make others feel better. And you do but I'm not so sure these days. I'm not sure if you're for real or whether you're just joking to make me laugh."

He kept his head down for so long that I began to wonder if I'd hurt his feelings. Especially if he was being serious. When he looked at me with a grin on his face, I smiled. He was only trying to make me feel better.

I said, "I can't stay here. After last night, I can just imagine what everyone's saying. I don't want them watching me, talking about me or feeling sorry for me. I'll leave on the evening train. I'm just not sure where to go. It's like I have so many choices, I don't know which one to pick."

He knew I was joking with the last comment but only a little sad smile played on his lips. He didn't answer me. Out on the water, I saw the flash of paddles. Mother and O were returning.

That evening, I said my goodbyes then set out in the canoe for Fred's cabin. I would return the canoe to the boat landing, pick up my suitcases and I then I'd be gone. This time, I knew I wasn't coming back. Nothing could mend this.

The Groundhogs took off after supper and didn't return. I was hoping they would help me with my suitcases but they were probably at the train station already. I got to the landing and was pulling the canoe up when I heard someone coming down the path to the lake. Who could that be? Not Fred! But it was Ron. He came and took the other side of the canoe. We pulled it up and turned it over. Without a word he followed me up the path to the cabin door.

I expected the door to be locked but it swung open when I pushed it. It was very dark inside. Ron struck a match behind me and lit the candle while I picked up my suitcases. They were exactly where I had left them. I had nothing else to take. I blew out the candle then turned to follow Ron out the door. When I felt his hands gripping me firmly on the arms, I froze. He pulled me against him and held me so tightly that I was barely able to breathe. I dropped my suitcases and started to push him away when I heard a whisper against my ear.

"C.B.T.M. Janine!"

His breath was warm against my cheek.

"Please, don't do that."

He slowly pulled my head onto his shoulder and gently ran his hand over my head and over my shoulders saying, "Oh, baby, I'm sorry. I didn't mean to scare you. You say you're leaving for good. I may not see you again for a long time and… It's just that I have loved you for so long but you were always out of my reach. I have tried to love other women, but I can't. I love only you. I have always loved only you. But, I know you don't love me. I know. You have told me that over and over again since we were kids . . . but I just want you to know that I will always love you anyway. Can you understand that? That's what I have been trying to tell you. Don't be afraid of me. I love you. My whole purpose in life is to do what I can to help you."

I had to get out of there right that minute. This was not the Ron I knew.

So, in a rather loud voice, I said, "Shhhh. Here they come. I sent the boys to meet me here. Now, I'll have to tell them it was dark inside the cabin and I kept bumping into you. Come on, let's go."

At that, he released me and went out the door. I picked up the suitcases and went out. He was in the clearing peering about, then turned and came to take my suitcases.

"There is no one out here, Janine," he said.

As gently as I could, I said, "Ron, it's okay. I will carry them. I don't want people saying things about you and me that are not true. And they *will* gossip if you are seen carrying my suitcases away from Fred's cabin."

His hand came up and gently brushed across my cheek but he said nothing.

I continued. "Thank you for all your help. Thank you for making me laugh. Thanks for being there when I needed someone. Take care and go back to your wife and be happy."

When he turned and disappeared down the path toward the lake, I walked on to the railway station. As soon as I came into the light of the store windows, the Groundhogs descended on me, running at full speed. They grabbed my suitcases then walked sedately, like they were in a procession behind the Queen, all the way to the train station. I smiled. That was our last bit of fun together. I knew when I was gone, they'd practice that walk.

When I boarded the train, I knew there was a slight chance that Fred would be on it, so, very cautiously, I went down the aisle and found a seat. I had just paid for the train fare to Sioux Lookout when Gook came up from behind and sat down beside me. What a wonderful surprise! She took my hand without a word and we sat like that for a long time.

Then, I smiled and asked, "So where are you off to?"

She glanced over and said, "Oh, Remy got sick when she was supposed to bring him down. Now I have to go get him because she's left already."

So Remy's annual summer visit was a bit late this year.

Then she asked, "Where are you off to?"

"Sioux Lookout," I answered. "I'm going to see how much money I have left in the bank and then I'll see how far I can get with it."

After a while, she said, "He called me this morning, just as I was leaving. He told me."

I didn't ask what he had said.

Then, as though nothing was wrong, she said, "We'll be coming back on the morning train. Why don't you come back with us? Spend the rest of the summer with Remy and me."

As if reading my thoughts, she added, "Oh, don't worry about Fred. I said some nasty things to him. He knows I'm really mad. He won't come to visit for a very long time."

I pressed her hand in mine. "It makes me so sad that I've caused this anger and sadness between you and Fred."

She squeezed my hand and said, "Life has a way of straightening itself out. Nothing or no one will ever break the love that ties two people together. He will always be my son. And you will always be a daughter to me. You know from that first minute I met you, I felt you were one of my own."

By the time the train stopped at Sioux Lookout, I had promised

Gook that I would join them on the morning train. When I got to the hotel room, I dumped out my suitcases to see what I actually had in there as I hadn't had a chance to open them at the cabin. I hoped my good pair of shoes was in them. I had on a pair of jeans, a tucked-in shirt and my old running shoes. I found all of my stuff in the suitcases and was pulling things out when an envelope fell out from one of the pockets on the lid.

I picked up the envelope and opened it. There was no letter or note, only some money and money orders that came to two hundred and eighty dollars in total. What was this? My severance pay? An incredible surge of anger filled me. I wanted to scream, to lash out and punch something (or someone) as hard as I could. I grabbed a pillow, pressed it to my face and screamed and sobbed while I rocked back and forth at the edge of the bed. Soon spent, I got up, filled the tub and soaked in a hot bath for a long, long, time.

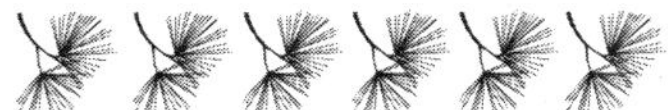

He was at the end of his rope. Why was she doing this to him?

She deliberately led him on and then turned her back on him with no explanation. He knew she was embarrassed about what was happening to her and had even started making excuses over why she was acting that way. But that only worked for a little while. That last evening at the trapline when he had seen Jason in the cabin, he just couldn't take anymore. He had left her in a miserably dark mood and had come back to hear her laughing and found a different man in the cabin with her.

Why didn't she ever laugh like that when he was with her? He had tried to make her laugh and joke around, but all he ever got were tears and the turn of her head followed by a run-and-cry episode. He was tired. He didn't know what else to do.

Now, he was reacting badly to the situations he found himself in. He no longer felt in control of anything and that everything was just happening to him. He felt as though he was being swept down the roiling river. Where had he gone wrong? What could he have done differently? He hadn't a clue. This situation was driving him crazy. He had even taken to keeping a close watch on Ted. The crazy guy was up to no good.

One night, as he was coming around the cabin, he heard a noise at the canoe landing. He ran inside the cabin for a flashlight and snuck down the path toward the lake. Sure enough, there was someone moving around. He crouched down, took one careful step after the other and suddenly flashed light on the moving shape. It was Ted. He lit up like a giant alien bug from outer space. He had discovered reflector tape in Sioux Lookout and had taped it over his hatband, across the shoulders of his jacket, down both sleeves, on his pants and even around his shoes. Damn! Did he ever look funny!

He burst out laughing as Ted yelled out, "Shut off that damned light! I'm trying to hide from the Widow Sue!" In a lower voice, he asked, "Where have you done with your damn canoe anyway?"

Even more ridiculous was that Fred had been trailing Ted earlier that day. He'd followed him over the hills and deep into the bushes beside the store that same afternoon he'd got off the train in the village. He had lost Ted and gone to drink at Bob's place but the party had soon moved across the tracks later in the afternoon. That's where Karen had come and whispered to him as she passed by the couch.

"Got your message. Can't come. Wait for you tonight."

Then she'd left the cabin. He hadn't sent a message to her. Where was she going to wait for him tonight? What the heck was going on?

The party moved to another cabin along the lake down by the dock before his bottles ran out. When he went to the outhouse he saw Ted's head disappear among the rocks. Wondering what the heck he was doing there, he had quietly followed him.

Ted was clearly following something and for a moment Fred swore he saw the head and shoulders of a man who stepped in front of Ted. Suddenly, Ted's body was thrown into fits and he began hitting at the air, thrashing about. He seemed possessed of the devil. It occurred to Fred that Ted must have knocked down a wasp's nest so he quickly got out of there. It was getting late in the afternoon when he got back to his cabin and threw himself on the bed.

The next thing he knew there was Charlie in the lamplight. He thought he was dreaming until he heard the door slam shut. He jumped out of bed and noticed Karen beside him. When had she come in? He'd rushed out to chase Charlie, although he knew there was no way on earth she would believe the truth. And, to add more pain to the misery, he didn't know why he'd said that Karen's two small children were his.

Well, that did it. That was the end of it all. She was gone now. Gone forever!

Chapter Twenty-Three

Several weeks after I had been with Gook, she came back from the store and told me that Jason had disappeared. Apparently, he'd been missing a long time and still hadn't been found. I couldn't think of anything to say. How could he go missing? People didn't just go missing in the bush. There's nowhere for them to go. And guides weren't supposed to get lost.

Near the end of the month, I was turning from the sink when Fred walked in. I was shocked to see him and dropped the cup I was holding as my knees turned to jelly. Without a glance at me, he walked right past me into the living room where Gook sat mending Remy's pants for the tenth time. I was shaking so badly. I did not want him to see me like this so I left the kitchen and went into my bedroom where I stayed for the rest of the evening.

Before I went to bed, I heard him leave. Gook came in and sat down beside me. She told me that yesterday they'd found Karen's body beside a woodpile in the bush. People thought that maybe she had slipped on something while she was carrying a log on her shoulder and that the log had crushed her head against a rock on the ground. Fred had found her that morning when he got off the train from Sioux Lookout and went over there. The police had questioned him and nearly everyone in the community but no one knew anything.

She added, "That's why he flew out here. He always comes here when he's upset."

My brain was numb as I heard myself ask, "Have they heard anything about Jason?"

She nodded. "Fred says they found his body sometime last week. He fell out of his boat and drowned."

An experienced guide like Jason falling into the water? Never. Someone did something to him. I lay down and looked at the dark ceiling after Gook left. Later, I heard Fred come in and I could tell he was sleeping on the living room couch. Oh, to be so close to him, yet be a million miles apart.

The next morning, I got up early and snuck around the kitchen fixing myself coffee and toast. When I thought he was waking up, I left and went to my bedroom again. Soon, Remy came in and crawled into bed with me as he always did in the mornings. The bed was already made, so I threw a blanket over his legs while he sat there eating my toast. We usually talked about birds, flies, fish, frogs, snakes and such. Why just yesterday morning, he wanted to know what snake pee and poo looked like but I hadn't a clue. I could hear Fred coming in and out of the kitchen and strained to hear his voice as he spoke with Gook. Then Remy was out the door. He wanted to spend some time with Uncle Fred.

Seconds later, I heard the front door slam shut. I thought Fred had left so I got up and looked out the window. There was Gook going down the path with her walking stick periodically pointing toward the lake and talking to Remy skipping along beside her.

The door opened and Fred walked into my bedroom without knocking. "We have to talk," he said. With his back against the door, there was no way for me to leave or to walk away.

As coldly as I could, I said, "I have nothing to say to you," and kept looking out the window.

He had not moved and his voice was hard, "Maybe you don't, but I've got a lot I want to say to you. And you are going to listen to me. Since you probably don't even know, I want to tell you what you have been doing to me."

I turned from the window to face him. "What? What I have been doing to you? I don't need to listen to this!"

As I strode toward him shouting, "Get out of my way. I don't have to stand here and listen to you any longer."

His arms came out toward me. I backed away. His voice thundered out at me."You stay there and you listen to me! You took my love and you used it against me. You used my love just so you could torment me. You are a selfish and heartless woman. You take and take but give nothing back!"

I was breathing hard now and shaking my head. "You've got it backwards. It was I who gave and gave but it was never enough. My love was never enough, was it? The only thing you saw as proof of my love was a baby. But even that was not enough, was it? Where were you when our baby died inside me? Huh? Where were you? And then, I gave you my love in a million other ways but it still just wasn't enough, was it? All you wanted to do was get me pregnant again. Why? What is one more baby to you when you have others from someone else? No, you wanted me to pay for being different, for not being the kind of hunter and trapper like you are, is that it? I gave you everything a woman could give but it just wasn't enough. There is just no way you could turn me into a Karen could you? My love isn't as good as hers, is that it?"

Exhausted by my tirade, I said quietly, "Go away! Of all the things that you have taken from me, there is nothing else you can hurt me with any more."

He let out a big sigh and put his head down briefly before he looked up and said, "I didn't mean that about Karen's children.

They aren't mine. She had a husband before Big Al and those are his kids."

I was near to breaking down and I heard myself shout, "What?" I couldn't take any more. As I struggled to maintain my sanity, I said in a trembling voice, "Shut up! Don't talk to me anymore about your filth and garbage!"

Then I said the first thing that popped into my mind. It was the only thing I knew would hurt him. "Murderer! That's what you are! You killed Jason didn't you? Why? Because he was the only person who saw me as a human being? And what did Karen do to you, eh? Did you catch that whore sleeping with someone else? Did you kill her too?"

I watched him standing as though frozen and his face turning grey. Through clenched teeth he muttered, "You *are* crazy. No. You're evil!" then turned to leave.

I threw one more question at him, "Fred, what really happened to Jason?"

He stared at me with his hard eyes before he said, "Don't ever come here again. This is my refuge. Mine. You hear me?"

Then he left, slamming the door behind him. I stood staring at the closed door and nodded stupidly. I had heard.

I heard the front door close ever so gently.

So, this is how it would end. I moved toward the window and watched him walk away. He went down the street and disappeared around the corner. I hadn't realized that I was moaning from the sharp pain in my chest.

That afternoon, I packed my bags that afternoon in a daze. Later, as I was leaving, Gook gave me a hug and put an envelope into my hand. I shook my head and tried to give her back when she said, "No, it is not from me. Fred said to give it to you. It's yours."

I said nothing. She seemed so frail and I felt the hard shoulder bones against my hands as I held her close to me. I kissed her forehead and whispered, "If I'd known how much pain and anxiety I would cause you, I would have died back then." Then I turned and went out the door.

I headed to the airport in the company of a dozen or so children. Fred had taken Remy for a canoe ride so I didn't even get a chance to say goodbye to the boy. My heart ached over that.

On the plane to Nakina, I opened the envelope and counted five hundred dollars inside. Where on earth did Fred get that much money?

Where could I go to start all over again? I did not want to go to Port Arthur. I'd been there. I wanted to start brand new in a place I had never lived before.

I went to Winnipeg and managed to find a secretarial job at a construction company. I talked to no one and I knew I was withdrawing again. So, in November, I started to volunteer at the hospital when I wasn't working.

Just before Christmas, on one of my evenings after work I came across Gook in the waiting room. Remy? I rushed to her and learned that he was okay. It was Fred who was in the hospital. She was there because of Fred. The doctors had just finished operating and he was in critical but stable condition. I was shaken by the news. What I could gather from Gook, Fred had been hauling wood all day to his cabin in the village. Bob found him later that night when he had gone to borrow the axe. A huge pile of logs had rolled down on top of Fred, injuring him terribly.

At my questioning look, Gook nodded. I went up to the intensive care unit and found the room he was in. He was bandaged up pretty much everywhere. The shock sent my knees shaking. I hurried out and tried to compose myself before I went back into the waiting room to sit with Gook. I visited him every evening after work, sitting by his bed, waiting for him to wake up.

One day, as I was looking out the window, I realized that he was awake. His face was puffed up and his eyes were mere slits amongst the bandages. They had also stitched up his scalp. He had several broken ribs; one arm was in a cast and his left leg was encased in bandages where the surgeons had patched up a huge gash.

Not knowing how he would react, I reached out and touched the free hand lying limply between intravenous tubes. I kept my eyes down but felt no answering pressure from his hand. I told him that Gook had just left but that she would be back later on in the evening and that Remy had also been there. Fred just closed his eyes and drifted back to sleep again.

A week later, he still had not spoken to me. But, he reached for my hand each time he woke so I knew he wanted me to stay. He made no attempt to talk to me. I left each time Gook came in and I'd hear him talking to her in a soft, weak voice.

Christmas day was spent at his bedside. To keep him occupied, I started reading a book, a chapter at a time, each time I came. When I had first begun, he turned his face to the wall but I continued to read. Now, each time I came in, he'd hitch himself up in bed for the story.

When work resumed again after the New Year, I came only in the evenings. On one of my visits, he had just come back from a shuffling stroll down the hallway and was sitting on the edge of his bed. He would be going home soon. Gook had already gone ahead to prepare the cabin and to wait for him there. He was so gaunt and weak I wondered how Gook would manage.

I set the juice on the table beside him and said, "Here, I brought your favourite drink."

As I sat down on the chair beside the bed and pulled the book from my handbag to read the last chapter, he asked softly, "Charlie, would you dance with me? I can do the shuffle real good now."

I couldn't stop the tears that spilled over my cheeks. I wanted so much to reach out and hug him, just to hold him to me. If he had died how could I have gone on in this world without him? Knowing he was safe and my anger at him had been the only two things that had kept me going as I struggled to find a new life for myself.

I put my head down and wiped my eyes and I heard him gently say, "Come here, Charlie."

But, then the nurse came in.

I managed to pull myself together in the time it took the nurse to get Fred back into bed and comfortably propped. When she finally left, I smiled and pulled up a chair.

"Well, do you want to hear the last chapter, or not?"

He nodded and closed his eyes as I began reading. I finished the story and, thinking he was asleep, began getting ready to leave.

I touched his hand as I stood up and his fingers clasped around mine. He whispered, "Jason must have seen something or someone, or found out something. I wasn't there. I could have helped him if I was. He was my friend."

I immediately said, "Shh, not now. I know. I didn't really think that. What I said back then. I'm so sorry. Let's talk some other time. Go back to sleep."

His eyes opened. "It wasn't me, Charlie."

I nodded and whispered, "I know, I know. I'm sorry I said that, I was so angry then, I would have said anything to hurt you. That was all. I'm sorry I said that. I know it wasn't you."

He whispered back, "I didn't hurt Karen either. I've never hurt anyone, except you."

Then with his hand keeping a firm grip on mine, he said, "The logs. Someone moved the logs."

I held my breath as my heart pounded in my ears.

He continued, "I had just come in with the last load. It was dark. I saw one log sticking up at an odd angle and I couldn't figure out how it got like that. And then, when I pulled it, the whole thing came down."

I was remembering my clothesline pole at the cabin but patted his hand and whispered, "Go to sleep, now."

He closed his eyes and I left.

I never saw him after that. I couldn't go to the hospital the next day. I didn't have a telephone and my landlord had said he was coming to fix the stove later in the afternoon. I had to wait for him. Also, I had to work the following day so I walked to the corner store to the phone booth and left a message with the nurse to tell Fred that I would not be coming that evening. When I arrived at the hospital the next evening, I found that he had gone home.

I had brushed up on syllabics during my visits with Gook those summers and now I wrote to her once in a while in them. It was April and she was back on the reserve. She wrote that Fred was back in the village, recovering nicely and was almost as good as new. She mentioned that there was something wrong with her heart and that she had been to see the doctor. Around June, her letters stopped. Since I had no other way to reach her, I called the postal clerk at the store in the village and asked him to tell Fred to be at the store at a certain time that evening and let him know I'd be calling.

That evening when I heard Fred's voice at the other end of the line, my heart jumped. I had to clear my throat before I said, "Hi. So, are you all mended now?"

His voice came back, "Yeah, I'm fine. Why? Are you thinking of coming back and doing more damage?"

I knew he meant it as a joke but I felt the rush of pain before I managed to say, "No. I was calling about Gook. Is she okay? She just suddenly stopped writing."

There was a pause at the other end before I heard him say, "I didn't mean that the way it sounded. It was just, when you used the word mend . . ."

I interrupted, "Do you know if she's okay?"

His voice came back in a colder tone. "Yeah, she was here. I took her home the other day. She wasn't feeling well when I left though. She had a cold but she should be all right now. I'll be going back there in a few days. I just came to get my stuff from the cabin here."

Still in an impersonal tone, I asked, "Can you call me around noon at my work number when you get back to her and let me know how she is?"

His response was short, "Yeah, sure."

I gave him the office number where I worked and said good-bye.

It was a week before he called. He said that Gook wasn't feeling well and that she was asking me to come and stay with her for the summer. He sounded like it was almost as an afterthought when he told me that he couldn't stay with her because he was going back to the cabin at the trapline to work as a fishing guide for the tourist camp. He was Jason's replacement. I hung up wondering what I should do.

I quit my secretarial job and took the train home to see my mother. All was well there. By all accounts, the Groundhogs were running wild in the community and O and Mother passed the time sitting on the wooden platform beside the door watching the evening sunset.

Soon after that, I flew out to see Gook. When I arrived I discovered that her Band had moved her to a smaller two-bedroom house at the end of the road, next to the Nursing Station. When I entered, a young man came out of the kitchen and his face lit up. I watched his face intently as he laughed and talked excitedly. He looked like Jere. Remy gave me a big hug and a kiss to my cheek before he was off and running down the street.

I had a wonderful summer with Gook. We went fishing nearly every day in the new aluminum canoe that Remy's family had bought for her. Fred had gone back to the trapline. Apparently, he'd been sober for almost a year now. At the end of August, Remy went back to Winnipeg and then September arrived. I knew I should have returned to the city long ago, but I couldn't leave Gook. Toward the end of September, I got a secretarial job at the Nursing Station and it suited me just fine.

One day, I had just finished taking clothes off the line after work, when I walked in and saw Fred at the kitchen table. My heart nearly jumped out of my chest. He looked back to normal. We spent the evening reminiscing and catching up on news. I noticed that we were very careful that we didn't broach subjects that might be painful for either of us. Throughout the evening I felt Fred and I drawing closer, but a gap was still there. There were a million miles between us.

I think I am getting very close! They just don't give up do they? My little lost ones are trying to make it home. Maybe in a little while... I still have that one last thing to do.

Chapter Twenty-Four

Around November at the Nursing Station, the nurse poked her head in the dispensary and said, “Someone here to see you.”

I turned around and stood looking at a tall, solidly built, man who smiled immediately. It was Ron. And he had changed. He entered and we shook hands.

“Hi,” I said.

“Hello.”

“How you doing?”

“I’m okay. And you?”

“Fine, I guess,” I responded.

This was not natural. How phony we sounded! We both burst out laughing. He pulled up a chair and sat down. In the small room our knees almost touched.

I asked, “So, what are you doing here?”

“Oh, just came to see you.”

I smiled. “I mean, what are you doing on the Reserve?”

“Oh, I work at the Band Office. Economic Development.”

“How long have you been here?”

“Oh, about a week now. And you?”

“Well, I work here as you find me and I’ve been living with Gook, I mean Amelia, since July.”

“I know. That’s how I found out that you were here. Somebody mentioned your name and that you were looking after the old lady. So, I thought I’d come by and say hello.”

I tried again. “Is your family here?”

“No. My wife left last summer. She’s married to somebody else now. On the next reserve east of here.”

“Any kids?”

"No. We never had any kids." He smiled and added, "Maybe that's why she left."

Just then Susan, the nurse, came by and Ron said, "Hey, Susan, you know what Channie here used to do for fun when we were kids?"

Now that didn't sound right.

"What do you mean what 'I' used to do? Why don't you say what 'you' used to do?" I said.

Then the laughter started. I sat down at the edge of the counter and watched Ron as he kept the whole clinic entertained for about an hour with stories about our outhouse gang: the Snake-tunnel Skaters, and those hell-bent Rump riders of the Toboggans. His hair was still long and he had it tied in a ponytail at the neck. He had always had long hair, long curly black hair. It was good to listen to Ron telling stories. I hadn't heard him do that in years. He used to keep us entertained all the time with stories when we were teenagers.

When he had gone, Susan remarked, "I never knew Columbo was such a good story teller."

I asked, "Why do you call him Columbo?"

She laughed and said, "Well, the first time he came here, about a year or so ago, he always wore an old brown overcoat."

I stood by the window thinking it would be like the one Fred used to have. The one he had lost and never found again. I shook my head. I didn't like where my thoughts were leading.

I hoped tomorrow would be a nice day. Fred was coming to visit.

All through the fall and into winter, Fred visited Gook and I regularly. We were making a great effort to bridge the gap that had grown between the two of us during the previous year. Gook was there, leading the discussion. We spoke of many things: some off-hand topics, some of a more philosophical nature, and those that set us to soul-searching. Some evenings, we just told jokes and stories. We played cards a lot. There was Cribbage, hearts and sometimes we just watched Gook play solitaire.

A few days before Christmas, Fred arrived at Gook's place although we had not expected to see him. It was a pleasant surprise when I came home to the sound of his voice in the living room and heard Gook's raspy laugh. I looked at him and saw the sparkle in his deep brown eyes. He had put on a lot of muscle and looked great. He was aware that I was watching him but I didn't look away. I figured that if I could ignore his close scrutiny of my body from my feet to the top of my head, he could take me looking at him. He had become a close friend, a friend I still loved very dearly. He smiled back at me.

That evening, Christmas Eve, we sat around the wood stove in the darkening living room until after midnight. We sat in the dark so we could see the lake better. When Gook went to bed, Fred came and knelt down in front of the chair where I sat facing the window. I was admiring the view of the frozen lake in the moonlight when I saw his hand holding something out to me. I needed to see what he was handing me, so he switched the light on beside me. The light blinded me for a second. In his hand was an engagement ring.

On impulse, I picked up the empty box, turned it over and pulled out the guarantee from the case. A receipt fell out with it. I read the date. He had bought the ring at the time when I was left stranded in the cabin with our dead baby within me. He saw that I remembered and was now realizing when he had bought the ring but he didn't say anything. My hand clenched the paper before I pushed it back inside the case.

Fred reached for my hand. I did not move as he slipped the ring on my finger. I knew that this had been a long time in coming and that he must have known that one way or another, I would be beside him again. I reached for him and we clung to one another. This was the first time I had touched him since I'd held his hand in the hospital.

It was around the middle of March when I returned from work to find Ron sitting at Gook's kitchen table. As soon as I walked in he said that Gook had gone to the store to get some meat for supper. I realized right away that Gook had had another reason for going because we had more than enough meat in the freezer. I sat down across from him and watched him fidget.

He smoothed the long curly jet black hair away from his forehead before he said, "There is only one way to do this and that is to say it straight out. Are you involved with Fred? If not, can I take you out? I mean, you liked me once, right?"

I looked him straight in the eyes, shook my head and said, "No, Ron. It never worked that way. Even when we were kids you were my protector, my older brother. You even protected me from people I loved. You'll never know how much I loved Jere at that time. I looked to you for comfort and protection, but that was all. There can never be anything between us, Ron. I am going to marry Fred."

I stared at the floor until I heard him move. I glanced up and a shock ran through me. There were those eyes again: cold, merciless and crazed. But in one shake of his head, he was back to normal, even attempting to joke and put me at ease. When he got up to leave, I said nothing as I watched him go out the door.

I talked to Gook but she didn't offer any insight other than to say that if I feed a wild animal, it would most likely come back for more. I said nothing to that.

When Fred came again around the middle of March, Gook was determined that this situation was going to be put to rest. She sat Fred down at the table across from me and slammed the door behind her. She was off to play Bingo.

We looked at each other for a full minute, then Fred asked when I had seen Ron last. I hesitated. What was I going to tell him? The truth? I named the date that Ron showed up here.

Fred sat with his head down for the longest time after I told him what Ron had said to me. He took a deep breath and began to speak in a serious voice.

"I have to tell you something. You must sit still and not say anything until I have finished. Do you understand? You promise?"

I nodded. What on earth was he about to tell me? I wasn't sure I wanted to hear what was coming.

He took another deep breath. "I have had the invisible man, our Weesquachak, out at the trapline several times since you have been here on the reserve. He seems to think I am some threat even though you are not actually there with me."

"What on earth are you talking about? What has he got to do with me?"

Fred glared and said evenly, "Didn't I ask you not to interrupt? Be quiet and listen!"

I took a deep breath and locked my gaze on my clasped hands on the table as he continued his story.

"It was just before New Year's, right after I left here, when I noticed the tracks. That was the very first time that I'd known him to come around the trapper's shack in the winter. Now that I had tracks to go on, we were on a level playing field. I knew I would catch him then. Anything that leaves tracks can be caught. Well, after about two days, I knew he was staying in the area so I made it look as if I were going into Armstrong. By my behaviour, I really made it look like that. Only I turned around about ten miles away and made my way back through high ground. As I approached the cabin from the inland peninsula, I noticed fresh tracks and tracked them right to the cabin. A blizzard had started to blow in late that evening, but I knew every foot of that land so it was no effort for me to reach the cabin. It was as I approached the cabin from behind the woodpile that I became aware of a man just in front of me. The snow was coming down thick and heavy that night and I was only about six feet behind him when he pushed the cabin door open. You know that four-foot stick I always have leaning against the door that I use to whack my snowshoes to get the snow off? Well, I picked that up and hit him on the back of the head. He went down inside the cabin. I stepped over him in the dark and lit a candle. He was just coming to when I yanked him up by the collar. I tied his hands behind him then tied him to the bed frame and sat him up on the bench. He wore a balaclava over his face so all that was showing was his mouth and eyelids. He was looking straight at me when I yanked off his mask. And . . . it was Ron."

My heart leapt into my mouth. "Ron! What? Why?"

A long, long time passed where we just looked at each other, minds going over the strange incidents that had happened to us over the years. Sick at heart, I acknowledged that it could have been Ron. Fred's eyes told me that he had no doubt that our invisible man and his attempted murderer was none other than friendly, gentle Ron.

"What did he say?"

He understood my hurt gaze and continued "I told him that I would keep his hands tied until I took him to the police. He said that he had only just arrived to ask me if he could court you. Then, he said that if I hurt him in any way, he would say that he had seen me coming down the path where they found Karen dead that morning. He was determined to accuse me of murdering Karen if I ever accused him of attempting to hurt me or you or anyone else. He also said that he would testify that I had tried to kill you that night on the lake when the whole community had witnessed the scene. He seemed very intent that no bad word should come to you about him. In return for my silence about my suspicions, he would keep his mouth shut about Karen and myself. So, I must tell you about that night. . ."

I took a deep breath to say that I did not want to hear it but he cut me off.

"No! Hear me out. I got off the evening train at that tourist camp about three miles west of the village and spent the night huddled by the railroad tracks, trying to figure out how I was going to approach you. You see, I had chickened out. I heard you were back in the village and I just could not go and not see you . . . and I was just not ready to face you just yet . . . you understand?"

Fred continued, “Anyway, the next morning, I walked the three miles to the village and you know Karen’s cabin is the first one at the end. It was there that I found her. I knew something was amiss as soon as I approached her cabin. I don’t care what anyone else thought of her, but to me she was always a friend. She always took very careful watch over her children and I saw her most of the time only as a friend. Only, I could not say anything since I didn’t officially get off the train, you understand? And, I didn’t know anything more than what everyone else knew. Anyway, there it was. Ron was describing how he had witnessed me meeting Karen and how I had smashed her head against the rock with the log because she had hurt you. Do you understand? How would he know exactly how she died if he didn’t do it himself? Now, he was trying to blackmail me, saying that he could say I was the murderer and that he was a witness to the whole scene. I felt that I just did not have a choice. Keep quiet or answer to a whole lot of questions that were going to cost me a whole lifetime and a lot of suspicion... and you! I just could not afford to lose you forever on a false charge of murder. That was the last thing I needed to come between us. As to all my suspicions about Ron, well, I still have absolutely no proof whatsoever. I don’t know if he was telling the truth, that he had only just arrived to talk to me, because then, the snow had covered up all the footprints. So, I cut him loose with a warning that if I ever saw him on my territory again, I would hang his you-know-what right beside the beavers’.”

I put my head down and let the information sink in. I could not decide whether Ron would take this as a threat for the future or whether it would put an end to the horror. There was no way to know. I looked at Fred and as honesty and openly as I could, I told him that I believed him. I also said that I had my doubts that Ron was that clever. I was inclined to believe that he had only just arrived to get Fred's permission to see me.

I looked at Fred. We had certainly come a long way. I hoped that our paths would merge from this time on. He was still sober after a year and a half. I had remembered to reach out without fear and he was right there with me.

We decided to get married during the annual spring Pow Wow in the community. I had never been to one at this reserve. Shortly after we told Gook of our plans, an Elder came to see us. He was a frail looking white-haired old man. Gook led him to the living room sofa where they sat talking until I brought in a cup of tea for each of them. Quite naturally, Fred and I sat down on the floor in front of him although there were armchairs behind us. He looked at Fred and said,

"Salamander, you know that your father and your woman's father were good friends."

Fred nodded and glanced at me.

I was still getting over the surprise that Fred had an Indian name. I knew that our fathers were friends, yes. So I nodded too.

Then the elder said, "I knew your grandfathers. They were good Medicine Men." Then he looked at Fred and said, "Your grandfather was a well-known Tsaki, a tent-shaker." He turned his eyes to me then and said, "And, your grandfather was a Nanandawe, a bone-sucking healer."

A shock went through me. I had not known that.

He turned his attention to Fred again, "You know your clan is the Sturgeon. Your woman's clan is the Loon."

That was also news to me.

He turned his eyes to me again and said, "I know that you do not have a name by which the spirits and your ancestors can know you by. But, I have seen you coming for many years now and I have a name ready for you to take into your heart. From then on, everyone will recognize you for who you are." I nodded, not being sure what that meant or how I was supposed to respond to that.

After the driver came to pick up the Elder, and we were washing the cups in the kitchen, I asked Gook, "Did you know my father too?"

She raised her eyebrows at me, "Oh, no. I never knew where my brother went when he left our lands. I never met any of his friends. I was married early and after ten years, my young husband died. We had no children and I never remarried. Fred became the only son I have ever known."

When she left to go to her room, Fred sat down at the table with me and we had a second cup of tea. I asked, "You never said anything. You are of the Sturgeon Clan." He smiled, nodded and took a sip of his tea. I continued, "And, I am apparently of the Loon Clan." Again, he just smiled. I rotated my teacup, saying, "The sturgeon and the loon are one of the oldest ancient species left on earth." He said nothing, so I continued, "The loon is about twenty-five million years old and the sturgeon is older than the dinosaurs. About three hundred and twenty-five million years old, at least." He took another sip of his tea and pursed his lips.

I said, "The sturgeon are the remnants of the boney-plated fish." He took another sip of his tea as I added, "Loons eat fish."

Suddenly, he sprayed his tea right across the table at me and said, "Sturgeons are bottom feeders. Loons don't go down that far," he giggled into his teacup.

While I wiped the tea off the front of my blouse, I asked, "Did you know about our grandfathers being Medicine Men?"

He glanced at me and said, "I knew about mine but I didn't know about yours."

It was the day before the wedding that I met the Elder again with everyone in attendance at the Sunrise Ceremony. After that, he held the Naming Ceremony for me. He told me that my name was Night Hawk Woman. I was startled to hear that. How could he know that? How would he know that?

The next day during a break in the Pow Wow, we had our wedding ceremony. I had not seen Fred that morning as I had been with Gook at the cabin where the women had prepared me for the ceremony. I was dressed in a leather dress with a fully beaded trim at the hem and collar. Crowds gathered around as Gook and I, with all the women behind us, headed to the ceremonial grounds. When we arrived, there, at the other end of the clearing, was a man in full Anishinabe regalia. I knew from the way he walked toward me, that it was Fred wearing a full traditional outfit that I had never seen him in. I knew that I had come home. I knew where I belonged.

That afternoon, Fred and I got married at the church just to make the paperwork legal. A wedding draws a crowd, so it was no surprise when we emerged from the church to find all the people lined up outside to shake our hands and wish us well. We were about halfway through the crowd when Ron suddenly stepped out in front of us. Without a pause, he pulled me into his arms and hugged me. When he turned to Fred, at that moment, I felt that the world stood still. They seemed totally oblivious to everyone around. The tension was almost visible and hung thickly in the air. Whatever had happened between them obviously had gone beyond me. Their eyes bore into each other until Ron moved. He bowed slightly to Fred, then turned on his heels and disappeared through the crowd. A raven swooped down, squawking and reeling crazily.

We never saw Ron again.

Shortly after, we heard that Ron was arrested for the attempted murder of Ted. This time there were witnesses and when the police came to arrest him, he bragged to them how he had killed Karen, Jason, and several other people who were getting in his way. They said he'd gone crazy.

In the stillness of the dawning light, I fold my wings close to my body and welcome the pungent odour of my wolf scent. It is the sense of smell that first invades my present form in the process of transformation. It is the smell of man that I find most abhorrent when I move from the wolf into the shape of a man... brrrr! The fur on the back of my neck literally stands on end. Only my stealth and senses shift when I move from dog to wolf. My mind changes most from any form to that of the raven. I am anything I want to me. I am he. I am she. I am it. I am. I shall rest now. A well-earned rest. My job is done. Goodbye my lost ones, for you are now found. They should thank me that they have found each other.

It was late June when we landed at Clay Lake. I had the little black puppy that Fred had presented me with on our wedding day. I held it against my chest as we approached the cabin. I saw that some things had changed. There was a new fish-cleaning shed with screening all around beside the dock. Over at the point was a screened-in shade over a picnic table nestled between the trees. The brush had been cleared all around, leaving the trees room for their branches to spread to the sun. There was no grass to grow but the ground was covered with low ground plants with their leaves weaving a green carpet six to eight inches from the earthy soil. The air smelled wonderfully fresh. Birds chirped in the trees and squirrels came chasing each other across the path in front of us.

I walked up the path and there was the cabin in front of me. It now had a porch with bug-screened windows on the top half. Beside a large covered woodshed, with steps leading up to it was a clothesline platform with another higher step in the corner for easy reach to the pulley.

I looked back to see a big smile on Freddy's face. How I truly loved this man. He held the cabin door open for me and I went in, stepping onto a "welcome home" mat by the door. The log walls had been covered with wood paneling and the floor had been covered with linoleum. A birchbark canoe with carpeted flooring came immediately to mind. My eyes settled on the two rows of books on a shelf above the bed.

I glanced at him. "Books?"

He threw his head back and laughed.

"Well, you got me hooked on books when you read that one to me in the hospital."

As I stood there admiring all the work he had put into this place, at each loving detail, I knew that words had their place and deeper knowledge was better left unsaid.

Fred came up, put his arms around me and whispered, "Welcome home, Charlie."

Printed in Canada by Gauvin Press in November 2005